Published in the United States by STARbooks Press, PO Box 711612, Herndon, VA 20171. Printed in the United States

Cover Design by Emma Aldous: www.arthousepublishing.co.uk

Herndon, VA

I0692925

BONE

By Sable Stone

Herndon, VA

Table of Contents

Chapter One

Nick knew a lot about color for someone who only wore black.

He knew that red triggered the body's hunger response, which was why restaurants like Chili's and Friday's and other chains with cutesy names ending in apostrophe-s used a lot of it in their décor, subliminally encouraging their patrons to order more than anyone should ever consume. A friend of Nick's had gained a lot of weight following the all-night painting party that turned her kitchen walls a sloppily-applied apple red, and a second party was thrown to cover it up, just as sloppily, inside of a month. Boudoir-wall ruby also signaled both rage and lust, emotions Nick found forever linked to the bedroom. While red in a traffic light or octagonal sign meant stop, the same scarlet, worn as lipstick or lingerie, got a lover ready-to-go.

He knew that yellow yielded anxiety, and that often the planned sunny scheme of a nursery was abandoned when the infant intended to sleep in it cried ceaselessly. Yet yellow was indeed a child's color to Nick: lighthearted and playful and decidedly less-than-adult. Exuberant yellow made most young – or young-at-heart – people happy.

He knew that blue was soothing and serene, like the sky and the sea. A blue bedroom was more peaceful than provocative, promoting sleep over sex. Blue was butch, masculine to a fault, precise and honest. Blue was trustworthy in a policeman's uniform, a banker's pinstripes, and a superhero's tights.

But Nick trusted only black. He flirted with other colors, fell in and out of aesthetic obsession with them all the time, and never had a favorite. At one point or another, he had loved them all.

Which is why when Nick first came to South Beach, where the neon lights of Ocean Drive impart their own ever-changing casts on the pastel celluloid surfaces of Deco architecture and the candy-wrapper skins of idling exotic cars, he knew he'd never get bored, and made it his home.

The rest of Miami, however, had disappointed Nick. He had counted on culture and found instead merely commerce. The interior design firm he worked at was in Design District, which before the real estate bust was believed to be Miami's Next Big Neighborhood, but until gentrification recovered would remain a place Nick didn't like to be after dark. Nick had expected the projects at that firm to be edgy and modern, colorful and bright, like both the District and Deco Drive, but discovered as the industry slowed that their most consistent work was in the Gables or the Grove: traditional and Mediterranean, neutral and conservative. Crossing the causeway from South Beach to downtown was like shifting from fifth into first, and Nick often joked that he didn't dare go so far as Hialeah without a Spanish-English dictionary and a passport.

# # # # #

"We have chemistry together," Mark shouted at Rob over the club's loud rock.

"What, dude?"

"Not you and me. Not that kind of chemistry. That girl and I."

"The fuckin' stripper up there? She's hot."

"We have chemistry together."

"Go for it, dude." Rob said 'dude' a lot. Mark never pointed it out. Mark was smarter than that, and smarter than his friend. He never pointed that out, either; Mark was smarter than that, too.

"Not like that. Chem-One-Oh-One. Nine-A-M Tuesdays and Thursdays in Lab Two-Oh-Six. Professor O'Malley." Just the thought of Professor O'Malley, with his Freud beard and short-sleeved shirts that exposed reed thin arms of dark reddish hair against pale ruddy skin, was enough to flatten both Mark's beer buzz and half-hard cock. Mark returned his concentration to the drinks and dancers to try to get them both back.

Rob looked harder at the girl onstage, seeing if he recognized her as she reached back to unhook her sparkly bra before jutting her arms forward and shimmying the loops of fabric along them, toward her hands and then off them, letting the top hit the floor. "You should say 'hey' to her," Rob said. "See what's up. Get in there, man."

Mark believed that Rob knew about a lot of things – how to avoid a hangover, how to pass a class without attending most of it, how to punctuate sentences with 'man' or 'dude' in place of a period or question mark – and for the most part, Mark thought Rob knew about girls, but about this one, Mark knew Rob was wrong. He shouldn't say 'hey' to her, not when he wanted to say so much more.

Girls like the one on stage right now, dancing in more makeup than clothing, were easy for Mark to spot on campus. If a pretty female student put effort into her appearance for class and campus events, wearing lipstick with her hair down to a lecture class or high heels just to study in the library – the distracting clacks of those shoes against the old hardwood floor there routinely met with the just-as-irritating insistent 'shh's of a hissing librarian – then Mark figured the girl had never been inside a strip club. If a pretty student instead hid behind glasses and ponytailed hair and wore loose jeans and sweats throughout the school, then Mark thought it was possible the girl stripped, and didn't want anyone to know. Those girls never raised their hands in class, never flirted with their male teachers to get out of trouble. They never came to a football game to see Mark play. Mark had an eye for detail but usually kept what he saw to himself.

"You should tip her, man," Rob said.

Mark didn't acknowledge Rob.

"Ask her out. Ask if she wants to study together, see if she wants to, eh, *bone up* on anything." Rob nudged Mark hard when he said 'bone.'

Mark didn't say anything, just stared at the stage, making the visual connection between the brainy student he knew was blowing the curve for everyone and the girl with glitter on her nipples sliding a middle finger down the front of her G-string. Though Mark knew the stage lights probably made it impossible for the girl to see the crowd, she seemed to be staring right at him. He was paralyzed, transfixed.

"You don't have enough game to be our QB, dude," Rob said. "You better man-up before spring break in Miami."

Chapter Two

Nick's boyfriend Andrew didn't know why Nick was going out with Ron tonight. Andrew always said Ron was a bad influence.

Nick knew Andrew was right. Ron *was* a bad influence. It was Ron who took Nick to clubs to dance and flirt with other men long into the night, Ron who always suggested that Nick walk out on his boss and get his own design company off the ground, Ron who had put three drinks into Nick before taking him to a tattoo parlor to get the company logo he'd designed for himself inked on the back of his hand between his right thumb and forefinger for what Ron called 'a handshake your clients won't forget.' The three drinks had rendered Nick not-drunk-but-tipsy; he hadn't felt much of it until the needle inked close to the bone.

A bad influence, indeed, Nick thought.

But that, Nick knew, was what was going to make tonight good for him. He hadn't been bad in a while, and it was definitely time.

The way Nick felt about the possibilities of the night – of how good it would feel to be bad – influenced what he picked out to wear that night. Night was when everyone else would be wearing his signature black, and he'd have to work hard to stick out. He took a shirt and leather pants from the closet and tossed them, still on the hangers, onto his bed. His coverlet was black, too; his clothes seemed to disappear in a satin swallow the second they hit the bed. Nick grinned as he opened his underwear drawer, and the grin widened when he found the film-thin boxer briefs he'd wear tonight, the sheer shorts' only modesty a contoured opaque panel in the front. Nick pulled them on carefully and checked himself in the mirror, turning slowly to take in all his hard work at the gym. The solid black seam in the otherwise transparent shorts' back cleaved perfectly into the crack of his ass, the panel in front bulged out with his sex, half-hard with the night's potential against the silk-smooth fabric. *Hot,* Nick thought to himself, as much to coax himself out of his usual self-criticism as to reinforce the reason for all his workouts, and as much about his body as the underwear. Even if no one else saw them, Nick would know they were there, feel them, and that would embolden him, make him feel sexy.

He hadn't felt sexy in a while. It wasn't that Andrew didn't try and hadn't once made him feel that way. But the effort Nick was putting into his appearance – and by extension, their relationship – wasn't being matched by Andrew anymore. Rather than change, work on himself or break up, Andrew allowed Nick a lot of freedom.

Reflecting on Andrew was killing Nick's mood, so he pushed those thoughts aside and pulled on the leather pants. The fit hugged his hips and fell straight down the legs, like a proper pair of jeans. They were from some no-name store and had a tag inside that proclaimed little more than their designer-less manufacture. Nick's shirt was Dior. Though the shirt had buttons all the way up the front, Nick closed but two of them, leaving a small upside-down V of his skin at his midriff and a much deeper V from his throat to his sternum. Even so unbuttoned, the shirt fit tight enough for Nick's nipples to poke and press against the cloth, the 'o' in the embroidered logo on his chest encircling the pointed peak of his left pec.

After pulling on socks and boots, Nick did another slow revolving cake for the mirror, gave his reflection an approving-enough look, and headed out.

# # # # #

The lobby at the Loews hotel was far more inviting to Mark than the room he shared with Rob. The door*man* had instead been a woman, a young and pretty Latina in a fitted burgundy uniform. Polished cream marble the same color as the sand of the beach outside poured its liquid sheen across the open floor from under the check-in counters on the left and beyond, funneling into a narrow bank of elevators before splashing up and into the two bars: alcohol and sushi. Doors were either glass or louvered wood, building on the breezy character of the heavily-trafficked ground floor. Railings and light fixtures were shaped like pineapples, lending a tropical vibe to the space that relaxed everyone in it. *Perhaps too much,* Mark thought, as the receptionist had told Rob, his eyes on a brass pineapple as he absently asked her for a Mai Tai as though she were a cocktail waitress, that the pineapple was the international symbol for 'welcome' in a way that suggested Rob had best not overstay his. After one of Rob's signature smiles, she forgave him with one of her own. Once up the elevator, the soothing neutral marble gave way to brightly-colored carpet, glass and louvers became opaque and private and locking, and the welcoming pineapples shrank in size and effect. The room itself, Mark knew, would be nothing special. Though Rob had splurged picking Loews for its location and reputation for hosting celebrities, he'd decided to get a room without a view and save themselves a bit. 'Drinking money,' Rob had called it. *'Stripper tips,'* Mark had known better.

Their room was surprisingly simple, and though Mark hadn't known exactly what to expect after seeing the lobby and hall, he'd imagined simply *more* for four-hundred dollars a night. Mark knew it didn't really matter, figuring the room would be nothing more than a place to build a nice minibar buzz before hitting the clubs and to crash after partying. Rob threw his duffel onto the bed closer to the window, claiming it. Mark didn't argue; it wasn't *his* four-hundred dollars.

After they'd each showered and dressed – Rob left the bathroom in just a towel and absently swapped it for a loose T-shirt and baggy jeans right in front of Mark, but Mark dressed in a similar outfit in the bathroom with the door shut despite the fact that they had been in the locker room with each other nearly every day all season – the men left, with Rob still talking about a Mai Tai and Mark looking forward to the reverse chivalry of the pretty Latina holding the door.

# # # # #

"Breakfast at eleven at night?" Nick asked across the clean-enough diner tabletop.

Nick's alarm was all for show; he liked Ron fine, but if he genuinely cared what Ron was putting in his mouth, he doubted his concern would start with *food*. And Nick liked the 11th Street Diner a lot as well, though the fact that the steel streamliner-style structure that so many characterized as 'True South Beach' was originally from Pennsylvania by way of New Jersey bothered him a little. The diner was more or less a dining car: silvery metal on the outside with a telltale barrel-vault on the inside that gave away the railcar origins of the style. It had been brought to South Beach in the early 90s, before

Nick had moved here, so his response to the structure as being less-than-native and inauthentic to the area was tough to defend when the crowd at the diner engaged in boisterous appreciation of their surroundings.

This happened often, and the diner, given its hard metal shell and smooth interior surfaces, frequently seemed louder from the street than the night club next door, and with its aerodynamic design, as though it could take off at any minute. The booths wrapped slick oxblood and white vinyl seating around aluminum-edged laminate tabletops, the bar had a stainless steel top on its stainless steel body, and the windows – rounded at the corners – had no curtains, so sound bounced around with nothing to absorb it. During the day, these reflective surfaces amplified the daylight in the dining car's bare windows; Nick never needed coffee to wake-up if he was having breakfast there. Nick always positioned himself in the diner to admire the hand-painted mural inside it, which traded the florid sensual stylizing of a Tamara Lempicka for the realism of the era's Hollywood efforts, the mural looking more like a colorized movie still than an Art Deco masterwork. "Best thing before going out, sweetie. Grease soaks up the alcohol," Ron answered back.

Ron peppered his phrases with 'honey' and 'sweetie' more liberally than he seasoned his late breakfast. Nick didn't mind, but the endearments always confused him, not knowing if Ron wanted more from him. "I thought that was for *after* you drank all night," Nick said.

"Heard of paying it forward? Thinking ahead?"

Nick rolled his eyes. "Greasy is right. That platter should come with its own defibrillator paddles."

"What, it's just scrambled eggs, four links of sausage –"

"One for each aortal chamber?" Something about being with Ron allowed Nick to abandon his usual reserve, crack jokes, and enjoy life. He stifled this part of himself at work – and with Andrew.

"That's two medical jokes in a row. Did someone watch an *ER* rerun after work?

"Just hoping to play doctor with someone new tonight."

"Trouble with Andrew?" Ron had never liked Andrew to begin with, and never minded when Andrew didn't want to go drinking or dancing or do anything that involved leaving his house, and when Andrew packed on ten pounds in his first month of dating Nick, Ron found himself encouraging Nick to dump Andrew nearly every time they spoke.

Nick and Andrew had been together for five months, time Ron measured instead as nearly twenty-five pounds. Nick certainly hadn't quit going to the gym in that time and was starting to resent Andrew, though Andrew had apologized for the weight and freed Nick to have just-sex with other guys so long as he stayed with him. Still, Nick defended Andrew, "You're one to judge someone for gaining a little weight, with that breakfast you've got there."

"Atkins. Sausage and eggs are okay. Fucking *lard* is okay. Just don't put any carbs near me."

"You know vodka's made from potatoes, right?"

"I'll sweat it off." Ron offered. Nick wasn't sure if he meant on the dance floor or in bed.

"I bet you will."

"We'll sweat it off."

Ron was always flirty with everyone, and Nick still wasn't sure exactly what Ron meant.

# # # # #

Mark and Rob hit Ocean Drive on foot, pressing and mingling through throngs of half-dazed guys and hot Latinas in stretchy minidresses, Rob occasionally risking a hand up a supershort hem. When the crowd was too dense, Mark saw that Rob couldn't move quickly enough to avoid his hand getting slapped away, but for the most part, it looked to Mark like Rob got away with it, the odd girl turning around and shouting "Hey" at him, then getting a look at Rob and not seeming to mind so much, smiling and waiting a bit before heading off again in the opposite direction.

Mark knew Miami would be hot, particularly this time of year, but didn't expect to sweat so much, or to have to push through crowds of similarly perspiring people, though the honey-skinned women with their foreheads misting and their eyeliner smudged were easier to take than the men with sweat-slicked hair, their light-colored shirts stained dark in diamond-shaped patches on their backs and heavy half-moons under their arms. Mark kept plowing into guys hard and wondered if that was why Rob was doing what he was to the girls, touching what he wanted on purpose to avoid accidental contact with what he didn't. Mark reminded himself to ask Rob how wet the girls were where he had touched them, hoping that whatever Rob said would replace the feeling of coming in contact with so many sweaty men on the street. After several aimless blocks in the heat, Mark was relieved when Rob suggested a cocktail.

Rob and Mark stopped at a bar without even checking the name of the place. Rob ordered Mai Tais for both of them only to be asked by the bartender, "What's in one of those?" Rob had a rule, and Mark thought it a good one, not to order anything the bartender couldn't make from memory, which may have accounted for how many times they drank nothing more complicated than a beer and a shot. On the flight down, when Mark had ordered a beer on the plane, Rob had stopped the flight attendant from cracking the can, telling Mark that they were on vacation, going away to do things they wouldn't normally do, drink things they wouldn't normally drink. Unable to decide on-the-fly in-flight, they had ended up with two miniature bottles of booze – one vodka, one tequila – and a plastic cup of OJ each. After downing his tequila sunrise and most of Mark's screwdriver – both bad, though Rob had predictably remarked that leaving anything in either glass was 'alcohol abuse' – Rob decreed that they would drink Mai Tais for the rest of the trip.

So far, Mark thought, *this wasn't working out so well.*

Mark searched the surface of the bar quickly for a patron with the most colorful drink in the goofiest-looking glass. "What's that?" he asked the bartender, thinking that it looked exotic-enough to sate Rob's on-vacation request and was, obviously, something the bartender could make.

The bartender answered while pressing down on his blender's on-off switch, the machine spinning and screeching, so Mark couldn't hear.

Mark responded with a peace sign. *V-for-victory*, he thought: *Two of those, please.*

Mark watched as they were assembled in the blender, whirred together, and poured in front of them, and paid before Rob could offer, all the while hoping Rob was distracted by something and didn't see that whatever Mark had ordered for them both, which was still a mystery, was made without the bartender ever touching a bottle of liquor.

Two virgin-whatevers later, they left the bar, Mark smirking when Rob announced he felt a little buzzed from "whatever that was."

"Whatever, indeed," Mark replied.

# # # # #

"I just don't understand how you can wear black all the time. Honey, it's so depressing," Ron started in. "I mean, this is Miami, sweetie. How about a little color?"

"It's slimming," Nick said, defending the color and still eyeing Ron's Atkins-approved but seemingly fattening meal.

Ron made a face at Nick. "That can't be the real reason. Tell me why, sweetie. I've always wondered."

Nick loved the mystery of black and wondered if he, too, should be mysterious, coyly dodging Ron's question, but he knew Ron wouldn't give up. "I guess it comes from being an interior designer. I make decisions about color all day long, so wearing all-black is one less decision I have to make. And, if I'm proposing a scheme with, say, a lot of green in it, I don't have to worry that I'm wearing a red shirt."

"Merry Christmas."

"Ha-ha. Or rather, ho-ho." Nick paused, then continued, "The point is I don't fret that I might distract or clash with my work. Plus, if I'm meeting two or more clients in a day, I don't have to change shirts between meetings to coordinate with the different concepts."

"Makes sense, honey – but wait, every project your firm does ends up –"

"*Beige?*" Nick asked sorely. Nick was bored at work, and Ron had struck a nerve.

"Well, yeah."

"You'd rather I wore all-beige?" Nick asked, pointing to the bone-beige oatmeal the man eating alone in the next booth was lazily stirring, the pathetic-looking diner staring at the waiter's ass as he traced its shape in the bowl over and over.

"Point taken," Ron said.

# # # # #

Rob and Mark tried to get in at a couple of the clubs Rob had researched before the trip. Mansion had a long line and a two-hundred dollar cover, both of which Mark guessed were likely due to the signboard above the brass-and-glass doors proclaiming that some C-list starlet with no spinning experience was going to be the 'Celebrity DJ' tonight. The girls in the queue were hot; Mark had never seen girls like this in-person before, only in the backgrounds of music videos and on the arms of his sports idols, naked in *Playboy* or wearing not much more in *Maxim*. Now here they were up close, their hair as glossy as the magazines' pages, metallic eye shadow sparkling above cold, lifeless eyes. The girls were draped over men sporting suits despite the heat, dress shirts unbuttoned past the point where Mark would feel comfortable, the deliberate exposure feeling flashier than wearing no shirt at all. Some of the men were lean, some muscled, some overweight, but the exposed Vs of their chests, alternately smooth or hairy but universally tanned, were nothing Mark wanted to see, and Mark doubted Rob was particularly at ease either.

"These guys are covered in girls, and they *still* look like queers," Rob said to Mark, likely louder than he'd intended.

Mark rolled his eyes back at Rob, thinking that a guy who looked like any one of these men back home would get his ass kicked for sure.

The biggest difference Mark noticed between this crowd and crowds back home wasn't in the way the men dressed or the women applied their make-up. It was in how everyone – men and women alike – paid little to no attention to Rob and him. Back home, the party didn't start until they arrived, guys greeting Mark with macho back slaps and women instantly fluffing their hair or checking their lipgloss at the first sight of Rob. Here, in a city all about its nightlife, they were invisible, ignored. Mark wondered if Rob noticed.

He had his answer when they walked away, north on Washington Avenue, stepping off the sidewalk and into the just-as-jammed street, cars crammed as close as the people in the crowd clustered, the fiberglass and steel of the expensive automotive bodies – curvaceous cars that, like the women in line, Mark had only seen in magazines and on MTV, never in real life – painted the same colors as the silk and sequins that stretched over the just-as-shapely bodies of the club's crowd. Rob tossed a remark over his shoulder about how the bouncer hadn't gotten out of their way, eased the velvet rope aside for the two of them like the bouncers surely would back home, were there ever a velvet rope there to be eased.

"It's the fish-pond ratio in action," Mark said wisely, watching Rob nod but doubting he understood.

They increased their pace up the sidewalk, dodging the homeless but not their smell, their accelerated speed making Mark's breath come quicker, so he inhaled unwashed street person steps away from taking in the overly applied cologne of men waiting to get into a club. Everything mixed like this to Mark, everything he could observe and absorb about South Beach coming at him rapid-fire as they all but ran past it, the sweet tomato sauce and pungent pepperoni of a pizza joint only steps away from the more refined but related smells from a nice Italian restaurant, the bright white lighting of a tattoo parlor pick-out-a-design-and-sign-here area next to a dark but colorful lounge, the black of a bouncer's tight T next to the women wanting to stand out, wearing every color *but* black.

Further up Washington, Cameo had a shorter line but not-as-hot girls in not-as-slinky dresses. Rob couldn't stand to be ignored by these lesser girls, too, and after waiting around a bit for anyone to notice them, spot them in line, wave them in and waive the cover, they trekked further along Washington to another club Rob wanted to go.

# # # # #

"Seriously, you're ordering a milkshake after sausage and eggs? If you're trying to kill yourself, there are better ways," Nick said. Nick couldn't remember the last time he'd indulged in a milkshake, but figured it was before he'd started taking his shirt off in public. No matter how good a milkshake might taste, Nick thought, it could never compare to the way admiring eyes felt on his body.

"Again, Atkins. Dairy's okay, provided it's not past its date-of-expy." Nick was always entertained by Ron's way of turning ordinary words and phrases into his own shorthand of a language: usually cute, uniformly effete. 'Expiration' became 'expy,' 'appetizers' became 'appies,' 'perfect' became 'perf.' Ron continued, "And speaking of things beyond their discard-by dates, how are things with Andrew going?"

When the conversation turned to Nick's dating Andrew, as it often did, Ron routinely reminded Nick that he was settling. Ron always said this, and also that he didn't know why. Nick wasn't entirely sure, either, but the more he thought about it – about Andrew – Nick knew Ron was right. Nick trusted Ron's opinions about a lot of things.

Though his decisions for his own grooming and clothing often yielded a response of 'physician, heal thyself' or forceful hands clamped on either side of his head to turn his face to a mirror, Ron was usually right about hair and fashion when it came to other people; this made Ron a good shopping buddy, forcing Nick to try on clothes that were incredibly different from what he'd pick out for himself, save for that they were invariably black, Nick's one rule. At dinners out, Ron boldly ordered for both of them, for the sole purpose of making Nick try something outrageous that Ron was convinced Nick would like; this made Ron a good restaurant buddy, and had expanded Nick's palate well beyond the range of his middle-class Midwestern upbringing. Though Ron was a screaming bottom and Nick was nearly all-top, Ron would never be a good fuck buddy for Nick, but Ron made a good wingman on nights when they were out, which was often, with Ron always pushing Nick to risk rejection and stop playing it safe with guys who he figured would say 'yes' and go after the ones Ron thought were completely gettable and Nick deemed completely out of his league.

None of their time together had served to answer the question of why Nick was settling with Andrew. Nick didn't see much of a future there, and Ron spent a lot of his time trying hard to break them up.

"He really is beneath you," Ron said.

"I'm the top. Sooner or later, they're all beneath me."

"Ha-ha," Ron said the words flatly. "He knows it, too."

"Knows what?"

"That he's beneath you."

"Actually, he hasn't been beneath me for a while. All that weight, I can't get it up to top him anymore."

"That's a long time without –"

"He still goes down on me, but I admit my eyes are closed the whole time." Nick's eyes darted around, looking for children or nuns or anyone else who might not like overhearing this. It didn't seem to him like anyone around was listening.

"Is that why he lets you go out with me?"

"What is it you think he thinks we're doing together?" Nick asked. Ron was a good friend, but he didn't want him getting confused about things or hoping that there would be anything more between them than friendship.

Ron didn't acknowledge the question. "Is that why Andrew lets you go to Twist? Find someone to close your eyes and think about while he –"

"Has sausage and eggs?"

Ron laughed hard enough that Nick feared he might choke. "You alright?" Nick asked when Ron's laughing-hacking-coughing settled down.

"No worries – no gag reflex, remember? Can't choke."

It was Nick's turn to laugh too hard. This attracted the attention of their concerned waiter, who in turn caught the eye of the sad oatmeal-eating man to their table. They switched to small talk for a while, which wasn't enough of a distraction to keep Nick from wondering what he really was doing with Andrew after all.

# # # # #

About a block up from where they were, Mark saw a glittering marquee winking the words 'Club Madonna.' Under the lighted sign was a giant velvet chair with an ornately carved gold leaf frame that Mark couldn't place from what he'd learned in his Survey of Decorative Arts easy-A-to-fulfill-a-history-requirement class as either Rococo or Baroque so much as capital-T Tacky. In it was a woman in an equally tacky dress of metallic lamé, sitting in a manner that suggested her feet hurt so badly in their nearly-six-inch heels that she didn't care how she came across anymore. Beside her was a thick black man in a tight black T, sporadically standing stiffly with his arms folded to intimidate the men in line, scare them out of doing anything that would get them thrown out before they were even allowed in, and then relaxing his arms and leaning toward the girl in the chair to smile at her and shrug understandingly. *Don't-even-think-about-it, I-know-I know, on and on, on and off.* Club Madonna, Mark guessed from Rob's over-the-shoulder "I think we're almost there," was their intended destination.

Club Madonna, Mark knew from the rest of the clues, was a strip club.

# # # # #

"When did you know you were gay?" Ron asked Nick in line at Twist, the bar next to the diner. In a town famous for its nightlife, and for cover charges often in excess of a hundred dollars per person, Twist was known for never charging at the door. Because of this, Twist attracted a wide variety of gay men: cheapskates who could cruise the crowd for nothing out-of-pocket; local gays who breezed in and out of Twist to see which of their friends were there and catch-up; drunks who'd rather spend their money *at* the bar than getting into it; hardcore partiers who made this their last stop of the night, a place to go when the scene at whatever bars they'd been at so far that night bored them and their money was almost gone. All, of course, hoped to hook up at some point inside Twist, leave with someone, whether they knew each other already or just met. Nick checked the crowd to see who made up the line: locals mostly, he surmised, there to see friends.

"I'm more used to straight people asking me that question than a fellow gay."

"Well...what do you tell all those straight people when they ask?"

"I ask them when they knew they were straight."

Ron laughed, as did a couple of guys in line near them. "But really, when did you know?"

"I blame –"

"Blame?"

"Go with it. You know I'm not 'out-and-proud,' I'm just 'out.' And I don't do the whole 'gay pride' thing, like the parades and stuff. I'm not out-and-proud, I'm coping. I'm gay-and-coping. And, the gay-and-coping parade doesn't draw a big crowd cause it takes so long, what with guys like me not so much marching as shuffling along, looking down at our feet." Nick mimed the movement he described.

Ron laughed easily, and more men in line seemed to be paying attention to – and entertained by – Nick's words and actions. Nick thought Ron *defined* out-and-proud.

"So I *blame* the '88 Olympics, as I'm sure do a lot of gay-and-coping guys my age." Nick paused, then added, "I'm dating myself here."

"You've dated worse, sweetie."

Meaning Andrew, right? Nick thought but didn't dare say and get Ron started again. "That year, we had Greg Louganis and Brian Boitano. If you were a boy who watched the two of them and there was even a *chance* you were going to turn out gay, there they were, in Speedos and Spandex. They did it."

"So not nature-versus-nurture," Ron said leadingly.

"Nope. Olympics versus watched-something-else-that-day."

"And *Brian Boitano?* "

"He's handsome, and I was, like, seven. I won't be judged by a man your age –"

Ron was sensitive about his age and raced a hand toward Nick's mouth to quiet him.

"– with a Justin Timberlake poster over his toilet."

# # # # #

It didn't take long for Mark and Rob to realize Club Madonna was nothing like the strip clubs back home.

Pretty-if-plain girls worked at the clubs Rob and Mark went to all the time. They had their reasons – not easily differentiated in the clubs' generally dim lights. Some needed the money for the college Rob and Mark attended, or for their families. Some were bored with life in the quiet towns that seemed to center on a single street with six strip joints within blocks of each other, and came to a place where no one would know them to, as they might put it if they were ever caught, 'live a little:' to 'walk' – or 'dance' – 'on the wild side.' For still some others, whose ample breasts outsized their education or intellect, dancing was all they could do for the kind of money Rob, at least, threw at them. This gave all of the women a different but unified appearance; they varied in age and motive, but the anxious look on their faces was shared. It was all they had in common, if not the reasons for it. Some feared being recognized, others dreaded the strung-out buzz that deadened them to reality wearing off, some surely were tensely totaling up the money they were making in their heads, hoping it was enough for their rent, their car, their kids. Whoever they were, and whatever their reasons, they were personable in the clubs despite the degrees of despair or panic in their faces, and conversed with the men as though there were nothing unusual about being naked in front of a fully-dressed stranger. Most were willing to perform a lap dance or three to the customer's completion in front of everyone, without making the men get up and head to a private room. They didn't seem to mind being touched, and often grabbed Mark's wrists when Rob had bought him a dance to place Mark's hands on their bodies, as though his trying to be respectful had offended them, or was at least unnecessary. Many of the girls were willing, for a hundred dollars or so, to follow a client to the parking lot and give him head – or more – in his car. Mark knew a few had found their way into Rob's car, and though Rob wasn't cheap and could easily afford it, Mark doubted he'd had to pay.

Club Madonna made every night at the clubs back home seem like Amateur Night. The clubs back home might have small lighted signs advertising in same-size font both 'Live Ladies Naked' and '$4 Lunch Buffet,' the buildings themselves were small, converted restaurants or ranch houses, the parking lots full of the clientele's pickups and the dancers' decade-old American-made convertibles. Club Madonna had a huge marquee like an old movie house, and a limo parked outside covered in decals of the bar's logo and images of the girls who presumably worked there: fenders and doors wrapped in close-ups of faces of dancers who were rarely seen as more than tits and ass. Though someone checked IDs at the doors back home, there was never a cover charge. Club Madonna was twenty bucks apiece for Rob and Mark to get in.

Another difference was made clear when Rob ordered the Mai Tai he'd wanted since they'd left Loews. Where the clubs near campus reeked of cheap draft beer served in overflowing mugs and pitchers, Club Madonna, the bartender told them, didn't serve alcohol. "You can bring it in with you, no problem," the man had said, his eyes locked on Rob, "but I don't stock it."

Had Rob not just paid forty bucks in cover for both of them, Mark figured he'd have left right then. Another twenty with tip, and they both had small watery Cokes.

At first, Mark thought the bartender must have felt bad for them, as he dressed up a glass of shaved ice and fruit juice with an enormous cherry-and-pineapple garnish for Rob. "Call it a 'Mock Tai,'" he said as he handed it across the bar. "A 'Mai Tai Lie,'" the bartender winked. "On me."

Rob could be charming when he wanted to be, and his All-American looks had netted him a lot of favors in life. Mark never thought Rob was particularly gracious about what people did for him, but given how the bartender had winked, Mark wasn't terribly surprised when Rob yanked the drink off the bar quick enough to cause some of it to spill over without a 'Thank you.'

"Fucking faggot bartender in a strip club – guy's got no idea how good he's got it on the job," Rob said over his shoulder to Mark, trailing behind him.

"Or what he's missing." Mark added, questioning his own sincerity as he eyed the girls on stage.

The girls at Club Madonna looked completely different from the ones back home. What Mark noticed first was the shared look on all their faces. The girls back home always looked as if they were about to get caught doing something. The girls here were blasé and covered their emotionless expressions with a quantity of makeup that most men might not notice but Mark found off-putting. Beneath the façades lay no trepidation about dancing: no doubt, no anxiety. They were alien and artificial, all exaggeration and affectation with spray tans and spike heels, acrylic nails and augmented breasts.

There were three round stages at Club Madonna, and two had poles. The girl on the left stage was more acrobatic with the pole than the girl on the right, though the one on the right was more Mark's type. The girl on the left was hardly a girl at all. She seemed to Mark a seasoned performer, easily in her mid-thirties, which made her old for this club, even if she stayed in shape and hid behind matchstick-width eyeliner and a head of what Mark reasoned had to be extensions for the way they hung from her head in wide, even ribbons. She was tan, with large round breasts above her prominent ribcage. The breasts didn't move much despite the tempo of her dance. The girl on the right was younger and, if Mark could admit it was possible in this setting, possessed a certain innocence, as though, though she blended well enough with the crowd at Madonna, maybe she hadn't been working there long. She wore her dark hair in a bob with bangs; there was a bluntness to the geometry of her hairstyle that played well against her softer features and natural body. Despite her exposed breasts and ass vying for his attention, Mark found himself taken in by the deep blue eyes beneath the light and thin brows that traced their roundness concentrically, each brow a pale half-moon. Mark wouldn't have been surprised if the dark bob was a wig. The girl leaned against the pole in the center of the stage when she wasn't ignoring it, choosing to lie against the floor and writhe in time with the music instead of spinning around or grinding against the rod.

Between those two stages was a platform with two girls dancing together: front against back, then back against back, then front against front. Their bodies mimed passionate mutual masturbation more than they did dance to the music, though their faces registered not even a hint of pleasure. They were zoned-out, zombies in greasepaint and G-strings.

Mark saw Rob swallow hard looking at the two women together. Though their movements were hardly animated or believable, it was an act he and Rob hadn't seen before; the girls at the bars back home certainly never dared pair up on stage. Rob seemed to Mark to like the show, downing the Coke in his right hand, eyeing the Mai Tai Lie in his left with more resentment than thirst.

Mark smirked at the drink, then him. "Whaddya gonna do?" Mark said good naturedly.

"When in Rome, I guess," Rob conceded. "But I don't want that bartender anywhere near me."

"When in hell, embrace the devil," Mark recalled the quote from an early General Education requirement.

"But I don't suck dick."

Mark nodded to the two women grinding each other on the center platform and joked, "Neither do they, I think they'd have us believe." It was impossible to tell what color the room was overall – it was so dark, and the changing stage lights cast the whole room alternately in blue, purple, and pink, when it didn't seem mostly black. There were a few women in the audience – Mark didn't think he'd ever seen a woman at a strip club back home if she didn't work there – but the crowd at Club Madonna was mostly male, and mostly ten years older than Mark and Rob.

Mark pointed to a table by the stage on the right, and they sat down. Mark was eager to get a closer look at the dancer with the bob, but the music changed and another dancer came on. The new dancer was black and beautiful, striking even, though she was hardly either of their types. Her shaved-short haircut confused Mark, though she'd pinned a silk flower in front of her left ear to balance the masculinity of her hair and frame. Her body was more muscular than they were used to – or interested in – with raised and rigid biceps and a flatter chest. She was a better dancer than the other girls – than Mark had ever seen at a strip club – but she too seemed to be lazily going through the motions of her routine, her athleticism on auto-pilot.

Mark reminded himself to take considerate glances at the dancer in front of him as he surveyed the crowd, though looking as indifferent to her audience as he was to her, he wasn't sure she'd notice or care. The clientele was tough to gauge, none of the men there looked at all like Mark or Rob. They resembled instead the bartender, or the guys outside Mansion, with manicured nails and flashily unbuttoned shirts, eyebrows waxed into crisp punctuation marks that raised questions with Mark, who was unused to this sort of grooming on a man, about the men's collective sexual proclivities.

Rob, instead, acted like he barely remembered there were other men in the room. He reached out to grab one of the dancers walking by – a tall and tightbodied Latina with long wavy hair and a pink leopard bodysuit – and bought a couch dance, suggesting that Mark join him while the dancer dodged the clutch of Rob's hand. The dancer initially resisted, insisting it would be more than the twenty-five dollar house fee for both of them on the sofa, but Rob assured her that she would only dance for him, that Mark would merely watch. Rob smiled at her, and she relented, leading them both to a plush pink couch in a corner of the club.

"You like hip-hop, *guapo*? R and B?" the dancer rolled her 'R' almost artificially.

"Whatever," Rob said.

"*Lo que sea*," she said back. "I am Marta." Mark thought Marta introduced herself with the same deliberate, distinguished authority his college professors used to announce themselves on the first day of class. *Here's the syllabus, don't forget to tip,* Mark thought, thinking also that all of the names the girls used at Club Madonna sounded like real names, even if they weren't the dancers' own. Back home, a girl Mark might know on the street or at school as 'Pam' or 'Jennifer' was suddenly called 'Passion' or 'Starr-with-two-Rs.' It was often tough for Mark to keep a straight face when a girl introduced herself as something ridiculous – *'Hi, I'm Petals'* – at the beginning of a private dance.

"Low–kuh–say–uh," Rob sounded out Marta's words back to her without realizing he'd dismissed her introduction, her attempt to humanize the exchange.

The dancer's first move was not the standard leaning into Rob's lap or bending over in front of him suggestively but a complete drop to the floor, on her back, her bent legs splayed in front of her. The carpet in front of the lapdance couches was also pink with black leopard spots, so Marta's bodysuit seemed to blend into it. There on the floor, she looked to Mark to be nothing but an arrangement of dismembered parts: Head, neck and bust; splayed arms; bent-backward legs; no torso. Mark wondered if the pink leopard bodysuit had been chosen on purpose to blend with the carpet: if a lot of Club Madonna's sober clients were amputee fetishists, devotees with dog-eared copies of *Boxing Helena* on their nightstands. Otherwise, the effect was more disturbing than alluring. The dancer was so slender, too, that the severed parts against the carpet looked to Mark like little more than skin and bone.

The dancer quickly pulled herself back up, reassembling her parts in Mark's mind. She quickly peeled the bodysuit down off her shoulders and let the armhole loops hang at her waist. *Skin, bone, and implants,* Mark thought.

Like a reflex, Rob reached out for her pointy exposed breasts.

"*No me toques,*" the girl ordered, her words brisk and breathy, and though neither of the men spoke Spanish, the meaning was clear to Mark.

But apparently not to Rob, who tried to touch her again.

"*No me toques,*" Marta repeated. "Look. Don't touch. Learn some Spanish. Learn some manners," the girl said, the sex in her voice surrendering to her irritation. "Sit on your hands, *Papi.* I only here to dance."

Though her words were intended to shoot Rob down, her movements stayed sexy and inviting, as though she were even daring him to try it again.

He didn't. She pulled the rest of her bodysuit off, revealing a pink G-string. And after another smack-down-to-the-floor bend – her body appearing fully intact to Mark this time – she pressed into Rob's lap and let her hair brush against his chest and neck.

"Take that off too, baby," Rob said, eyeing her G-string.

"Not for twenty-five. *No puedo.*"

Her protesting the price made Mark wonder what else was negotiable, but he didn't think Rob seemed into her enough to find out.

Marta's dance ended, and though Rob had paid in advance, she thanked him. Mark thanked her back for him. Neither man tipped her or requested an encore. Marta left without trying to talk them into another dance, looking slightly dejected but mostly unsurprised.

Just as the men were about to get up, a petite blond with saline C-cups and sea-green eyes strutted over to Rob, leaned a knee between his legs, and cooed, "Why don't I finish what Marta started there, baby." She was talking to Rob without looking at his face, gazing instead at the growing erection that she was already more responsible for than her coworker.

"Twenty-five for a dance, right?" Rob asked the question but was already sold.

"Twenty-five was for Marta. I'm Angel, and it costs more to get into heaven, baby." Angel's voice managed to make her money-grubbing entendre sound like harp music.

"For more I get more," Rob said.

"How much more do you want, baby?" Mark noted that Angel ended every phrase with 'baby,' and that Rob had dropped 'dude.' "How much more can you handle?"

"Baby," Mark couldn't resist muttering under his breath. Neither Rob nor Angel seemed to hear him.

It was Rob's turn to talk while eyeing his crotch. "How much can *you* handle, Angel?"

"Try me, baby. For fifty, you can try anything."

Rob reached behind him for his wallet and pulled out three twenties. Mark hoped Rob knew better than to ask for change.

Angel was out of her white lace bra before she started dancing. Most of her moves consisted of angling her chest into Rob's cheeks, and Rob was only too happy to lean in further, burying his face in her cleavage. "Can I touch them?" he asked.

"Sure, baby."

Rob's hands were inches away from her nipples before she answered, and now were all over her, pawing her buoyant, liquid breasts and marveling at how they felt. "Mark, you gotta feel these, dude."

Angel shot Mark a look, but spoke to Rob, her voice still saccharine sexy, artificially sweet, playing him. "Huh-uh. Just you, baby. It's okay if he watches, but he can't touch."

"But, I can touch," Rob said, seemingly forgetting Mark and leaving his hands on her chest.

"You can touch me there, baby."

"Can I touch you..." Rob drew out the vowels as he moved his hands to cup her ass, "...*there?*"

Angel was completely in Rob's lap now. "Sure baby."

"Can I touch you..." Rob didn't move his hands from her ass but locked her eyes with his, and then glanced down at the front of her lacy G-string, "...*there?*"

"You want to get into heaven, baby?" Angel taunted. "It takes more than sixty dollars."

"She's a fucking televangelist," Mark was still under his own breath but thought he could shout it out and be equally ignored. "Give 'til it hurts."

"How much?"

"You gotta *earn* your wings, baby." Angel's wily wordplay shifted gears, "You wanna get me all wet?"

"Yeah, baby." Rob said 'baby' completely differently from how Angel did, his voice deeper and more imploring.

"When in Rome, when in hell..." Mark said, knowing Angel was setting up Rob.

"Shower show's a hundred bucks, I lose the G-string," Angel paused, adding, "Your friend can come, too."

"Hundred bucks, we better *both* come." Rob was willing to pay to see what a 'shower show' entailed. None of the clubs back home had anything that sounded at all like it.

Angel led Rob to the shower room, and Mark followed, knowing he was welcomed by Angel more than he felt invited by Rob.

The shower room was small, and Angel entered through a different door than the men. Once inside, this put her on the other side of a floor-to-ceiling sheet of glass from them. Mark and Rob weren't the only men in there, nor Angel the only woman, and while the men didn't dare so much as acknowledge the presence of one another, the women interacted with each other. Angel did, indeed, remove her G-string, and was smooth there, as were all the women but one. The dancer who wasn't totally shaved smooth looked as if she had a full white bush, the liquid soap the girls used on themselves and each other lathered full and bright white in the hair between her legs. The hair on her head was darkened by the water. Mark returned his attention to Angel who, soaking wet now, was going at it with another girl. They were the dancers from the center platform, Mark realized – he hadn't recognized Angel from the stage without her partner. The girls continued to shower without engaging their audience, and Mark grew listless. The room itself was distracting, the shower wall behind the girls set with as much exposed foam-white grout as shards of ceramic tile, choppy black waves of small square tile separating fields of larger angular chips of amethyst and putty, light blue and terracotta. Mark knew that he was supposed to be looking at the girls, not the wall behind them, but those girls, despite their nudity and playful soaping of each other, weren't doing anything to pull his focus.

Rob was growing agitated. Mark wanted him to remain calm, not do anything that would get them thrown out, though he figured they were leaving soon anyway.

Mark knew Rob was as disappointed as he was. He could hear other customers' disappointments, too, summarized by one older man saying, "Ten dollars for a Coke while I watch two girls get sprayed with a little water. We're the one's getting hosed."

# # # # #

Twist was laid out to make the worst possible first impression. A stairway to the right led to a dance floor for those in-the-know, but if you hadn't been before, you were more likely to stay straight ahead, where on the same level was a dark, moody bar frequented by dark, moody old men. When Nick had first come to Twist, he figured since the club didn't have a cover, this initial bar might be the extent of the club, and sat and had a drink there. Though the bartender there was about his age – and hot and shirtless – there wasn't much else to look at, and had Nick not followed some guys closer to his age straight out the back door, he might never have seen the rest.

Beyond that initial dark bar was a door to a courtyard, with a small building so packed with guys and bass beats – both throbbing – that men and music spilled from its doors. This small glass-walled building was Ron's destination tonight – it always was. Nick went along, but didn't really like it in there.

They pushed their way in and nearly into a dancer on a small stage. Nick didn't always use the term 'dancer' for the guys who worked this bar, and they certainly didn't need to dance well, just parade through the crowd, bump and press their white-underwear-clad buff bodies into the guys at the bar or lining the walls, soliciting tips and standing lapdances. For this, Nick usually just called them 'milkmen,' for they were dressed – if barely – in white and promised – if vulgarly – to deliver cream. But the guy on stage had moves, and Nick found himself admiring the guy's rhythm as much as his physique, the way he used juts of his ass and crotch toward the crowd to mark predictable beats in the music, remarkably keeping pace with the fast song and smiling the whole time.

A bullhorn-loud voice announced that the dancer's name was 'Orlando' and that, for twenty dollars, he'd 'dance just for you.' Orlando then hopped down from the stage to work the room, and without missing a beat, another man in white briefs jumped up on the platform and began to gyrate and preen for the crowd.

"Okay if I leave you in the 'dairy case?'" Nick asked Ron, shouting over the music as it changed from upbeat Latin pop to heavy hip-hop, marking the change in the dancers' ethnicity and body type: Puerto Rican and peppy to black and endowed.

"What?"

"I'll be upstairs. Don't spend too much on the straight boys." Nick advised, knowing Ron was an easy mark for the milkmen, and that one had already squeezed Ron's nipple and ground a few bucks out of him. Nick took it as a compliment that the milkmen all-but ignored him, as though he obviously didn't need to pay for their hollow attentions, though he supposed they could just as easily think he was broke – or worse: cheap – or otherwise off-putting.

"Dairy case, milkmen, I get it now." Nick knew Ron was willing to admit he was slow and routinely blamed it on alcohol, whether he was drinking at the time or not. "Your very presence is *curdling.*" Ron added.

"Good one." Nick said, though Ron's delivery was clunky. *I'm the clever one,* he thought, *ha-ha.* "I guess you already made the joke about how my relationship with Andrew is past its expiration date. A *cheesy* joke at that." *Not* that *clever, I guess.* Nick wondered why he defended Andrew so much, given that things weren't working and he was waiting for the right time to officially break it off.

Nick climbed the outdoor stairs to the rest of the club and went in, past the line for the restrooms – mostly men comprising the queues for both the gents' and the ladies' – to the long bar in front of the low lounge furniture. Nick stood still for a while, feeling the crowd's eyes on him and sizing up the pack in return. The built and bald stud whose every breath strained the stitching on his tight tank was hot but familiar; the man was there every time Nick went to Twist, which Nick figured wasn't that often considering its location and lack of a cover. Nick always wanted to go for it with the guy but did the math and stayed away, since the guy was there every time he was, and with a different guy every time, not that Nick blamed anyone with him for enjoying at least a fun few hours with so much meat, but Nick wondered just how many such lucky SOBs there had been. Nick stayed away even more out of fear; just because the guy could have anyone and everyone – and seemingly had done just that – didn't mean he was interested in Nick.

Nick searched the crowd for anyone rivaling the baldie, who had settled into a white sofa and was already occupied with a slightly-built boy of a man for the night, not that that kept three similarly-built man-boys from hovering in case the boy bored him or refused to do what he asked. Nick was usually in control of things sexually but knew he, too, would surrender to the guy if given the chance. No one else at Twist interested Nick much, though he scanned the mass of men for anyone who could at least distract or amuse him for a while.

Nick made eye contact with guys at the bar and knew any of them would buy him a drink if he chatted with them for even a minute but didn't want to bother with what would feel like a lie, pretending he was interested in anyone there but the guy with the shaved head and muscles everywhere. Nick bought his own gin-and-tonic – "easy on the tonic," he'd ordered – and stepped toward the dance floor, half-hoping he seemed attractive enough that someone would ask him to dance, half-hoping no one would. After downing the drink, Nick stepped onto the low-ceilinged dance floor on his own and let the first drink of the night hit him.

Nick nodded and tranced out in time with the others dancing, knowing that, though they looked a lot like him, they were all wasted on alcohol or Ecstasy or worse and that he was more-or-less sober. He stayed for a few songs, absently wagging his body left and right to the beat, letting his head clear of all thoughts of Andrew, of the disappointingly bland current projects at his once-creative firm, of the guy with the shaved head who he wanted so much. Nick's presence on the dance floor drew out some of the better-looking guys in the club, dancing near-enough to Nick for him to know they wanted his attention but all seeming overwhelmingly similar: handsome-enough, well-groomed, gym-built.

Neither the music nor the men at Twist were holding Nick's interest much, and he left alone, not bothering to track down Ron and let him know he was leaving, trusting that Ron was having a fine time without him.

# # # # #

Mark and Rob left Club Madonna both hopped-up and disappointed. All the bars and clubs were still open, which wasn't surprising to Mark after midnight, though the fact that the dirtier-looking shops that sold cheap sunglasses and T-shirts printed with juvenile puns showed no signs of closing up for the night was.

"Souvenir to remember the trip by?" Mark asked Rob.

"I'm already trying to forget, dude," Rob answered, but went into a shop anyway. Mark spun the postcard racks and fingered the beach towels for a while, waiting on Rob to wade through the black-white-and-teal-logoed Marlins merchandise, eventually settling on a wooden bat Mark had no idea how Rob would get on the plane.

Chapter Three

Nick felt it before he heard it, and then heard it before he felt it.

He felt the presence of the two men behind him as he turned onto the alley behind the club. *You're paranoid,* he thought to himself. South Beach was always busy and loud, and though the block of alley that he walked as a shortcut on the hand-back familiar way home was usually deserted, the sounds of the occasional drunk pissing or couple fucking were nothing out of the ordinary. He kept walking without turning around.

Then he heard it. "Hey faggot," a male voice behind him called out, stressing 'fag' above the other syllables, getting Nick's attention. *"Fag-got"* the voice repeated. SoBe's large gay population made 'fag' more familiar as a term casually exchanged by two gay men inoffensively and inclusively referring to each other, like 'niggaz' used among black men; Nick hadn't heard the word said like he'd just heard it since high school.

Then Nick heard something else, the whoosh-whistle of air moving toward him fast, followed by a loud whap.

And finally he felt it, the gust of the fast-moving air on his face and the sharp sting of the baseball bat against his shoulder. The hit knocked Nick to the alley's asphalt, where the pain in his shoulder pulsed before radiating out. Nick turned his head to see his assailant and couldn't stifle a moan as the feeling from his shoulder reached up to his neck to grab him.

"He's moaning with pleasure. The *fag*-got likes a little action from the straight boys."

Nick saw the two men poised over him, one fanning the baseball bat in front of him, his curled right hand waving the bat into the open palm of his left, the other man posturing with his arms out like parentheses around his body, as though his chest and back were too broad for his arms to hang straight down. Their bodies were developed little different from those of the better-looking men in the club,

31

although rather than bared or hugged by tight shirts, their pumped chests hid behind looser T-shirts that skimmed pecs and pointy nipples but could have hidden perfect six-packs as easily as slight beer guts. *Tourists.* Nick thought. *Frat guys. Fucking hot frat guys.*

"Don't fucking look at us, *fag*-got." The one with the bat was doing all the talking, before swinging the bat from low to high, like a golf swing, smacking against the dimple of Nick's cheek like the dimples of a golf ball. *Fore,* Nick thought, chastising himself for cruising the guys who were assaulting him, and tried to picture their faces instead of their bodies as he struggled to touch his right cheek with his left hand. *Broken,* he thought. *Both men have dark hair. The one talking has dark eyes. The one with brackets for arms has lighter eyes. Blue? Green?* Nick doubted he would be able to describe his assailants later to the cops beyond their physiques and tried to inch his body away from them.

"You don't wanna play with the straight boys? What kind of *fag*-got are you, *fag*-got?" Nick was paying attention to the voice now, hoping to notice some identifiable accent or stutter, but heard instead just the blurring liaison of the 'f' from 'kind of' into 'faggot' with its stressed, taunting first syllable. "Like the *fag*-got'd really try to get away from a couple of studs like us."

Not normally, no, Nick admitted to himself. He felt the air whir and whiz onto him as the bat came down hard against his ribcage. All he was now was pain, shooting to his chest and back.

Nick cowered and curled into the fetal position, all of his right side exposed but his left protected, as the blows from the bat struck and broke his bent leg above and below the knee, his arm above and below the elbow as he hugged himself, trying to comfort himself, willing the pain – and his attackers – to stop, to go away. Each blow of the bat yielded a hard thud on the surface of Nick's body and a softened snap deeper inside him.

The pain was unbearable, but Nick had to get another look at his attackers, identify them beyond 'the man with the bat' – *'Batman'* – and 'Bracket Arms.' He could hear his bones resisting the turn of his neck, feel every part of his body tell him to stop.

"It's like a drug, dude. Take a hit." Though the man with the bat was much further away than the other, Nick could make him out better, seeing him toss the bat from his swinging arm to the other and punch the air with his newly free hand as he said 'take a hit,' signaling his friend to do just that. To Nick.

The strong, silent one knelt down and swung his fist against Nick's right eye. The ring – a gold class ring with an oval blue stone – on his hand tore into Nick's skin, and Nick fought to keep his eye open as blood drained into it.

"Feels good, right?" Batman asked his partner-in-crime, then asked Nick, "Like having him close to you, eh?" Strong-and-silent Bracket Arms wasn't speaking for himself; the only voice was from Batman, still standing over him. "While you're down there, man..."

The light eyes of the man kneeling over him were blue, Nick noted, before the man's face turned to look at his friend with the bat, see what he wanted.

"...take down the *fag*-got's pants."

Nick suddenly remembered his choice of underwear for the night and regretted it.

Bracket-Armed Blue Eyes flinched away from Nick as Nick curled away from him. Nick could feel hands fumbling with his pants' button and zipper, his ass revealed and cold against pavement and cool night air.

"*Fag*-gots's got his fuck-me panties on for us, eh?" The man's voice shifted from tease to bark. "Black and see-thru. Pull 'em down."

Mark's ass tensed, but Blue Eyes did nothing.

"C'mon, you know it's what he wants. And what the *fag*-got wants, the *fag*-got gets."

Nick felt his underwear pulled off him without feeling Blue Eyes' fingers so much as graze him, as though the man were scared to touch him if he weren't hitting hard.

The guy with the bat handed something to his friend, who seemed to know what to do with it. He certainly didn't ask what his friend meant.

Nick struggled for a look at the object in Blue Eyes' hand. Amber-brown, half-conical, half-cylindrical, shiny, translucent: a beer bottle.

"Give it to him. Give the *fag*-got what he wants."

Nick tried to say 'no' but only grunted. He tried to scream but only breathed out hard. Nick cringed as the blue-eyed man inserted the beer bottle, conical-end first, into his ass. Every movement he had was a wince now, a flinch. Every feeling he had was pain, humiliation.

The guy with the baseball bat stomped the bottle further into Nick. Then he swung the bat, the golf swing action again, into it, breaking the bottle off so it stayed inside Nick with nothing but jagged shards poking out and into Nick. Satisfied, the guy tossed the baseball bat aside.

Nick was crying now, tears mixing with blood and running out, tinted red against his purpling bruised face.

"Oh, the *fag*-got's crying now. Sad it's a bottle and not my dick, eh? You want this dick? You wanna see this dick? Here, let me take it out for you." When the guy wasn't talking, the alleyway grew quiet enough for Nick to hear the teeth of the guy's zipper pull apart, the rustle of denim, the guy's heavy breathing and his own. When the sounds ended, when he heard just his own breath, Nick figured the guy had it out. "Traded one baseball bat for another, eh, *fag*-got?" The man shifted his weight, spread his legs a little, posturing. "Look at it. I know you're dying to. Look at this dick. Show me how much you want it."

Nick didn't want to look, but wondered if the punishment for resisting and not looking was worse than that for doing what he was told. It was dark, and the man didn't trim his pubic hair, but there in the nest of shadows and wiry bush was his soft penis. Nick looked up into the man's face and tried to focus on details. The dark eyes he noted before were warm chocolate – the night sky and the blood in his eye would have obscured and greyed-out a less-rich brown hue. There was a slight cleft in his chin. A thin stripe of skin in his otherwise thick eyebrow. No scar connected to it, the man must have shaved it in.

"Fuckin' *fag*-got's lookin' at my face." Nick noted the g's falling away from the man's speech as the frat guy slipped from cocky college boy into barking brute. "I'll give you something to see," the man said, as a stream of yellow urine curved from his soft penis onto Nick's eyes.

Nick closed his eyes against the piss that hit him.

"Keep 'em open." The man ordered without stopping the flow of urine. "Open your mouth too, *fag*-got."

Nick didn't know why his mind flashed to the image of a woman applying mascara, opening her mouth to keep her eyes wide open, the connection between jaw and eyelids.

Nick obliged, and though the man might have been aiming for Nick's mouth, and plenty of piss found its way there, urine covered Nick's face. Nick breathed it in, wet and pungent.

"Your turn," the voice barked, not at Nick but at his friend.

"Fuck yeah, take this, you faggot." Strong-and-Silent's only words were tentative, like he was trying on his friend's brash persona like a borrowed shirt: seven deadly syllables as a hesitant near-whisper. He unbuttoned and unzipped and took out his cock. The arc of piss he released shot high in the air before raining down onto Nick's fetal-prone body: the guy's penis was erect.

So was Nick's, a fact that devastated him, his body betraying him like that. *Faggot,* he thought to himself just before consciousness left him. *Fag*-got.

Chapter Four

Beep.

Beep.

Nick tried to turn his head but couldn't, trying to turn off what he thought was his alarm clock. He couldn't move his body enough to see or reach where the sound was coming from. *Not my alarm clock,* he realized. Nick woke to the sound of the machine monitoring his every heartbeat.

Beep.

Not my own bed, with its upholstered headboard and thousand-thread count. Nick felt the metal support braces of his hospital bed through its thin mattress, the sheets feeling more like paper than cloth.

Beep.

Not my own foot, leg, hip, side, arm, hand. All the appendages on his right side were replaced by puffed-up cloud-white versions twice his size. *Plaster casts,* Nick understood.

Beep.

It hadn't been a dream.

The hospital room was proof to a designer like Nick that blue-green was an easy color to get wrong. Greyed-down and neutralized, the hue could achieve a silvery sage color that would be soothing to someone waking up in an unfamiliar hospital room, even under the harsh fluorescents overhead. It would be serene and evocative of the ocean. Instead, the color on the walls was intense and shrill, an aqua that Nick, having never been in a hospital before, had still rightly always called 'institutional.'

A window to his left let in too much of the intense Miami sun, though he couldn't tell if there was much of a view. A curtain to his right warned him that he wasn't alone, that this was a shared room. *Great,* Nick thought, *I haven't had a roommate since college.*

Suddenly, the curtain moved, pulling toward him and widening the expanse of shrill institutional blue-green paint on the long wall opposite him. The curtain's movement had startled Nick, but his reflex recoil was made impossible by so much bandaging and who-knew-what prescription painkillers.

Nick shuddered as though it were all happening again, only worse.

"You're up," a voice Nick didn't recognize said, though from its nasal musicality and lacking masculinity he assumed *gay male nurse.* It didn't usually bother Nick to see – or hear – gay men who were more effeminate than he was, but right now Nick was wondering why *he* got gay-bashed with *this guy* walking around, and he hated himself for the thought. "I'll get the doctor." The voice left before Nick could get a look.

Or perhaps before the nurse could, Nick reasoned, figuring he probably wasn't much to look at right now. *Things couldn't be all that bad,* Nick thought, *if my biggest worry is that I'm not getting cruised in a hospital. Who would look good under these fluorescents anyway?*

Beep.

The beeping sound had sped up a little, filling the room intermittently without leaving such a long silence in between. Nick had gotten used to the sound and didn't notice its tone so much anymore, only its rhythm, its pacing. *My pace,* he thought, feeling a connection to the machine.

"Mr. Akram"

"Nick," Nick tried to correct the formality but, bandaged and doped-up, his name came out more like the strained "neck" he had.

"Nick. I'm Dr. Monroe."

Shit. Dr. Monroe was cute. There was no way the nurse would be checking me out with him around. "Nice to meet you, I'd get up and shake your hand, but..." Nick smiled at the good-and-good-looking doctor and thought, *I'm flirting. Shit.* Then he asked what he was wondering: "How do I look?"

"Why don't I just review your injuries for you, and we'll leave how it looks out of it for a while."

That bad.

"You should heal fine, and I expect a full recovery."

That's better. Not great, but better.

Dr. Monroe then listed nearly every bone on the right side of Nick's body, and followed each impressive pronunciation with the word 'broken.'

"Oh God." Nick had meant to merely think that, not say it aloud. "What *isn't* broken?" Nick followed up.

"Basically, everything on your left side. You have some minor scrapes and bruises there, but otherwise everything's fine. Beer bottle we removed left you with fairly significant rectal bleeding..."

Nick was surprised at how breezily the doctor mentioned this and moved on, as though rectal bleeding were nothing uncommon for a gay man like Nick. Nick couldn't tell if he was being judged or sympathized with, and wondered – wishfully, he admitted to himself – if his good-looking doctor might be gay.

"And a broken coccyx, which is it for right down the middle. Any of these blows to the center of your body – spine, neck – could have killed you. You'll be in casts for a while, then rehab while we re-train your body to stand and walk."

A bit lopsided. "What about my face?" Nick didn't ask out of vanity. He always figured his body was better than his face; he'd put in effort at the gym toward making that the case, and worried what being unable to workout for a while would do to the body he'd worked so hard on. Nick wondered if he'd bother with his body anymore if his face were off-balance, destroyed altogether.

"Well, Mr. –"

"Nick. You removed a beer bottle from my ass; I think a first name basis is in order." *Shit.* Nick knew he always got shy or bitchy when he liked someone. *Shy would have been an improvement,* he thought. Trying to save it, he asked, "Am I going to be asymmetrical there, too?" Nick paused, "And are we talking Katie Holmes or Lyle Lovett?"

"Katie Holmes?"

"You never noticed she talks out of whatever side of her face is facing the camera? It's disturbing."

The doctor smiled, "Actually, there was a plastic surgeon in-hospital when you were brought in. Your zygoma – sorry, that's 'malar bone' or just 'cheekbone' to anyone without 'M.D.' after their name – was broken, and your nose, and there were significant cuts and bruising to the right side of your face, but in a couple of weeks, it'll be less noticeable. The fat lip should pass in a few days."

"So there's no awkward marriage to Tom Cruise in my future."

"It'd be no more awkward than his marriages so far."

Maybe the good-and-good-looking doctor was gay, Nick thought hopefully.

"There's a police officer here to ask you a few questions about the incident. You should know that we performed a standard S.A. – sexual assault – kit when you first arrived."

"He didn't rape me." Nick paused, corrected himself, *"They* didn't rape me."

The doctor's otherwise clinical voice turned soft and sympathetic. "It's called 'object rape,' and yes, you were. I can send the officer away if it's too soon or –"

"It's fine."

"And, I can go or, if you want –"

"Stay." Nick tried to shake his head, but it wouldn't budge, "I mean please. Please stay."

"Very well." Nick could hear the doctor's smile but couldn't see it, like sharing an amusing anecdote with a friend over the phone. *I should call Ron,* Nick thought, then realized that thinking to call Ron before Andrew meant that Andrew meant nothing to him.

The officer was uniformed – *stifling in the Miami heat,* Nick guessed – and all-business. He seemed to have enough information to only ask questions.

"Did you get a good look at your attacker?"

"No," Nick answered.

"There was more than one," the doctor chimed in.

"Doctor Monroe?" the officer asked.

"You said 'they' earlier. *'They* didn't rape me,'" the doctor paused, "and *they* did."

"Just with a bottle," Nick added, as though that made what had happened to him somehow better, okay even.

"How many were there? Did you get a good look at them?" The officer didn't seem to realize he was repeating himself, but Nick did, and figured the doctor did, too.

"Two. Couple of frat guys."

"What does that mean?"

Of course the officer wasn't fluent in hot-male types, Nick thought. "White guys." It suddenly dawned on Nick that he was talking to a black officer. *Oops,* he thought, then corrected himself. "Caucasian. Male, early twenties, *built."* Nick stressed the last word without meaning to. "Liked calling me 'faggot.'" *Fag-got,* Nick recalled, grimacing at the memory but apparently on enough morphine to feel the memory more than pain.

"'Built' meaning muscular?" the doctor asked, helping things along.

"Yeah, jocks." *'Jocks' was a tough word to say with your face half-bandaged,* Nick thought, resolving to make a conscious effort to choose words that didn't make him sound like a bad actor playing at mentally challenged.

"Even with the UM guys hitting the clubs on the weekends, we don't get a lot of hate crimes reported in South Beach." The officer was writing in a small notebook while he was talking, not looking up at the doctor or Nick. "It's likely they were from out of town."

The officer was right, Nick knew, and most of the University of Miami football team was pretty well-behaved in South Beach, glad that the presence of so many gay men made the local women comfortable in degrees of undress that would be unreasonable elsewhere. Nick added details as he remembered them. "One did all the talking. Educated-sounding voice, but he got off on the power. He had brown hair and eyes."

"Did you make contact with them, fight them off at all?"

The doctor answered for Nick. "We scraped under his nails for trace. There was a lot of dried blood there but not much else. We swabbed his wounds – everywhere – for foreign DNA. One or both of his attackers urinated on him, so there are samples of that as well. Your lab should have them by know, and what was left of the bottle, for prints."

The use of the term 'we' made Nick uncomfortable, as though a dozen strangers had poked and prodded him, as though this handsome doctor didn't want to do it himself.

More writing from the officer, seemingly unable to look at Nick. Nick again wondered what he looked like now as he recalled the appearances of his attackers.

"The other one also had brown hair but blue eyes. Didn't say much. Only hit me when the other guy told him to. He was the one who used the bottle on me. And only after the other one told him to do that, too."

"Like I said, it's very likely that these guys were from out of town." The officer looked up, finally, though he spoke more to the doctor than to Nick, confirming Nick's fears that his current appearance was tough to stomach. "I'll send a sketch artist out to see if you can work up possible faces. We'll run the bottle for prints, hopefully they're in the system." Nick noticed the officer said 'hopefully' without much optimism in his voice. "But without more to go on, I gotta tell you, it's unlikely that we'll catch these guys."

"What more can I do to help you get them?" Nick asked, the question as muffled by bandages as by the revelation that it was doubtful he'd know any justice, any peace.

"There's not a lot you can do, I'm sorry to say," the officer offered. Nick didn't doubt his sincerity but still wasn't comforted.

Doctor Monroe seemed a bit surprised that Nick's prospect for a day in court that even then could go either way was so much lower than his potential for recovery from such a brutal attack. "So, short of one or both of them finding Jesus and coming in to confess –"

The doctor found himself interrupted by Nick's my-sense-of-humor-is-my-coping-mechanism laughter. "I think when you find Jesus in Miami, Doctor, you have to pronounce his name 'Hey-Zeus.'"

# # # # #

Healed, Nick found his way back to the club. He was wearing the same outfit, the same sheer underwear. He saw his attackers at the bar.

They, too, were in the same clothes they had worn before, the night they followed him into the alley. Tonight, he saw them differently. Casually hot, without trying too hard, the way so many of the men at a gay club do. Human.

It bothered Nick to view men so violent as human, their actions as understandable, as potentially understood and forgiven.

Still, he couldn't stop looking at them, despite the men on display who were closer to him and obviously interested in him: the tight-bodied Louganis lookalike who gyrated against him wearing nothing but a Speedo, the tight-pantsed boyish Boitano whose every elegant move was betrayed by an ass that stuck up and out wantonly, the scruffy doctor-type still in his hospital scrubs and Clark Kent glasses, not trying very hard and looking cuter for it. Nick noticed the three men and admired them, but his focus was on the boys at the bar.

And finally, their focus found him, too. They smiled and even shared a laugh upon seeing Nick, as though they knew him, but when they faced him, their faces were menacing.

Menacing and sexy.

Nick nodded to them, and one nodded back. The other raised his beer toward Nick, an across-the-bar salute.

The amber beer bottle in the frat guy's hand made Nick both nervous and aroused.

Nick nodded toward the door and walked out, knowing they would follow him.

They did. He felt them behind him, getting closer, within reach. Nick fidgeted with his cell phone, as nervously as purposefully.

"Hey Faggot," he heard. "Fag-got."

Nick spun around, aimed his phone at the men, and snapped their photo before the men began beating him down.

Nick went through the motions of protecting himself unconsciously, clutching the camera-phone in his left hand as he went down, tucking it under him and coiled himself around it, like a child with a favorite doll or blankie, all of the value in life housed in something so small and inanimate and precious to him.

The frat guys, too, were revved-up and reenacting their abuse, slamming into Nick with the baseball bat, pulling his pants down and off, inserting the beer bottle, pissing on him.

When Nick thought they were through, the quiet one who had inserted the beer bottle and spoke in little more than a whisper leaned back down to Nick. "One last thing," he breathed out, reaching under Nick's body before kissing Nick on the cheek. Nick looked into the man's blue eyes as he groped under Nick and pulled away.

"Hey-batter-batter," the man whispered to his forty-feet-away friend, his near-silent voice getting his attention as though he had called out for him by name.

"Swing," he whispered, and pitched Nick's cell phone to the other man, who connected with the phone, shattering it along with Nick's hopes for justice.

"And the crowd goes wild," the man whispered to Nick before walking away, eyeing Nick's exposed ass and cupping his own cock.

# # # # #

Beep.

Beep.

It had been a dream, Nick realized, though no relief accompanied this realization. He was still in the hospital, still swathed in papery sheets and plaster casts.

And still erect.

Chapter Five

Back in their hotel room, Rob had gone right to sleep, though his snoring was not what was keeping Mark up in the next bed, staring at the blue-banded coffer in the ceiling. Mark couldn't lay still. He couldn't even hold just his head motionless, and everything he saw as he surveyed the room was slightly blurred. The room itself was small and sparsely decorated, a relief from the loud patterns and pineapple mosaics of the public spaces of the hotel. The walls and bed linen were off-white, save for the rectangular navy pillow that had been placed on the center of each bed when they'd checked in; those pillows were now on the floor with last night's clothes. The drapes hung in two layers: opaque royal blue over standard hotel white sheer. He and Rob hadn't pulled those drapes shut when they'd returned to the room, so when the sun had come up, Mark gave up on his fight to sleep and took a shower.

The water pressure at the hotel was better than at Mark's parent's house, or at the fraternity house, or at the dorms where Mark had showered more than a few mornings after hooking up, so Mark stayed in a long time, using half the vial of hotel shampoo on his half-inch-long-hair and soaping up his body three times, everywhere. He was shaking hard, and dropped the shampoo once and the soap twice. There was no sensuality to his shaky caress of himself, even when he soaped up his dick, despite the unstoppably jerky motions of his hand there and how similar they were to jerking-off. Mark turned off the water and discovered he was still soapy in the places where his body hair was densest, turned the water back on and rinsed his underarms and cock again. He toweled off, raked his fingers through his wet hair, the usually straight-back motion a zigzag with his uncontrollable hands, wrapped the towel around his waist, and opened the bathroom door to let some of the steam out to clear the mirror.

Rob was still snoring.

Mark pulled on jeans and a white T and pocketed his cell phone. He grabbed his wallet, checked to see that his hotel keycard was

47

still tucked into the slot between his license and ATM card, and was careful to shut the door quietly behind him.

Mark went down the elevator to the lobby, tripping over the change from the elevator cab's carpet to the lobby's sand-beige marble. He left the hotel to walk the street.

South Beach looked completely different to him this morning; Mark thought the expression 'night and day' could have been coined by the city's first visitor. The few people up and walking about looked confused to be doing just that. Like Mark, they were without sunglasses and squinted in the bright sun reflecting off plate glass storefronts and quartz-white sidewalks. Mark saw a girl coming at him dressed in a gold sequined mini dress carrying her high heeled sandals by their thin straps as she walked barefoot across the hot street. Mark caught her eye as she passed him. She shrugged at him and smiled, looking both self-conscious and smugly satisfied.

Most of the stores were closed, but Mark found a small *bodega* and went in, the bells above the front door barely audible over the loud Spanish ballad playing for the benefit of the shop's two customers, neither of whom looked up from their newspapers at Mark. Mark ordered a coffee.

"*Café Cubano?*" the man behind the counter asked Mark. Mark looked at the man blankly. "Cuban coffee?" he asked, this time rolling his eyes.

Mark nodded. He'd heard of Columbian coffee – Juan Valdez and a donkey in cheesy television ads – and didn't know if coffee from Cuba was different or better or how so. To Mark, coffee was coffee, and though he ordered it, needed it, he didn't like it much to begin with.

The man behind the counter – who looked to Mark like the actor who had played Juan Valdez in those TV spots, short and full-cheeked with black eyes and a moustache – handed over the smallest Styrofoam cup Mark had ever seen. Mark figured it was like espresso, hot and strong, and guessed it was good enough.

Mark tried to steady his hand but couldn't. He hadn't realized how much he'd been shaking all night, and after splashing the hot coffee all over his fingers and the floor below him, Mark looked at the tiny cup in his hand like a gun that had accidentally gone off.

"Mira," Juan Valdez said to Mark, trying to hand him a half-inch stack of paper napkins.

Mark wordlessly accepted the napkins and dabbed at his hand. He ignored the floor. Embarrassed, Mark turned to leave.

"Usually the gringos are jittery *after* they drink my coffee," the man behind the counter muttered over the bells that jingled at Mark's exit, his accent tripping on 'usually' and 'jittery' but pronouncing 'gringos' perfectly, a dismissive reflex.

Mark was back to the sidewalk, squinting in the sun. Most of the cars on the street were taxis, half searching for someone to take home from last night's wild time, half already full with such fares. The occasional black-and-white police car salt-and-peppered the streets, with the rest of the cars as brightly-colored as the Italian exotics that had lined Washington Avenue last night but were instead inexpensive American rentals. It had bothered Mark last night that the outrageous and audacious cars, for all their bulging engine covers and swooping spoilers, never got over fifteen miles per hour on the crowded streets of South Beach. They were all flash, like the unbuttoned shirts of the over-tanned men and ease with which they paid the clubs' exorbitant cover charges, their capacity for speed never needed, never realized. *The class valedictorian flipping burgers or stripping after graduation,* Mark thought: *a thoroughbred pulling a wagon. A waste.* The scene on the street was so different this morning. Only the rentals slowed for yellow traffic lights, with cops routinely following cabs through the red ones but not bothering to pull them over and cite the driver. The occasional horn blast was just as likely to express frustration at the rental in front of a taxi for yielding to a yellow as to startle that driver's eyes up from the map or off the sights and back onto the road ahead the instant red turned to green.

Otherwise, it was quiet, quite a contrast from the bustle of the night before.

Mark turned back to Ocean Drive and stepped off the side of the street lined with boutique hotels to walk through Lummus Park to the sand. At night, the multicolor Deco hotels and boutiques won the battle of nature-versus-neon, but by day, there was no contest for Mark, who had never seen the ocean before this trip. He kicked off his flip-flops and walked toward the water, carrying his sandals the way the woman crossing the street had held her heels, the sand already hot underfoot.

Mark stared hard at the ocean, the sunlight that grazed its surface brightly searing his eyes as he thought about last night, the bat in Rob's hands, the man he'd sodomized with a bottle. The man had done nothing wrong, Mark thought, it was just a wrong-place-wrong-time thing, catching Rob at a moment when his temper and testosterone had flared. Mark looked down at the sand in front of him and vomited.

He walked further, into the water, the waves lapping at his feet, his ankles, soaking his jeans to the knee as he ventured in further and deeper, vainly hoping Macbeth's hopes: to wash off what he'd done. But it would forever stain him, he knew, and he headed out of the rising surf into the crumbling wet sand, then to the dry sand that clung to him like a one-night stand in the morning – irritating and everywhere he didn't want it – then threaded his toes through the grass of the park.

A street musician was setting up there, fanning out thin jewel cases of his amateurishly recorded CDs and turning an oversized stereo up to full blast to play his wares. It was a danced-up, energized mix of a song Mark knew, its lyrics a somber and sad chiaroscuro with the rapid beat and elevated key, the contrast like the optimism of the ocean against Mark's doomed mood, how low he felt despite the high energy of South Beach.

Mark grabbed another coffee at the Starbuck's a block from the hotel. The person behind the counter looked incredulous that Mark wanted just a coffee, not something with an ersatz European name of three words that all ended in vowels and too many shots of too-sweet flavored syrup. Mark was incredulous in return, at the fact that an order for plain coffee seemed to take longer than the impossibly complicated – in name and composition – drinks for those in line after him. But his coffee was produced eventually, in a normal-sized cup, and Mark sat in a worn purple velvet chair and looked out past the park to the water as he drank it, trying to keep his hand steady when he brought the cup to his mouth.

Mark's mind raced with remorse and the risk of arrest. He and Rob were leaving town today, on a flight booked a month ago, and

Mark didn't know if that would make them look guiltier-still if this ever caught up to them. Not that they weren't both guilty, Mark knew.

When Mark came back to the room, Rob hadn't showered or packed, but was awake, flipping channels at heartbeat-speed. *Bum-bum* fitness product infomercial. *Bum-bum* maybe-reality-maybe-scripted MTV show. *Bum-bum* hotel channel focusing on Loews amenities and Miami tourist spots.

"We gotta check out in fifteen-twenty." Mark said to Rob. "Grab lunch, see the rest of town before we get on the plane."

Remote control still in hand, Rob wordlessly got out of bed and passed Mark on his way to the bathroom. Mark didn't think Rob was purposely avoiding eye contact, but he didn't meet his stare, either.

# # # # #

"You know we can slip a little caffeine into your IV if you're used to coffee or Red Bull to get you going." Groggy as he was, Nick recognized the doctor's voice and perked up immediately.

"I lived half my life checking every drink I've ever been handed, afraid some guy would slip me something and I'd end up in a hospital for taking it – now you're telling me I can get slipped something while I'm actually *in* the hospital?" Nick was glad that his behavior around the doctor had gone from bitchy and blunt to more charming and breezy, though he was sure the doctor had him figured out, the way a boy at the schoolyard would sooner kick a girl in the shins at recess than tell her he had a crush.

The doctor laughed good-naturedly. "I wasn't offering anything stronger than caffeine to get you high. Although if you only knew what kinds of painkillers you were on right now, you'd have checked in a long time ago."

"I'm not that kind of partier."

"I ran your bloodwork; you didn't need to tell me that, I already knew. Besides, the kind of shape you're in, it's clear you keep an eye on what goes into your body."

"It's a temple," Nick sing-songed cheerily.

"You're Jewish?"

Nick wondered if he should joke about the doctor checking to see that he was circumcised but thought better of it. *Maybe he checked already,* Nick thought devilishly. "Have I been complaining that much around here?"

The doctor smirked. "Hardly. Everyone here loves having you around, though you're healing nicely and we're going to be able to release you sooner than we thought."

Nick hoped Dr. Monroe's 'everyone' included the doctor himself. "I promise to write."

"That's a lost art: letter-writing. I haven't written anything but prescriptions in I-don't-know-how-long..." the doctor's voice trailed off with the tangent.

"Maybe you just haven't had anyone to write to," Nick said.

"Maybe," the doctor said.

Nick still didn't know if the guy was flirting, only that he was himself, and not as successfully as he'd wanted. Nick watched the cute doctor with his scruffy I-started-my-rounds-yesterday growth of beard and hair that was curiously matted in some places and spiked in others turn and walk out of sight, checking out his ass through his shapeless scrubs as he went.

# # # # #

Rob and Mark had gotten lost cutting through downtown trying to find Coral Gables and the airport, ending up in downtown and getting a look at a Miami that didn't resemble postcards or television. Tall buildings stretched to the sky, allowing no sun to the street for blocks at a time. The density of tall buildings was broken up by construction, the sunlight brightest there, blinding Mark as he navigated the carved-up roads in an unfamiliar rental car. They'd found Bayside and stopped, paid ten dollars just to park and get out of the car, try to get their bearings, catch their breath and a few last rays.

It was clear once they'd gotten out of the car that they were next to the causeway that could take them across Biscayne Bay, back to where they'd started the day, as the slender stacks of condos and growing neon glow of South Beach were visible from Bayside even at midday.

"Never again, dude," Rob said.

"What?" Mark had heard Rob fine but didn't know exactly what he meant. There was so much that Rob could never want again. He could never want to go back to South Beach, never want to get back in the car with Mark and his failing navigational ability, never again want to attack a stranger in the street.

"Never going back there."

"Nothing there for us," Mark added.

"Nothing there but *fag*-gots."

Mark swallowed hard at Rob's words. Bayside held little interest for them, and they walked about in near-silence, taking in instead the music blaring from the restaurants there, the décor as loud and tacky as the by-the-door-in-large-font proclamations that eighteen-percent gratuity was added to any order, the tourist shops that sold the same cheap merchandise they'd passed up in South Beach, the displays of exotic birds or domesticated snakes you could have your picture taken with for ten dollars. They stopped for lunch at the Hooters upstairs, where Mark ordered a Coke and Rob told the waitress no, that they'd each have a Mai Tai.

"I'm sorry, we're out of pineapple juice," the waitress said, bringing her elbows together in front of her chest, increasing her cleavage by way of apology.

"International-symbol-for-welcome-and-hospitality my ass," Rob said to the waitress as much as Mark, straining to scope out the girl's ass in her Hooters-uniform-orange short-shorts.

"How about margaritas?"

"Sure," Rob said, resigned.

"Frozen or on the rocks?"

"Whatever."

"*Lo que sea.*" To Mark, the waitress looked and sounded a bit like Marta. "Salt?" the waitress asked Rob more than Mark, though Mark answered with a nod.

"Low–kuh–say–uh," Rob repeated, unknowingly discouraging the waitress from continuing to flirt. Mark wondered why the waitress bothered to work them so hard if a set gratuity would be added to their tab anyway.

An order of buffalo wings, two burgers and fries, and four margaritas later, Rob and Mark left Bayside with the waitress's 'can't-miss-it' directions to the airport.

Mark and Rob didn't talk much for most of the day, and Mark realized any meaningful conversation would be up to him. He gave up hope for this and tried for small talk on the plane, telling Rob about his morning walk, and the girl in the gold dress who'd walked by him on the street.

"Walk of shame," Rob said. "Probably had her panties in her purse. Fuckin' Miami. Don't see anything like that back home, right dude?"

Mark knew they didn't see men like the one they'd beaten down in the alley back home either, and realized Rob wasn't going to talk about what they'd done anytime soon, if ever, unless maybe he was drunk and bragging to his buddies. *Their buddies,* Mark reminded himself. Mark knew that, around their friends, he'd better keep his mouth shut and his head down, at least for a while, and keep his thoughts – like he always had – to himself. The man in the alley was just like the girl in the street, some foreign and freak-show-strange exhibit they'd never imagined back home: inhuman. They were just freaks to be knocked at, to knock down. Mark was all-but certain Rob was never going to talk about attacking that man – admit it, even – but less certain that Rob even thought it was wrong.

"Right," Mark said, surrendering his guilt to an in-flight Mai Tai: the first of their trip and the last thing he wanted.

# # # # #

54

Nick was obsessed with his X-rays. The doctor had an orderly wheel in a light box so he could show Nick exactly what had happened to him, what was going on under all that plaster he was wearing like armor against an attack. *Too late,* Nick thought.

"This is the lower half of your left leg, below the knee," the doctor started. "You can see where both the tibia and fibula were broken, but the break in each was clean, like they were everywhere, so there was no need for any grafting. It was like you were hit in one spot one time and then your attacker moved on, not striking the same place twice."

"Like lightning."

"Exactly."

Nick nodded, though 'tibia' and 'fibula' meant nothing to him. He did appreciate that the X-ray didn't show any skin or muscle; he had always thought his calves were too skinny.

"Here, above the knee, you can see where the femur was just cracked. I've seen this bone get pulverized by repeated blows. You were lucky, it looks like they only hit you there..."

Nick felt the doctor catch himself; no one attacked in this manner was 'lucky.' "It's okay," Nick said, and when the doctor smiled at him, Nick thought *I* do *feel lucky, to have such a cute doctor.* Then more wistfully, Nick thought maybe all this happened for a reason. It was Nick's turn to catch himself, stop mooning over Dr. Monroe, return his focus to the X-rays and explanation of what happened to him.

"Notice the black triangle in the bone, the clean break, the pointy tips of bone jutting out from where they should be. When a bone breaks, the tips of the fracture point like two little arrows in the direction the blow came from, like accusatory fingers indicating blame."

"You heard the officer, they won't catch them."

"But your body knew to point at your attackers. To shame them, at least," the doctor let his words hang for a while before swapping the X-rays on the box. "You can see the same thing here, in your upper arm, the humerus –"

"Excuse me?"

"Humerus."

"What happened to me wasn't funny," Nick teased, hoping that flirtatiousness and an ability to take things lightly were desirable qualities to Doctor Monroe.

"It's Latin. Do you speak Latin?"

"Pig."

"Jerk."

"No, Pig Lat–" Nick smiled so wide it hurt. "Oh I get it, you're playing with me."

"Who's humorous now?"

"That's mine, up on the box," Nick was quick to retort.

"Right. It's broken clean, too."

Now Nick wished the picture on display *did* show his flesh and muscle; he liked his biceps a lot and wondered if the doctor might, too. Nick flexed as a reflex just thinking about his biceps; his left one tensed and bulged fine, but the plaster around his right wouldn't allow the proud swelling.

"In your forearm, only the radius is broken. You must have used your arm to shield your face for some of the attack. Your ulna was intact."

"Oh good, I was so worried about my ulna," Nick said sarcastically.

It was the doctor's turn to smile. "I think I have an Aunt Ulna on my mother's side."

Nick laughed.

"And speaking of sides," the doctor started saying, while replacing X-rays, arm for torso, "two true ribs –"

"Say that five times fast."

The doctor smiled. "That-that-that-that-that. Two of your true ribs – those that wrap the sides of your body, for those who aren't so good at Latin..."

"Oink."

"Ha," the doctor deadpanned before losing control and actually laughing. "Cracked. We had to wrap your entire chest, but the extent of the damage is localized right there. I hope you don't think my bedside manner is like this with all my patients."

"I was going to ask if the hospital had some sort of 'comment card' I could fill out with my complaints." *My one complaint: 'bedside manner' means you're not in here with me,* Nick thought.

"We did establish before that you were a letter-writer."

Nick pictured a letter in his mind:

Dear Dr. Monroe,

I want you.

XOXO, Nick

"The wrapping," the doctor returned to task, "extends to the iliac crest." The doctor shuffled X-rays again, so Nick was looking at his hip bone, wondering, *where's my dick in this picture?* "We reset the crest to connect back with the rest of your pelvis. You clearly protected yourself there, too. Masculine response, protect the goods," the doctor cupped his crotch as he spoke, and Nick got hard immediately. "My guess would be you rolled over."

And exposed my ass to get bottle-raped, Nick thought, *though it was probably better than what could have happened in front there.*

Nick looked at the X-rays for some time and smiled, though it wasn't the images of the bones that interested him. Though they read as glowing and white when placed on the light box, on the X-ray film, Nick knew they were clear, transparent, almost not there. This made the focus of the X-ray, for Nick, not the bone but the black that surrounded it, engulfed it. On the film, the bones looked as though they were protected by so much black, steeling them against the assault that had occurred, allowing him now to heal.

Nick reminded himself to ask to take the X-rays with him when he was released, planning to buy his own light box and display them in his home like art, to make something beautiful from so much pain.

"And that's pretty much all the damage that's still healing. You'll be in the casts for another eight-to-twelve weeks; some may come off before then, depending on how you heal. Most of the cuts and scrapes were fairly minor, all things considered. Swelling's already gone down significantly. Cut-wise, nothing in your face should scar, and the rest will just give you a good story to tell."

"All things considered, Doctor Monroe, I'll likely make up another story."

"Just write me into it, okay?" the doctor tossed over his shoulder on his way out.

# # # # #

Back home, Mark and Rob cleaned up at the frat house and went straight to the strip joint. There was alcohol flowing, willing girls dancing like it meant something to them, and a crowd that seemed like it belonged there.

"There's no place like home, dude," Rob said.

Mark thought a Judy Garland reference was a bit odd from a gay basher. *A* fellow *gay basher,* Mark corrected himself.

Things they had taken for granted were suddenly appreciated. Their draft beers were five dollars for the pair, with tip. The dancers onstage were focused, enjoying themselves and the response they elicited from the crowd. The music was familiar from current radio rotation or classic rock status, not off-putting for being hipper than Mark or foreign to him in its style or language. The girls dancing wore lingerie recognizable to Mark as being from the Victoria's Secret catalogue, and most wore street shoes with scuffed soles and modest heels.

"Ready for the test tomorrow?" Mark hadn't recognized the voice of the girl he knew from chemistry class, and also hadn't remembered that Dr. O'Malley had scheduled a test for the first day back from spring break. Mark had intended to cram on the plane, but couldn't focus on anything but the memory of what he and Rob had done to the man in the alley.

"I forgot all about it," Mark said, more or less the truth.

"Must have been a hell of a time in Miami, then. Just be sure that all play and no work didn't make Mark a dumb boy. All I've done for a week is study for that test."

"You weren't here at the club, too?"

"I was, yeah. Nights. Work, go home, study all day, work, go home, study..."

"If you were here every night, I'd have had a better time if I'd stayed in town," Mark said what he felt, then realized how much it sounded like a line.

"You have no idea," the girl taunted, then took her turn on the stage.

She was announced as 'now on stage, Diamond,' but Mark knew from class that her name was 'Carrie.' She'd chosen a rather fast song, with a driving beat and not a lot of melody. Carrie hit every percussive beat with her body, jutting her hip or thrusting her chest out in time with the song, turning around and shaking her ass, each movement aimed at Mark, pointing to him with every part of her body that could be used for sex.

Chapter Six

Dr. O'Malley's test was grueling, half the questions making so little sense to unstudied Mark that he didn't even know where to begin in answering them. He stayed until Dr. O'Malley called time, 'pencils-down,' but spent most of the time combing the questions he'd left blank for even a single familiar-looking word. He knew he'd failed and wondered if he should even bother handing it in, if his score would be discernibly higher than a zero. Without handing it in, at least, he could pretend he'd missed class altogether, maybe preserve his dignity and not lose face in the eyes of an instructor who might grade his future assignments and tests differently seeing how unprepared he was today.

"Hell of a test," Mark heard Carrie say behind him as he walked down to hand it in.

"I bombed it," Mark said over his shoulder, then turned to face Carrie to ask, "You?"

"We'll see on Thursday, if he's graded them by then. I'm exhausted, though. You have a class after this? I'm going to bed."

"I don't have a class, no."

"Wanna come with me?"

"You just said you were going to sleep."

"No, I said I was going to bed," Carrie smiled. "And I asked if you wanted to come."

Mark smiled back at Carrie's cunning come-on. He tried to read Carrie's face, to see if she meant it, and it seemed she did. "You come on pretty strong for a Tuesday morning."

Carrie treated Mark to the same smile-and-shrug the girl in the gold dress had given him in the street in South Beach. "You've already seen me topless. Why beat around the bush?"

"Haven't seen that."

"Don't make me laugh," Carrie said, but it was too late for that, for both of them. "I'm serious. This test *ruined* my spring break. I deserve a little fun. I don't have to be at work for, like, five hours."

"What you have in mind doesn't take that long." Mark instantly regretted his words.

"That sounds less-than-promising. But we can try, can't we?"

Nick dreamed of his attackers every time he slept and always woke up feeling weak. Nick had worked out so much never to feel weak and took little comfort in the fact that it had taken two attackers to bring him down, to do this to him. Nick reasoned that had there been but one guy, without a weapon, he could have taken him. Nick was solid alright, hard all over, as resentful of the erection that remembering his attack always yielded as of the months of bed rest that lay ahead for him, guaranteed to make him soft again, weak, an easy mark.

The medication coursing through Nick messed with his cognizance of what was going on around him; Andrew, Ron, the hot doctor, the effeminate nurse, and who-knew-who-else coming in and out of the room as he came in and out of consciousness. Whenever Andrew visited, he always arrived out of breath from just the short walk from the elevator to Nick's room, his breathing coming heavy and out of tempo with the machines monitoring Nick's, their hearts pointedly, poetically, meaningfully out-of-sync. Nick rolled his eyes at how out-of-shape Andrew had gotten, though Nick knew his injuries would preclude him from exercise in the coming months and might leave him in similar shape.

The doctor had let Nick keep some of his X-rays in the room with him, and Nick had asked a nurse to tape some of them over the window. Nick was sure everyone thought it was rather morbid to surround himself with the images of what had happened to him while he healed, but for Nick, it was about blocking some of the light in the window, and of course, adding his trademark black to the room. Nick thought of the old decorating wives tale: you need a little bit of black in every room. This wasn't exactly true; it only meant that a particularly light décor scheme needed something to anchor it – a dark wood floor, or an antique tobacco leather trunk – to keep it from looking like a little-girl's room and feeling like it could float away, but Nick was glad enough, in most spaces, to let the 'little bit of black' in a room be his smartly-dressed self.

"Hell-*o-oh!*" Nick heard a voice croon out exuberantly, stretching 'hello' to three syllables, and knew without turning from the X-rays in the window that it was Ron.

"Hello." Nick could never match Ron's enthusiasm for life and, wrapped in plaster and hooked up to who-knew-what machines helping him heal, wasn't about to try.

"How you doin' in here, honey? Getting enough..." Ron drew out the punchline, *"...pain medication?"*

Nick was almost glad Ron's line had fallen flat. "I know you're here to cheer me up, to take my mind off things, but I need to talk about something serious before we do. After that, please, cheer away. Is that okay?"

"Of course it is, sweetie." Ron was usually all-for-laughs, but in times like this, times when Nick needed someone to be there for him, Ron was a good listener and a true friend.

"Good. Thank you," Nick breathed out, trying to find the words to start.

Ron waited him out, then asked, "What's on your mind, sweetie?"

"Everyone's been so direct with me about everything. 'These bones are broken because you were hit with a pipe or a bat. You're cut on your face from where they probably punched you.' But no one's talked to me about what happened..."

Though Nick had instructed Ron to be serious, the sight of Ron understanding what Nick meant and making a Betty Boop face, then borrowing the comic coquette's mannerisms to point at his own ass, was enough to get Nick to crack a smile.

"No one's probably able to understand what's going on because they don't know you. They think *gay man, something shoved up his ass, no big deal.* But there are tops, and there a bottoms," Ron paused, sighing slightly, "And you're a top."

"Unless your dick resembles a beer bottle, apparently," Nick could tell Ron didn't know how to respond. "Look, I have everyone here – the nurses, my hottie of a doctor, Andrew – all trying to be delicate and sensitive about the whole thing. But this is us, okay? I count on you to be irreverent and make me laugh, even if laughing right now makes my insides hurt like hell."

Ron took a while to respond, his gaze narrowing from wide-eyed concern to razor-sharp to match his tongue. "Of course it hurts, sweetie. What have I told you about bottoming without the appropriate lube?"

Nick rolled his eyes and smiled, grateful that Ron was talking to him normally. *Normal for Ron, that is,* Nick thought, and smiled even wider.

"I always told you the experience of bottoming would make you a better top."

"If experience as a bottom makes a good top you must be the best top on earth by now," Nick fired back, grateful to be talking about something other than plaster casts and object rape for a minute.

"Inside every top is a bottom just waiting to get out."

"Wait – don't all bottoms wish a top were inside *them?* Sort of a chicken-in-every-pot kind of thing."

Ron laughed for a while, then stopped and took a deep breath. "Okay, you asked me to be serious, so all kidding aside – and that means no jokes from you, either, Mister – let's be serious. The damage there is probably pretty minor."

Nick didn't say anything but looked at Ron curiously.

"Look, sweetie, I've let guys do some pretty wild stuff to me back there –"

Nick started to speak, but Ron interrupted him to continue.

"– and I remind you, no jokes."

Nick made a sheepish I'm-sorry face.

"Dicks, dildos, sometimes a dick and a dildo at the same time – I've always wanted to try two dicks at once, but I never met the right –"

"*Dicks?*"

"Guys." Ron gave Nick a mock-indignant look. "I've had objects in me, too. I guess a champagne bottle is as close as what happened to you."

"Champagne," Nick mused. "Classy."

Ron shot another look at Nick.

"Sorry. Again. Please continue, oh-wise-insatiable-bottom."

"The point is it's tough to do any real damage back there. You can be stretched wide enough to drive a Volkswagen inside, and an hour later, everything's back to normal, nice and tight and ready for more."

"Remind me never to let you borrow my car again."

"Seriously, sweetie, if there were any real permanent damage back there, I'm sure they would have told you. The doctor, the nurses. It's their job to let you know how you're healing."

"But it still feels –"

"Look, I'm sure it felt awful – well, I guess I might have liked it fine, honey – but what you're probably feeling is more like phantom pains. The violation of it, the memory, more than any real physical issue."

Nick waited a minute then said, "Thanks."

"Oh honey, don't mention it. But, I thought you said we needed to talk about something serious. We could have a real laugh riot talking about what's been up my ass."

# # # # #

From the short drive to her building – Carrie drove stick and drove aggressively, both points that excited Mark – to the three flights of stairs up to her apartment – Carrie leading the way, never looking back to see if Mark was still behind, never smiling back at him half-embarrassed or encouraging 'it's just one more flight' – to the beer she handed him without asking if he wanted one – domestic and still unopened in the bottle – one thing was clear to Mark; Carrie was in charge. None of this surprised Mark at all.

What was surprising to Mark was the way she undressed. After seeing her on stage so many times, teasingly taking her time with things, slowly pulling the zipper down the back of her costume or taking her time with a front-close bra and playing peek-a-boo with her breasts behind the cups, watching Carrie yank her sweatshirt over her head and ball it up to throw it in her own hamper faster than he could twist off the bottle cap was a bit of a shock. The speed and force of the action had ruffled Carrie's straight bob, but she made no moves to smooth it back in place, completely unselfconscious. Mark cracked open the beer while she squatted on the edge of a chair to unzip her flat boots and pull them off forcefully, letting them bang to the ground before kicking them to the corner. He took his first sip as she went for the zipper of her jeans and peeled them down her legs; she was perched on the chair again, rolling off her socks before he swallowed. Mark had seen Carrie's feet encased in high sandals with ankle straps when she danced; here in her apartment, the sparkly polish on her toenails was the only part of her feet recognizable as belonging to the girl she was at the club. Now barefoot, the high arches of her feet flattened, and the smooth skin of her legs was embossed with the ribbing of her socks.

Also foreign was the underwear, the strip club's padded-and-seamed corsets and push-ups of colorful satin or black lace traded for a simple flesh-colored bra, white cotton low-rise panties in place of a thong or G-string. While Mark took his second – and last – sip of beer, Carrie reached back to unhook her bra and tossed it toward the hamper.

Mark set the beer down on a table by the front door and raced to touch Carrie. His hand was cold and wet from the bottle, and she jumped, but he held her firmly, and they both got used to it, the cold giving way to each other's heat.

"This feels all too familiar," Carrie said.

"What?" Mark asked, fearing maybe it was familiar to her because she brought a lot of guys home with her.

"I'm topless, you're fully dressed..." Carrie let her voice fade out leadingly as her not-quite-green-not-quite-brown eyes darted between Mark's blue ones and the wide stripe of white T-shirt visible between the sides of his open jacket.

"Oh. Sorry." Mark paused, relieved, realizing he was still even in his jacket. "Let me catch up."

Mark shrugged the shoulders of his jacket over his delts, then tugged the sleeves down over his thick arms before pulling the jacket, now bunched and accordioned at his wrists, completely off and, not knowing where Carrie might want him to put it, tossing it toward the front door. Mark pulled his shirt up and struggled a bit to get it over his head, maintaining his sexual proximity to Carrie and trying not to elbow her as he wrestled it past his neck and finally off. It fell to the floor and their feet, and Carrie absently kicked it toward her own hamper.

Mark wondered if she intended to do his laundry afterward or keep his shirt as a souvenir.

Mark's hands trailed down his torso to the button and zipper of his jeans, and he undid them without looking down, though he struggled to look Carrie in her eyes and not just stare at her body. Her body, at least, was familiar to him; at the bar, a long stare over her breasts or ass was expected, understood, forgiven, but Mark had rarely met Carrie's eyes.

They were hazel, glinting tiny green-gold halos around the pupils, which now reflected Mark's I-still-can't-believe-this-is-happening face.

His jeans were loose and fell to the floor without any more work from Mark than just unzipping them. Mark thought to pull his wallet out of his jeans before they were too far out of reach, then a condom from the flap. He kicked himself for not kicking off his sneakers first, but managed to remove the shoes, then the jeans, with a few shuffles of his feet and a step forward, toward Carrie.

Carrie – in just her panties – and Mark – boxers and socks still on – made their way to Carrie's unmade bed with Mark leading clumsily and Carrie backing into it, both of them seemingly trusting it was there to catch her fall if he got ahead of her. They kissed and groped as they inched along, connected, two people moving as one four-legged thing with one goal in seemingly one mind. Carrie fell back on the bed with her hand inside the back of Mark's boxers; she pulled him down with her, on top of her.

"Right where I want you," Mark said. "Right where I've always wanted you."

"You never made a move," Carrie said.

Carrie was right, Mark knew. It was usually easy for him to go after girls he liked: frivolous girls who cheered at his games, either from the sidelines in short pleated skirts or from the stands, bundled in coats and drinking coffee or beer to keep warm; girls who were in college because that's where their parents had put them, with some-growing-up-to-do more than to learn any real marketable skills for a future profession; girls at school to find themselves – or find a husband; girls who danced at clubs – be they 'night' or 'strip' – grinding and writhing under colored lights to get Mark's attention at its most basic level. But Carrie had never worked at getting Mark to notice her, never came to any games that he knew of, was at the head of the class in her every class with little interest in the distraction of husband-hunting, and left her job at the strip club every night with more money from the men there – Mark included – than any other dancer.

"I prefer watching *you* move," Mark recovered, realizing he'd spent too long thinking about just how much he wanted this girl rather than just showing her.

Carrie squirmed under him to get comfortable, and Mark fought a laugh at her timing. A little more squirming from Carrie and her panties were down her legs, looped around one ankle, then fully off.

Mark lumbered up in the bed to get above her, kneeling over her, the condom still in its packet, pinched between his thumb and forefinger. His cock, in turn, protruded through the fly front of his boxers like a flagpole jutting off a wall, angled up high and proud. Mark waved the foil wrapper at Carrie like a flag, letting her respond to it as she liked. There were girls Mark knew he could have without protection: naïve girls who hoped they'd marry the school quarterback after letting him fuck them raw on the first date, maybe get knocked up and force his hand to take theirs. When Mark waved the condom at them the first time, white flag-like, some of the girls surrendered, said that it was okay, they were on the pill, they trusted him. Loving the feeling of skin on skin, of wet pussy around his bare bone, Mark always obliged, always still knowing that it was those girls who were obliging him. Carrie wasn't one of those girls; educated in the classroom and the club, she was anything but naïve.

Mark brought his fingers toward his mouth, tore the package open with his teeth and rolled on the rubber sheath. "Ribbed for your pleasure," he said, then put the wrapper back in his mouth to free both hands to ease the elastic of his boxers over his erection and down, below his ass. Mark tried not to wince at the bitter and numbing taste of the small amount of condom lubricant that entered his mouth.

"Don't think it'll do all the work for us," Carrie countered, kicking his knee to one side playfully.

Mark was kneeling over Carrie, his arms free; he knew if she kicked him again, and he didn't brace his weight with his hands on the bed, he'd topple either onto her or to the floor, depending on what she wanted. He was on top, but she had all the power. "I'll go down if you kick me again."

"You'll go down if I ask you," Carrie said suggestively, and barely nudged Mark's knee off the bed, "but not today."

Mark fell onto and then into her, his condom-wrapped cock sinking into the quicksand of her vagina, her movements below him pulling him deeper and deeper into her, so he was all the way in on the first thrust. Mark knew Carrie wasn't like any other girl he'd been with before, but still expected to tease her with his dick just a bit first, rub it against her slit, put in just the head at first, make her ask for more before giving it all to her. But here he was, balls-deep in her, and it was up to him to pull himself out, if only to be pulled back in seconds later.

But Mark could barely move, Carrie's grip around him was so strong. Carrie moved her hands down to Mark's ass and left them there, Mark felt the delicate pressure of them on his skin, how the pressure changed as his ass tensed and clenched, trying to pry himself out of her tight sex. When Mark felt he was wrenching himself out of her any more than an inch, he felt her hold on his ass strengthen, pulling him back in, forcing him back inside her.

She was wearing him out, Mark knew, the sweat of exertion dripping on his face, the strain like that of weight lifting – anaerobic, his heart not racing at all – just exercising sheer force.

"You like a strong man, huh?" he asked, huffing, out of breath.

"*Big* and strong," Carrie said, stressing the first word, Mark wondering if she were signaling to him that his size was doing more for her than his strength so far, or if he was just that big. Mark was endowed and hoped she wasn't just stroking his ego, capable of handling – or even used to – even more.

They wrestled like this for a while, Carrie easing up on the pressure around his cock and ass occasionally, just enough to sucker him into thinking he was winning. When she let him get ahead, let him pull most of the way out, she squirmed again under him, letting him fall out of her, letting the sound that made – almost a pop – distract Mark enough for her to take control, roll him over, for her to get on top.

Mark surrendered all control to Carrie. He barely caught his breath before the sheer sight of her, naked and on top of him, took it away again. He fought her to bend at his waist, using the strength of his abs to do a sit-up under her, bury his face in her breasts, suck her nipples lightly, but she pushed him back down against the bed again. He did these erotic sit-ups under her again and again, each time Carrie letting him spend just a little longer suckling on her full breasts before pushing him back down again, playful but punishing.

"I'm used to doing push-ups on top of a girl while I'm fucking her, but not sit-ups under her."

Carrie laughed at him. "Who said *you* were the one fucking *me?*" she asked, and sat down on his dick.

They both let out loud sighs as she began to rock and ride on top of him, wrapping her womanhood around him nowhere near as tightly as she had when he was on top of her, just letting him glide into her naturally and gently until she was all the way down on him. Then she clenched her sex around him like a fist, pulling herself back up, so tight around him she nearly took the condom with her.

Mark's hands gripped his dick, the ring at the end of the condom, and rolled the protection back down tight.

Carrie didn't miss a beat, her rhythm rocking up and down on Mark's shaft.

Mark occasionally sat up, licked Carrie's nipple or nuzzled his face between her breasts or in her neck, but she always pushed him away, back down on the bed, and pinned him again, so she could just ride.

Carrie kept going as though Mark didn't even need to be there, under her, she was flying so high. She tightened and released her grip on him as she rode, until Mark could feel how close she was to coming, and pulled her down for good, the entire length of him pulsing inside her as she spasmed uncontrollably around him.

Mark exploded inside the condom, feeling his come beat back against his cock, still inside Carrie.

She eased off him, and his cock fell out of her with a wet slapping sound, the sound mimicked a millisecond later as his rigid, damp dick slapped back against his own abs, the stretched and filled condom seemingly looking up at Mark expectantly. Carrie climbed off him but stayed in bed, lying next to him but not touching him. Mark liked her even more just then because of it, that she didn't wrap an arm around him or lay her head against his chest; she wasn't trapping him. Mark grabbed his dick and removed the condom before remembering he was at Carrie's place and didn't know where a wastebasket was, much less the bathroom. Naked, Mark got out of bed and looked for the bathroom. When he opened her closet door, Carrie said, "It's the door on the right," before closing her eyes.

Mark made as little noise as he could in Carrie's bathroom, flushing the condom and peeing, flushing again, washing his hands and wiping off his dick before drying off on the only towel in the bathroom. Mark turned off the light before opening the door and inching past Carrie, who looked to be asleep, on his way to find his clothes. He pulled on his underwear and jeans, then knelt to pull his shoes back on.

Mark eyed his crumpled T-shirt near her hamper and decided to leave it there, find his way home bare-chested under his jacket; let Carrie do what she wanted with his shirt.

The last thing Mark saw before trying to shut the door as quietly as possible was his abandoned beer bottle, the condensation crying down its amber glass face.

Chapter Seven

Nick hadn't been a particularly active child, choosing drawing and painting indoors over fighting and playing outside. As such, he had never needed stitches and had never broken a bone. He didn't know what to expect when the casts and braces and wraps came off him, but figured he'd be weaker on one side and need to rely heavily on the unharmed side of his body while he adjusted to the reduced functions of the other.

Nick's lack of activity and experience had left him unaware of the body's simple truth; after a bone breaks, it heals back stronger.

It surprised Nick to be able to put all his weight on his right leg right after the casts that had immobilized him for so long were removed. He hopped on it, increasing the pressure on the bones and joints, and discovered he couldn't tire himself out in the hospital's rehab rooms; he was never sore from even trying. Nick found his right arm, already the one he favored for everything from simple load-carrying to beating off, didn't strain under the weight of increasingly large dumbbells – even the largest one available still seemed tiny compared to what he could handle before – or his laptop when he tried to check in on things at work. All worry that his right hand – the one he wrote and, more importantly, drew with – would be rendered useless, and that he would have to find another vocation – one that didn't require him to convey his ideas graphically on the page – left him, and he found he trusted his sketching ability more, drawing one smooth line where he would go back over the same line again and again before, the hesitant and worried strokes making every line he used to draw seem hairy and rough. Nick felt more creative as well, the uniqueness of what he imagined – expressed in these newly-crisp drawings – amazing him, forcing him to reflect on what it meant to be right-brained, and stronger there, too.

But, Nick was indeed weaker on one side: the side that hadn't been hit, that was shielded by his positioning and the pavement under him.

At first, Nick had thought it was the medication; that whatever he was on for pain had specifically targeted his injured right side. But that didn't make sense, even to him. Medication or no, he was stronger on the side that had been hit and healed, and according to the hospital, he was strong enough everywhere to be released. He wouldn't miss the food, the awful aqua walls, or sharing those walls with another patient, but he would miss the hot doctor and was quick to take the doctor's business card on his way out and shove it in his front pocket, nudging his dick on purpose as he did.

Ron had collected him at the hospital and was going to look after him for a while. Like any interior designer away from his home too long, Nick missed being surrounded by his own things greatly, but Nick reasoned it would be easier to deal with Ron's one story walk-up than his own ten-flights-high location in the event of an emergency, and a good idea to have Ron to look after him. Ron was already over-cautious, fussing about positioning and buckling Nick into the passenger seat and driving home well below the speed limit.

"It's the pedal on the right, Grandpa," Nick joked to Ron.

"I just wanted to be on the safe side, after all that you've been through."

"I wasn't in a car accident. I got beat up," Nick had never said it aloud that way, and didn't know that it covered all that happened to him or sounded too dismissive, so he added, "beat up but good." Removing any mention of an object rape from his recounting of the events would soon, he hoped, remove it from his memory. "Two guys. A baseball bat. No car."

Ron didn't say anything, but sped up.

"And, I think if we ran into them on the road now, just plowed into them, even in your little bare-bones rustbucket, I think we could take them."

Ron smiled, and sped up a little more.

# # # # #

For Mark, there was usually nothing to feel after taking a girl to bed but smug satisfaction. He rarely bonded with women beyond what was base, and even that sense of carnal connection usually left him after he'd showered, working his dick into a lather under the water little differently from how the girl had, washing away any trace of her the morning – or mere moments – after he was done with her.

When the girl he bedded was a stripper, there were a lot of things Mark could feel as well. Sometimes, it was embarrassing, the girl deemed not on his level, though she relied on her body in the club little different from how Mark needed his on the field. Other times, it was a triumph, finally bringing a girl all his buddies had talked about wanting back to the frat house, making sure enough guys were up and about when she had to brave the hallway to use the bathroom or sneak away home, knowing the conquest would do even more to boost his reputation than it had to sate his libido.

Mark had never felt the way he did now; he was completely torn. Getting Carrie was a complete coup; she was beautiful and smart and the kind of stripper all the guys at the frat had noticed, and he kind of wanted to brag to them about having been to bed with her. But he also wanted to have her to himself, protect her, not let anyone else in on what this amazing girl was really like.

After the man in Miami, Mark wasn't sure he could keep another secret.

# # # # #

With Nick released from the hospital in a wheelchair and to Ron's care, Ron promptly brought him to his own place, not Nick's: a second floor apartment in an Art Deco building without an elevator. Ron had to enlist the negligible muscle of the guy he'd tricked with the night before to get Nick upstairs.

Ron's apartment was a hodgepodge of pieces he'd picked up in various ways; the sofa that had been left in place by a previous tenant, genuinely good art and accessories Nick had given him from the homes of clients who were redecorating for the sake of change if not notable improvement, perverse trinkets Ron had picked up in South Beach at shops that sold everything from women's G-string underwear printed with vulgar slogans like 'I have the pussy I have the power' and 'Lick it before you stick it' to, Nick sullenly reasoned, souvenir baseball bats.

Though Ron's building was an architecturally interesting-enough example of the low-rise Deco-era housing of the area – apartments that used to house older residents at low cost and reasonably high fashion and now charged their younger tenants far more despite little in the way of restoration or improvement – the interior was pretty generic and did little to pick up on the style of its exterior. The walls were all rental-apartment-beige, known to Nick's trade as 'builder-beige:' a generic not-quite-ecru-not-quite-taupe shade that seemingly all landlords, contractors, and developers used to cover the walls and make spaces appear neutral enough that just about anyone could envision living there.

Anyone but Nick.

On the offending beige walls were scads of glossy pages ripped from everything from beefcake calendars to workout magazines to the International Male catalog to hard-core gay porno magazines. Nick understood the porn but not the rest; he knew Ron too well, and Ron, like so many bottoms, was all about dick.

The collage was easier for Nick to look at than the beige. It, at least, inspired him to heal, to get back into the gym to start looking like the guys on the wall again, if only to start bedding guys who looked like that again, too.

So Nick lived for weeks surrounded by images of what he once was, and what he wanted. At first, he worked out with the weights Ron had purchased for himself years ago on impulse and just as quickly abandoned. When his strength exceeded their sizes – Ron had nothing more than an adjustable set of dumbbells that maxed out at forty pounds if Nick loaded all the disks intended for both weights onto a single grip – Nick sent Ron out for more equipment: Velcro-wrap leg weights, larger dumbbells, a chin-up bar he could mount to Ron's frustratingly beige doorframe and lift his face closer to the just-as beige wall and air vent above the door. When Nick saw how excited Ron was by his trip to the fitness store, he let himself get excited for a minute, too, thinking how Ron was finally 'getting it,' that he'd start working out as well, be not just his restaurant buddy and shopping buddy but his workout buddy or more, but the excitement was short-lived. Ron returned with the tools and as many stories about what shopping in a sporting goods store had been like for him. Sure, some of the shoppers were paunchy, some were female, but some of the men shopping there – and all of the store's staff – were the kinds of men Ron delighted in looking at: young and tan and fit. The packaging of the workout equipment was littered with images of tight-bodied men – invariably sweaty and stripped to the waist – caught in some maybe-accidentally-maybe-purposely provocative pose meant to demonstrate the steps of some strenuous exercise. *Step One: Grip the weight like it's your cock. Step Two: Bend over with your ass to the camera. Step Three: Lift weight near your face and eye it longingly, like it's no longer your cock but someone else's. Execute as many reps as it takes to get you off. Smile for the camera, exhausted and satisfied.* The names of the equipment were also provocative to Ron in a way that made him wonder if the easy entendre of the classic brands 'Everlast' and 'Everhard' or newer products like 'The Squat Rocket' or 'Butt Master' was intentional or not. Ron also marveled at how helpful the attractive employees had been, but Nick assured him, they weren't flirting. They knew to assist him – and fast – on-sight.

"Of course they were helpful. Look at you. You were either lost or shopping for a gift. And I'm sure your presence made them – and their customers – rather uncomfortable." Nick wondered if his words stung Ron a bit too hard, but Ron just shrugged, and was back to looking longingly at the product packaging without another word.

When Nick worked out, faces flooded his mind. He pictured his attackers, sure, how getting stronger might help to even the odds. But, more than anything else, he pictured his doctor, thought about asking him out, thought about how the doctor might respond to seeing his worked-out body fully healed.

# # # # #

For weeks, the frat house had been abuzz with the news that the girls of Phi Delta Somethingorrather – the houses, and the girls of those houses, had always seemed the same to Mark, and even more homogenous now that he was starting something with Carrie – were throwing a coed party. Tonight, Mark surprised everyone by not going.

The frat house felt like a different place with no one in it. Rooms that usually spilled over with fratheads and roughnecks spilling frothy white-headed beers were suddenly empty of both boys and brew;

the still and quiet were foreign. Mark hadn't felt ready to socialize with so many of his peers yet – namely with Rob – and used the night to throw six weeks' worth of laundry, colors comingled, the mass of it reading mostly as the school's colors of red and white, into the washer all at once. Mark flipped on the main room's outsized flat panel to kill time, and cranked the volume when the out-of-balance washer got loud, spazzing and shaking violently.

After surfing through the house's nearly twenty ESPN varietals and finding nothing, Mark settled on Spike, which was running a *CSI* marathon Mark hoped he could get lost in for a while. Mark knew he couldn't have picked a worse show to watch when Sara Sidle – whose plain-but-pretty looks and extraordinary science-smarts Mark found totally hot, and unique to boot, given that the actress who played Sara was tall for a woman and that an interest in science was an historically masculine preference – started spewing what usually sounded like fictitious forensic gibberish about fingerprints and blood evidence and DNA. Now, having attacked that man in the alley, the gibberish sounded real, and really damning.

After keeping his head down since returning from Miami and avoiding any real questions about how the trip was – all the guys, many of whom had never left the state and all of whom envied Mark's relationship with Rob, the frat's alpha, were so jealous – Mark had gone from aloof to suddenly panicked. And he knew, he admitted to himself, that he should have been more worried about all of it sooner.

Mark's mind raced with the details of the night, and what he'd left behind. His prints would be on the broken beer bottle he'd shoved in the guy's ass. Mark had cut his own hand working the guy over: the knuckles frayed from punching the guy's face, the palm torn up from the jagged edge of the bottle. *For fuck's sake, I pissed on the guy,* Mark fretted. Urine, CSI Sidle had taught him, was loaded with DNA.

Rob, if Mark remembered correctly, hadn't made much contact with their victim at all, and had taken the bat with them; Mark knew the bat was now upstairs by Rob's bed, as much a trophy to him as the much-notched headboard it leaned against. It had been Rob who'd pissed on the guy first, but Mark wondered if his own urine had washed all traces of Rob away, like a beer chaser after a strong shot, or had mixed with Rob's like the clothes in the wash, red with white, bleeding into what had once been pure. The idea that there was mostly evidence of his own being there, not Rob's, when it had been Rob's idea in the first place, was enough to get Mark out of the frat's favorite recliner and off to the Sorority Row party to confront Rob.

Not so fast, Mark thought, getting up too quickly and catching a whiff of himself. He'd have to shower first.

# # # # #

When Nick had gotten built the first time, it had been about two things.

The first was getting laid. Nick understood that, just as he was attracted to guys who were solid, yoked and diesel beyond even the point he had pushed his own musculature to, getting that way himself was going to appeal to a lot more guys than his design prowess or sense of humor. Guys could discover those later, after, if they hung around. Nick had a big dick, and did fine getting laid before he started working out in earnest, but he did a lot better after.

The second was control. At work, his boss was in charge of a lot of the decision-making: which jobs they took, what kinds of projects they were, what direction to take those designs. Nick had no influence over what he worked on all day, required to channel his creativity into something he did not genuinely take ownership or charge of, could not fully craft as his own. In his personal life, he never made the first move, only ever sleeping with the guys who hit on him first, ending up in relationships with the ones who stayed the night and then some. It had been that way with Andrew, and with all the others before him. Packing on muscle was something he could control.

That was what had made being attacked so hard on Nick. It wasn't the physical pain of the blows, or the swelling and surgeries and the healing. It wasn't the humiliation, the shame, the shock of being bottle-raped and pissed on. It was the inability to control the situation, to turn the tables on his attackers. It was also the inability to control his dick, which was hard the whole time he got attacked and got that way again whenever he thought about it.

Nick had gone into architecture because he was gifted at art and happened to be good at math; he had gone into the gym the first time the same way. He had an obvious appreciation for the aesthetics of the well-developed male form but also understood that there was math behind it as well. Beneath the sweat-glistened skin and sexy sinew, it was all numbers: X number of calories equaled X amount of energy to lift X amount of weight X number of times in a row for X number of sets. Art and math were in the architecture of the human form, Nick discovered; bodies, like buildings, were *built*.

Rebuilding his body added another number to the mix. He knew how long it had taken him to beef up in the first place and figured it would take as long or longer, though he didn't know how much longer – the extra time added to nurture his wounds – to get back what he had lost. *X equals unknown.*

Rehab, and the time he spent in the hospital leading up to it, had been about those things and so much more. Nick had spent much of the time in his cast wondering what damage was being done just sitting there, the horror of being sedentary, of not maintaining his hard-earned muscle while his bones mended, of going soft under all that plaster and losing what had made him appealing in the first place, he suffered through that feeling far more than he had suffered through the attack.

It hurt Nick more.

What also hurt was surrendering control. Before the attack, he set goals in mind: how many reps of how much weight for how many days per week, regardless of how he felt. Now, he worried that he couldn't control that, and would have to listen to his body, take its cues, not push himself too hard on his way back.

It was punishing work, and though Ron worried Nick was pushing himself too much, too soon, or even not dealing with the emotional repercussions of what had happened to him, Nick pushed through, and pushed hard. As he did, he found he was stronger on one side than the other, and not the side he expected.

Nick's attack had been one-sided, half of his body protected by the way he'd been positioned against the pavement. The side that faced up, faced his attackers, had been broken, but was healing back. He felt strong on that side, stronger even than on the side that hadn't been hit, had been protected against the asphalt. He didn't need to favor or baby it but instead found himself wondering how to make the other half of himself feel like the half that had been broken, the half that was now stronger, so he could take on more weight and grow stronger still.

# # # # #

In the shower, Mark thought about how hard he'd worked at being Rob's friend. The work had started long before they met.

Mark grew up with just-enough money in a suburb where just-enough *wasn't*. He was shy and kept to himself, always noticing details everywhere he went, observing and making mental notes. He picked up on the social hierarchy among his peers, what was important to them and why: brawn over brains, a lax attitude about academics over caring about grades, labels giving status to whatever they were sewn onto. Quiet introspection hadn't served Mark well on the playground, where he was bullied until he figured out a little more about life and how to make it easier. He'd never have the latest sneakers or even a brand-name backpack, and those facts alone had gotten his ass kicked once or twice, though he never so much as asked his parents for new clothes when the ones he wore were worn out. He started changing things for himself in junior high.

Every day after school, Mark would wait out the football or baseball team in the locker room and then have the coach let him in to the gym's weight room, which he then had to himself. He would lift for as much as two hours, as much weight and as many reps as he could take, until nearly eight o'clock at night, when he'd go home and shower and start dinner before his parents came home. Mark got a paper route and kept his grades up, so they never knew what he was up to those nights, and, hiding the changes that were happening to his body under oversized sweatshirts and baggy jeans he'd bought with his delivery earnings, no one else seemed to know either, until his freshman year of high school.

Three local junior highs funneled into Mark's large high school, so two-thirds of the kids there didn't know him from before, and those who had gone to the same junior high as Mark hardly recognized him. Mark's sweats were traded for polo shirts, collars popped like the veins of his arms, biceps stretching the cuffs of the shirts' short sleeves. His jeans stayed baggy, the tops of boxer briefs peeking out over denim waistbands, and he found that girls were peeking there, too, trying to get a glimpse of his ass or the happy trail growing in from his abs south. No one pushed him around anymore, and no one ignored him, either.

Mark had gone out for the football team and made it easily. He made fast friends with most of the team but hid from them who he was. They would never know how perceptive he was, how he noticed every little thing. He couldn't hide his grades from them, and when it became clear that academic achievement would threaten his new popularity, he let himself slide to a C-average. The ease with which his superficial changes had made him popular hadn't surprised him, what had surprised him was the fact that his parents hadn't noticed any of it – the changes to his body, his grades, his attitude – distracted instead by the details of their divorce.

Mark went to college in a small town, but his high school's suburb had been smaller still, and as such, Mark's popularity reached the school's summit. There was no top dog to try to befriend and help him on his ascent; with the changes Mark had made, he was his high school's alpha. Its king. And its Homecoming King. Prom *King*. The yearbook's Most Popular, Best Smile, Best Body.

College had been so different; all the traits Mark had hidden in himself were suddenly accepted when revealed by others. Quiet, introspective types found other quiet, introspective types to hang out with, and instead of getting pushed around, were for the most part left alone. Still, Mark kept his observations to himself.

What wasn't left alone at State was any guy who appeared to have any stereotypical gay attributes. That was an ass-kicking-punishable offense, but that fact was understood, and no one really dared to attract that sort of attention. There were no reported instances of gay-bashing here, because no one dared let on that they were gay.

Which, Mark supposed, had left Rob even less prepared for how to deal with seeing openly gay men in Miami or anywhere else.

Mark had kept his observations to himself and, with his commitments to the frat and the football team taking up so much of his time, combined with the fact that his college courses were simply harder for him than high school had been, had no trouble maintaining the C-average he had slid down into so favorite-chair comfortably. In high school there had been no one who was more of a leader than Mark, but in college, the leader was clearly Rob, and Mark prized his right-arm relationship to Rob. In a lot of ways, Mark was along for the ride; Rob always had more money than Mark, who was at State on an athletic scholarship and thus had even more reason to maintain that C-average. It was Rob's charm that had opened doors for him with most of the girls Mark had been with, girls who had been drawn to Rob initially but swayed by Mark's still-quiet manner and occasional slipped-out sensitive observation, or girls who had tagged along with a friend who was afraid of being with Rob alone, so they had doubled with Mark, only to end up just as seduced by Mark as they feared their friends might have been by Rob. Rob's charm had gotten them out of a lot of trouble, although it was usually Rob's mouth or his fist or his lead foot that had gotten them into that trouble in the first place. It was Rob's money that had paid the negligible cover at any club they went to, and that had covered most of the Miami trip, which Mark supposed meant it was Rob's money and influence that had gotten him feeling the way he did now, about everything. Mark knew that challenging Rob would risk everything he'd worked for since junior high, but he had to talk to someone about what they'd done, and he wanted to do that without anyone else finding out about it. Rob was his only choice for someone to talk to.

Still in the shower, Mark soaped his musculature self-admiringly, pride in what he'd accomplished with his body and life getting him half-hard. He went soft when he remembered details about what he and Rob had done in the alley.

# # # # #

Twist was packed, and Nick was unable to navigate the crowd without pressing his body against other men's, which Nick admitted was for the most part enjoyable in and of itself. He debated just planting himself in place and letting the passing men bear into him, but was on a mission himself, needing to get somewhere, to the two college-aged guys at the bar who had tipped their beer bottles at him after they'd made eye contact.

He pushed on toward them, but the crowd was too dense, the motion of the men in it almost entirely in the opposite direction, as though they were all inexplicably trying to get away from the two young hunks at the bar, fleeing from them. Nick noticed a man in loose hospital scrubs that hid his frame, his bright eyes behind glasses, his handsome face camouflaged in several days' of beard growth, as though the man were purposely masking his best features, letting Nick discover him like a secret no one else knew. Nick reached out for the man, who seemed to try to connect with Nick, but the pull of the boys at the bar was too strong, and Nick found himself led by his dick, compelled toward them. Nick would take a step toward the two young men only to be carried away from them by the crowd until, like being swept out with the tide, Nick found himself forced through the club's exit and into the street, where the wave of men continued to rush in one direction. Nick stepped into an alley to avoid being carried further and, knowing there was no way to fight the crowd back into the club, tried to figure out the route home.

"Hey faggot," voices shouted down the alley, toward Nick. "Fag-got."

Nick turned and saw the two guys from the bar at the mouth of the alley where it met the street. One was wagging a bat at Nick like an extra-long finger, shaming him, the other stood a bit behind, puffing out his chest but looking a little lost. The men ran down the alley, the one with the bat swinging it into Nick. Nick hit the ground and the men were on him, pounding away at him with the bat and their fists.

"Hey!" Nick heard. It wasn't the voice of the man with the bat. Is this what the other guy sounds like? *Nick wondered, but the voice was too far away.*

"Hey!" Nick heard again, and turned to see the cute scruffy guy in scrubs entering the alley, half a block from him and trying to break up the action by shouting.

"Think he's gonna rescue you from all the way over there, do ya, fag-got?*" the man with the bat taunted Nick. "We'll be done with you before he even gets here."*

Nick, who hadn't dared to speak since the men started in on him, managed to get one word out, loud enough for the doctor to hear: "Run."

The man with the bat was still on Nick, alternately beating into him with the bat and his fists. The other one kept calling him "fag-got, fag-got," too, but the word sounded hesitant from him, as though he was only repeating what his friend had said. The man holding him down grabbed Nick a little tighter and shook him gently, trading 'fag-got, fag-got' for "sweetie, sweetie..."

When Nick sensed that the hands on him weren't his attackers' but were instead Ron's, he woke from his nap abruptly.

"You were dreaming," Ron said.

Part of Nick wished the whole thing had been a dream, that he would wake up and the attack would never have happened. But it had, and another part of him was growing glad of that.

"It's time to get you back out there," Ron said.

"Look at me, I'm still a monster," Nick said, though he knew that the cuts had healed and the bruises had lightened, and he was more or less back to normal, only his lower leg still in a cast.

"Okay, it's time to get *me* back out there. I haven't had sex since I brought you back from the hospital. That guy who helped me carry you upstairs."

Nick remembered that man and thought what an awful prisoner's-last-meal he probably was for Ron, skin and bones and an alcohol-gut. Nick also tried to remember the last time he'd had sex himself, before the attack, and realized it had been a while for him, too, and that it had been with Andrew, perhaps a worse last meal, though Nick wondered just how far he could go in his condition, how much exertion would prove too much.

"How about Twist?" Ron asked.

"I'm not ready to go back there," Nick said, despite the fact that he dreamed about being there, and walking home from there alone, every time he closed his eyes.

"Score?"

"Really, I don't feel like seeing anyone I might know. I mean, look at me," Nick paused. "How about someplace out-of-the-area?"

"Azucar?"

Azucar was definitely *out-of-the-area,* Nick thought, but just picturing the club, with its high-energy Latin music and standing-room crowd with no place to sit down made Nick feel tired. Still, the men at Azucar, Latin like the music and just as hyper-lively, were great to look at and occasionally, take home like souvenirs from out-of-the-area. The men gave Nick an idea.

"Let's just be honest here; we want to go out and look at pretty guys."

"Duh."

"Preferably wearing as little as possible."

"Double-duh, sweetie," Ron said automatically, then understood. "I'll get dressed."

"Hang on a second."

Ron stayed in place.

"There's something I don't understand."

"What's that, honey?"

"Andrew visited me in the hospital every day, but I haven't heard from him since I got released."

"You have, actually," Ron said, then flatly added, "Whoopsie."

"I'm sorry?"

"He called here right after you got here, and I answered. I don't remember if you were asleep and I didn't want to disturb you or if I just – saw an opportunity and took it."

"An opportunity to do what, exactly?"

"To tell him you didn't want to see him anymore, honey. To tell him you never wanted to see him in the first place."

"Why's that?"

"You closed your eyes. You said you have to close your eyes to be with him."

Nick nodded.

"Right now, after all you've been through, your eyes should be open, sweetie."

Nick understood. His eyes should be open to be alert against another attack, though he figured it was as unlikely that he'd be attacked again the way he'd been attacked in the first place. *Lighting striking twice,* he thought, remembering his X-rays. But he also understood that his eyes should be open to observe and appreciate everything around him, in a way he hadn't before. Nick also figured there was a third thing Ron could have meant: to keep his eyes open to what was right in front of him, to see Ron as more than a friend, but Nick dismissed the thought.

Nick didn't know whether to pretend to be mad at Ron for deciding-without-asking to break up with Andrew for him or to say 'thank you,' so he said nothing at all.

# # # # #

Mark hadn't known which house was throwing the party and didn't really think he needed to. Sorority Row was lined with large, traditional houses – from a distance quite similar to the frat Mark lived in but, up close, far better-kept. And Mark had seen them all close up, in the morning light, sneaking out of some girl's room by way of an open window or back door before the house mother could catch him. Though there was some degree of rivalry among the houses, it was hardly akin to that among frats or football teams, and Mark figured he'd know where the party was on-sight because the other sororities wouldn't send out photocopied invites – invariably on pink paper – for a party to be thrown on the same night as another house's.

Mark walked the two blocks from the frat to the Row. Sure enough, though some lights were on in all of the houses, only one seemed haloed in a glow of excess light, music and men. Still, it was clear that the party was already dying down.

Mark went in anyway, accepting a Solo cup of flat beer from a stranger and smiling good-naturedly at the girls who smiled at him, ducking the girls who, likewise, were dodging him after spending the night – just-one-night – with Mark. In less than a minute, Mark realized that there were far more girls at the party than guys, which meant to him but one thing; flirty as they were, the girls were all-talk, had put on a good show for the guys but were looking like too much hard work to guys already spent from spending the day in their books or in the gym. The guys, Mark surmised, had moved on to surer bets. *To a strip club.* *Somehow,* Mark thought, *I bet they're where Carrie works.*

# # # # #

Nick felt self-conscious about his bruises and bandages at Johnny's, but when he looked around the bar, he felt better. Men so young their bodies were just budding with muscle and hair danced in underwear for men long past their prime, liver-spotted hands tucking singles into the elastic waistbands of black- and bright-colored briefs.

In the club, Ron wanted a table front-and-center to be close to the action, that action for the most part limited to the dancers who stepped onto a tiny runway of a stage to roll their hips and fan their arms in front of a starburst of LED light. Nick wanted to be in a dark corner, against one of the red walls lined with posters of upcoming and past events – always announcing an on-premises porn performer with 'Live in the Flesh' – all bordered in wide carved wood frames sprayed flat-black, or in one of the booths curtained-off in crushed red velvet; there, he figured, his injuries wouldn't be on display to the crowd like so much male flesh. They compromised on a table to the side of the club, still close enough to the stage for Ron to signal over each passing dancer for a better look. Ron got Nick settled and propped his crutch on the chair between them, indicating to the dancers that though they might have arrived together and sat at the same table, they could be approached separately.

"Remember the five-second rule," Nick ordered to Ron.

"What's that, honey?"

"You know when you're cooking in a clean kitchen and the food you're working with falls on the floor?"

"Yeah."

"The five-second rule is that if you pick it up off the floor inside of five seconds, no harm no foul, just rinse it off and keep going.

After it's touched the floor for more than five seconds, the food on the floor is thought to be too dirty to eat."

"I've heard that, sweetie," Ron said in a way that also implied *how-exactly-does-this-apply-here?*

"Look at the dancers, how they interact with the other customers. If a customer touches a dancer, and the dancer whisks his hand away in five seconds or less, that dancer's got some self respect, they're clean enough for us to be interested in. If the dancer lets one of these guys touch him for more than five seconds, lets his fingers linger or even places his own hand over the customer's to guide it over his body, that dancer is..."

"Dirty."

"Like the food on the floor." Nick paused. "And nothing you should be putting in or anywhere near your mouth."

Ron laughed.

Johnny's made its name employing thin twink-type guys who looked barely legal and barely a hundred-thirty pounds as they bared most of their bodies – they worked the crowd in their underwear, not really 'stripping' since they couldn't take anything off, and were allowed to flash their asses, but nothing up-front – for tips and to be bought drinks, grinding on anyone who seemed halfway interested in them wherever he sat, not taking a guy to a more private spot, so anyone near the guy paying was treated to more or less the same show that guy had purchased, *gratis.* There were plenty of such young, lean dancers working tonight, but Nick noticed a bit more welcome diversity than he'd expected, the odd thug and jock sticking out in what were still mostly over-thin dancers, the thug- and jock-types looking all the better by contrast.

From the look of things, Nick didn't think Ron cared who danced for him, so long as they were close enough to touch and teased him with a by-law-forbidden glimpse down the front of their briefs. Nick knew that was why Ron liked it better here than at Boardwalk, where the men were much more Nick's type; here, the guys would do pretty much anything, any desperation you could pick up from them obscured by dim lighting and Drakkar.

Nick noticed the most filled-out guy working there, a plump-lipped *Cubano* with a thick-muscled body. The crowd didn't seem much into him – part of the appeal for some of the clientele, Nick figured, was fantasizing that the guy dancing for them was younger than he was, even underage, and this guy had a developed body and hair under his arms – so just feeling Nick's eyes on him was enough to get him to meet Nick's stare and smile, to come over and dance for Nick without being asked to.

"I should see the other guy, right?" the dancer flirtatiously asked Nick, his hand close to Nick's face but not touching.

"I *am* the other guy," Nick said. He'd all-but forgotten his fading bruises, but this guy was pointing right at them.

"Oh. You deserve a lap dance."

"I don't need a –"

"On the house." The dancer grinned, his full lips parting to reveal crooked teeth before adding, "Just take it easy with me, okay. I'm bigger than the guys these men come here to see, but I'm still not as big as you are." The dancer pulled off the double entendre perfectly; talking about the size of Nick's muscles while aiming his eyes at Nick's crotch.

The dancer started in, and Nick kept his arms folded out of respect, not pawing at the man the way the other patrons might. This, apparently, was not necessary. "You can touch me if you want," the dancer said.

Nick obliged only to be polite, using his left arm to cup around the dancers body and pull it toward his still-healing right side, where he knew he was more sensitive.

"Yeah, that feels good," the dancer said, as much a statement of his own feeling as a question, checking in to make sure it felt good to Nick, too.

Nick pulled the man closer in, so his abs pressed into Nick's right hand. As a reflex, Nick gave the guy a squeeze.

The dancer flinched away fast. "Whoa, easy there, man."

Nick had seen the clientele of the bar grab dancers' asses and crotches without so much as a raised eyebrow, so Nick wasn't expecting the guy to pull away from a touch to his torso. Still, Nick apologized. "Sorry," he said, not knowing why.

The dancer kept grinding into Nick, and Nick unconsciously squeezed again, his grip on the guy surprising even him.

The man stopped dancing for Nick. "Look, don't make me get a bouncer, alright?" The dancer didn't pronounce the 'l' or the 'r' in 'alright,' and broke away from Nick.

With his right hand, Nick made a fist and released a couple of times. "I guess I don't know my own strength," he said to no one in particular as the dancer walked away briskly.

The strength of Nick's muscles had always amazed him; he worked out solely to attract and arouse his partners, not to lift heavy objects or do manual labor. He knew he'd have to be careful now as sensation and dexterity returned to his right side, not accidentally hurt someone he wanted to get close to, and was glad to have learned the lesson with a stripper he was touching more to be polite than out of any real desire to, rather than someone he might want a future with.

"What just happened?" Ron asked Nick, yelling over the bar's loud music.

Nick made another fist and held it, figuring if he was strong enough to hurt a guy, he was ready for a little independence. "I think I'm ready to move back to my own place," Nick said, grinning.

Ron, who was tipping the guy dancing for him enough to seem intent on taking him home for the night, grinned right back.

"After all, three's a crowd."

# # # # #

Mark hadn't been to the club since coming back from Miami – or from bedding Carrie – and wasn't quite ready to deal. He didn't know how to look at or treat Carrie when she was working, now that he'd been intimate with her. He also didn't know what to say when he ran into Rob, who he'd been avoiding lately, but Rob took care of that, approaching Mark and saying, "Dude, you look like shit."

"Failed my Chem test, I'm sure of it," Mark said, and though this was likely true, he'd hardly thought about the test and wondered why he was talking about it now.

"Dude, get a lap dance. Take your mind off it."

"It's hardly been on my mind at all." Mark said it because he was thinking it, not because he cared if Rob knew.

"Good for you, man, put it behind you," Rob paused, "but dude, if that's not what's bugging you –"

"I'm worried about what we did."

"What?"

Mark couldn't tell if Rob had asked because he didn't know to what he was referring or because he just couldn't hear in the loud club. Mark continued as though Rob had heard him fine, though he got quieter as he continued.

"In Miami."

"Man, that was off the chain!" Rob said, and Mark wondered if Rob was fronting, or if beating the shit out of someone was indeed an 'off the chain' good time for Rob. Sometimes, he knew, they couldn't be more different. Rob continued, "That strip club, that was hot."

Fronting, definitely, Mark thought, fighting a knowing smile against the grave nature of what he wanted to talk about. "I barely walked in and out of that sorority party tonight, and I got further with the frigid girls there tonight than either of us did with the strippers in Miami." Mark knew never to call a stripper a 'dancer' to a guy, and never to call a dancer a 'stripper' to a girl.

"Agreed, they were pretty Amish," Rob said. *'Amish:' Rob could be pretty funny sometimes,* Mark thought, but tried not to let Rob charm his way out of this. "So, if the strippers in Miami were so uptight, why are you worried about what we did with them?"

Rob did hear me, Mark thought.

"The guy. In the alley. I'm worried about what we did with him. *To* him"

"Whatdya mean 'what we did?' With him, to him. We gave a little faggot the night of his life. Maybe we got a little too rough with him, but man, check us out some time. The way the girls look at us – dude, I know you've seen that – he was looking at us the same way, I'm sure of it. Probably creamed himself just looking at us, or at least when you put that bottle up his ass, dude."

Only because you told me to, Mark thought, but Rob was talking salesman-slick. If they'd done anything wrong, it wasn't going to stick to them. *Or, at least, to Rob.* When Rob got like this, Mark figured Rob could sell dick to a dyke, provided it was *his* dick.

"I don't think he liked it much. And, if he decides he didn't and reports it," Mark winced, certain the man didn't like what they'd done to him, couldn't have, "there's evidence of us all over him."

"Did you switch majors to Forensic-Sci when I wasn't looking, dude?"

He shifts from 'slick' back to 'funny,' or trying-to-be, Mark thought. "What we did was wrong," he said.

"Don't go getting any bone-headed ideas about right and wrong. Being a *fag*-got is wrong. Two guys together, that's wrong. That girl up there..." Rob's voice trailed off as he ogled the girl on stage. Mark followed his eyes. It was Carrie. "Man, that's so right."

Mark put a firm grip on Rob's arm and tensed, trying to shake Rob out of his sales pitch. "Don't laugh this off, Rob."

Rob pulled Mark's hand off him, quick. "Whoa, dude, don't you ever touch or talk to me like that again. And, don't you ever say another word about what we did to that *fag*-got. To me or to anyone we know. Ever."

Another shift, to top gear. It was clear to Mark that Rob had no problem living with what they'd done, and that, consciously or not, Rob had chosen not to give it much thought. *It's amazing what you can live with if you don't think too hard,* Mark thought, wondering how hard it would be to push his thoughts of what they'd done from his mind, or even if he ever could. Mark had fought for so long to be friends with someone like Rob, someone like the guys who had pushed him around as a kid. And now, here Rob was, pushing him around again, but closer-up.

It hurt Mark more.

Chapter Eight

Most of the experience of living in the fraternity house was exactly what Mark had anticipated, but there were a few of surprises.

Mark had expected a fridge full of nothing but beer and condiments, and aside from the odd pizza box on the rare instance when a guy couldn't finish his own large-with-everything-on-it – and getting called a pussy for it – had gotten exactly that. Even in the shared spaces, walls were plastered with pin-ups of topless girls; the girls in the pictures were bottomless only in the collages inside the frat's bedrooms. Coffee tables covered in shoeprints and drink rings, mismatched leather sofas and recliners anywhere one would fit, contests to see who could go the longest without showering or shaving, purposely not concurrent contests to see who could get the most girls in his room in a weekend; Mark had expected all of it and, the showering contest aside, enjoyed and participated in it completely.

It had surprised Mark that Rob, an upperclassman footballer and clearly the most popular guy at the frat, and by extension, throughout campus, wanted to share a room, choosing a twin-extra-long for each of them shoved against the room's two long walls over a queen bed in the center of a larger room just for him. Rob's status meant he could easily clear any room in the house just by walking into it and ordering 'Out' to whoever was in it, regardless of what they were doing; privacy wasn't usually an issue, but Mark still wondered why Rob hadn't wanted a room alone with a larger bed for sex. As his roommate, Mark learned Rob could position himself to fuck in a twin-extra-long just fine, and could do so with Mark in the next bed without a problem. Later on he learned why Rob preferred the bed's size and proximity to a buddy; the girls he was with – two or three a week, never the same girl too many times – never got too comfortable next to him in bed or in the room with another guy, never tried to stay when Rob was done with them. At away games as well, when the beds in their shared hotel rooms were queens, Rob could still fuck all night and throw the girl out, go to sleep and wake up the next day and do the same thing again, fuck with Mark in the next bed. He never invited

Mark to take a turn with the girl, though; that privilege, Mark learned, was for the guy in the alley alone.

Every time he thought about Rob, he thought Rob could probably do it again, over and over, like fucking. He could beat a man down, go home, go to bed, wake up, and beat on another one. There was no remorse, no sentiment. Only code.

Rob had no shame and no secrets from Mark. He returned from the hall bath in a towel and dressed right in front of him. Rob never checked to see if Mark was asleep before beating off in the middle of the night. Rob didn't even seem to mind grooming himself in front of Mark, shaving- and tweezing-in the thin scar in his eyebrow that he thought made him look tough; to Mark, having seen Rob worry over it in the small mirror over their dresser, it would always look fake and affected, manicured macho posturing.

All this had made it hard to avoid Rob since they returned from Miami, and harder still to keep Rob from figuring out that he was avoiding him, but Mark managed by only being around Rob when someone else was there too: usually a girl, one Rob was quite thoroughly preoccupied with fucking. By being there when Rob didn't necessarily want him to be, Mark figured, Rob wouldn't seem to miss him much when they would have otherwise had the room to themselves.

# # # # #

Nick had taken great care in creating his home. The first step had been finding the right condominium to purchase. Since it had been the Technicolor of Ocean Drive that had lured him to the area, he knew he wanted to see the Strip close-up from his home. He also wanted to see the ocean.

There were two buildings that would allow for that – for both views – each on opposite ends of Ocean Drive. The building on the southern end of ocean was rather dated, and all the condominiums there were small one-bedroom units. Though that made them less expensive, Nick always hoped he'd be sharing his home with someone soon enough, and wanted to ensure that they – himself and the planned-for man-in-his-life – would have enough space. The view from that building also started at Ocean at Fifth, meaning that in the foreground of the view Nick wanted so much was a giant T.G.I. Fridays. Nick hated to admit that Friday's had the most consistent bar on Ocean, and went there often, always hoping the same friendly and cute Latino bartender with his seemingly permanent smile would be behind the bar pouring strong and slipping sippy-cup shots of Jägermeister – one for Nick, one for himself – between each round, and despite the chain not having the same personality as the one-off bars lining the rest of Ocean, Nick really liked it there. Looking out at it every day would make him admit that to himself every day, Nick reasoned, and opted for the building on the north end.

Architecturally, the building often came off as nothing special in its Deco Drive setting – just another bright jewel in a brilliantly pavéed setting – despite 1500 Ocean's attachment to the visionary and prolific architect Michael Graves. But Nick made the interior of his apartment there incredible and wasn't the least bit surprised when an editor from *Miami Home* magazine called him directly to feature the property and its designer as a cover.

Nick had been warned that all-black interiors were hard to capture in a photograph, but *Miami Home* had done a fine job of documenting the work Nick had put into the place. The black marble floors gleamed mirror-like on the magazine's matte pages, reflecting the view from the floor-to-ceiling glass near-perfectly but with white veins, so though the photographer had been there on a clear evening, the Ocean Drive view reflected in the floor looked shot with lighting. The alligator-embossed leather sofa from Fendi Casa shone as well, winking out from the pages and making it almost-worth Nick's dealing with the rude sales associate at their Design District showroom; she had gotten nicer when Nick expanded his order to include six boxy chrome-based leather dining chairs and a croc-print console. The infill items from Cassina and B&B Italia looked worth every penny in the pictures, the mirror-like chrome of the coffee table polished enough to reflect the photographer, his image narrowed and wrapped around the tubular leg, turning a close-up of the living room into his avant-garde self-portrait.

It had been Nick's strategy in designing the interior to create a space that was a completely neutral backdrop for the strong colors of South Beach, and moreover to focus on the fact that the Strip somehow got more colorful at night by covering everything in his signature black. In a way, it was how he approached all his design jobs, staying essentially neutral and letting the view or the art or a particularly colorful client to, once in place, pull the focus.

The reality of living with an all-black interior was something the magazine failed to capture, and Nick was rather happy about this. The black lacquer kitchen was beautiful enough for the Snaidero rep to call and ask if the company could use images of the installation for their own marketing, but the cabinets – and their Absolute Black granite counters – yielded a space so dark Nick was afraid to so much as chop a lime wedge in there for a second G-and-T. His most graceful of friends had all walked smack into walls they could barely see, a fact blamable as much on Nick's trademark black palette as on the strength of his signature Singapore Slings. Nick had worked closely with a lighting specialist to create a solution to what he always knew would be a problem, and though the ceiling had been silver-leafed to maximize reflected daylight off its nine-foot height, Nick felt as if he always had the lights on. This coupled with the fact that the space faced the south, and gathered nothing but direct Miami sun all day – which radiated off what would otherwise be a cold marble floor any day he forgot to close the drapes before work – made for a fairly substantial monthly energy bill.

The all-black environment was even harder to navigate now, on a crutch, his eyes so used to the overly bright fluorescents of his hospital room or the beige and bodies on the walls at Ron's apartment. The black marble floor, with its white veins in jagged and feathery broken lines, looked to Nick the way his X-rays had on the light box in the hospital, and he was newly fascinated with the movement in the patterns the tiles made, enough so to be distracted and dizzied by them. Barely three steps into the glamorous apartment he had worked so hard on, Nick stumbled to the floor.

# # # # #

"Hut hut hike!"

The center pitched the ball right to Mark's hands, but Mark made no move to catch it, and the ball went flying, arcing off his fingertips to the field, where it bounced and lumbered against the grass.

Mark took a knee and let the coach berate the team for its performance, but he knew it was all-him.

So did his teammates, who shot looks at Mark throughout the coach's tirade that let him know he was going to get it in the locker room.

# # # # #

Even with the crutch, Nick felt stronger than ever and was eager to return to work.

There was nothing special about the remodel he resumed design on, and that bothered him. It would turn out beautifully – his projects always did – but it too closely resembled projects already in his portfolio and revealed neither the client's personality nor his own.

What this meant was that the project was a new construction meant to mimic an old Mediterranean villa. The decisions involved in most interior design projects were like dominoes. Stand the dominoes upright in a row and push the first one down, and other decisions fall into place in line as if programmed to do just that, following the same direction of that first decision. Plan a project on the water, and certain soft shades of blue usually find their way into the interior. For a project situated among a lot of trees, green naturally enters the interior design in much the same way. A contemporary exterior begets a cutting edge interior; a genuinely old house gets its weathered brick or stone walls filled with antiques. Once the bones of a structure were in place, a lot of what followed was simply automatic. A boring exterior, sadly, left little room for the interior to excite and inspire those within it without that interior effort feeling incongruous. The architect of this project had fingered the first domino with stone and stucco and a clay-tile roof. Nick had merely come along and completed the job, filling the house with floors of tumbled travertine tiles and oak planks that had been newly finished to look centuries old, the manufacturing process including gouging pits into the wood and dragging a heavy chain against it to simulate years of wear. Nick had secretly taken great joy in describing the process to the fifty-ish female half of the married-couple-client, who had obviously had a facelift and countless injections to fill in the wear of her own years.

With his free hand, Nick waved 'hello' at the installer on his knees working on the wood floor of what would eventually be the den, and the man said something genial back in Spanish. *Guess I really just waved 'hola,'* Nick thought. Nick smiled at the man but didn't test his high school proficiency with the language and took a moment to collect himself, steadying his weight against the still-uneven floor. The workman resumed his rhythm with the tongue-and-groove of the floor, tapping the boards into place with a mallet.

The kitchen cabinets had received a similar aging treatment to their alder wood faces and were topped with honed granite. Nick had visited the site today to survey the work being done on the master bath, so he slowly crutch-climbed the curved staircase – stone treads, wood risers, and a serpentine tangle of wrought iron rail – to check its status.

The door from the master bedroom to its ensuite bath was blocked by all of the boxes of products being installed in the bath, proclaiming their contents in brown ink on lighter brown cardboard, little attention paid to the pointed caution arrows indicating 'this end up.' Nick hoped the box marked 'fragile' with the arrow pointing back downstairs was empty.

Just as the design scheme of the space was disappointingly neutral to Nick, so too were the manufacturers' descriptions of the toilet and taps that would comprise that scheme. *There are only so many ways to say 'beige,'* he reasoned, although the warm and dark metal finish for the faucets, called out as 'oil-rubbed bronze' on the box, always elicited a giggle from Nick.

Nick poked the rubber-tipped end of the crutch through more boxes – more beige – and saw that the toilet that arrived was a different color – a different beige – than the sinks he'd specified for the his and hers vanities. They were supposed to match, and it upset him that the general contractor hadn't caught that they had different color names printed clearly on the box, so Nick had his cell phone out fast as a reflex to call the GC and straightened his posture, preparing to speak sternly to the man who'd missed the mistake. Nick then thought of a better way to handle it, and with the phone still ringing, relaxed his stance.

Nick thought anyone who would knowingly name a toilet color 'biscuit' or 'bone' had no sense of bathroom humor or anatomical entendre, and that surely the contractor would respond better to a joke about those names than to Nick yelling at him, which even Nick knew came off a bit queeny and hard to take seriously to the routinely straight male contractors. It occurred to Nick that, before he'd been attacked, he would have yelled into the phone without waiting for answers or an explanation. He knew it would never have occurred to him before to make some engaging remark to charm the straight man on the phone before plainly stating the problem and pleasantly pointing out that, as it was the contractor who had ordered the fixtures, he would need to be the one to fix this, and soon.

"What's the difference?" the contractor asked. "Beige is beige."

"I'm going to forget you said that," Nick said, though with the monochrome monotony of neutral throughout the house, Nick wasn't entirely sure he blamed the man, though he was disappointed but unsurprised at the contractor's lack of accountability.

"Seriously, the toilet's behind its own little door – I'll switch 'em out, it's what you wanted, but I don't get why it's a big deal to you."

I am never working with this contractor again, Nick thought, but instead said, "We gay men like our 'bone,' okay?"

Nick pulled the phone away from his ear to dampen the GC's hearty laughter. "So you don't want the toilet left in 'biscuit?'" the contractor clarified.

"Not unless you want to find a 'biscuit' left in the toilet."

The contractor laughed again. "You know I did that once. Didn't realize the toilet wasn't hooked up on a jobsite before I used –"

"TMI," Nick interrupted.

"I think my doctor called it 'IBS,' not 'TMI.'"

"No. Not Irritable Bowel Syndrome. Gross, by the way. TMI: Too Much Information. An overshare. Do you need a Gay-to-Straight pocket dictionary, or are you going to be okay?"

Nick could hear the contractor smile against the phone. "I'm okay. Got it. 'Bone' it is. Anything else?"

"That's as far as I've got. I'll call back if anything else comes up."

The contractor laughed lightly into the phone. "Anything else like your 'bone,' right?" he said.

I work alone, Nick thought. "Your floor guy's already on his knees – why would I need to call *you* for that?" he said, and snapped his flip-phone shut. It occurred to him why he liked the flip-phone for business, the way it was similar to the closing clack of a powder compact after a woman touched up her face: a delicate but authoritative marking of a completed task, an accomplishment.

Nick eyed the cabinetry and countertops in the bath and found *them,* at least, satisfactorily beige, and went downstairs, pleased both with how the phone call had gone and how much easier it was to go down the stairs with a crutch than it had been to go up. *There's one contractor who will take my calls from now on,* Nick thought, and wondered why he'd waited so long to be more like himself – catty and clever, charming and effective – on the job.

On his way out, Nick saw that the wood floor installer had taken a coffee- or cigarette break – *café o cigarillo,* Nick thought, half-guessing at the Spanish – and left his tools out among the uneven lets-draw-straws lengths of oak that fingered out against the plywood subfloor. Nick bent down, leaning against the crutch to keep from falling the short distance, and smoothed a hand over the distressed finish of the wood before pocketing the installer's rubber mallet.

The rest of Nick's day had gone well enough, though driving in his condition proved as much of a challenge as he'd expected. He'd raced through most of his meetings and a design caucus with his boss with the image of the swiped tool he'd stashed in his glove box flashing intermittently in his mind with solutions for an attic's awkward ceiling angles and another home's combined butler's pantry and wine tasting room. In each meeting, he let more and more of his own personality come out, watching his revealed humor and easier-than-ever manner startle and then please his boss. After his last meeting, Nick practically broke into a run on the way to his car before it hit him that he still needed the crutch; he winced as he landed too hard on the side of him that was weakened but strangely felt stronger than ever.

Though he knew it was just an irrational irritation in his mind, Nick had never felt the elevator at his condo building move so slowly. Even his own pace down the hall and coordination with his key disappointed him. Everything was in the way – it seemed to him – in the way of him improving himself.

Once inside, he didn't change out of his work clothes, didn't make himself his customary end-of-business drink, didn't turn on the television to keep himself company as he usually did. All he did was squat toward the floor until he could softly fall against it, his ass landing with a soft thud against the cold hard marble. He pried off his left shoe and pulled off the sock, and let go of both to instead grab the mallet.

Nick aimed a few practice taps against his exposed big toe, deciding how hard he'd have to hit.

Nick had walked many jobsites while construction was underway. He was used to the sound of a hammer hitting a nail and driving it into wood – the solid pounding or banging of hard against harder. But the rubber mallet against his own bones, hard enough to break them, was different, like crunching into the thick layer of peanut husks on the floor at Raffles Long Bar in Singapore, or trying to get at the meat of any kind of crustacean. The pain was strong, and he figured it would be nothing compared to putting any weight on it, particularly with the other half of him helped-out with the crutch. But he could hide it and no one would know.

Nick swung at it again to make sure the bone was broken, smiling at pain that would have before made him cry, before crabbing his body toward the computer and running an internet search on how to wrap his toe and grow stronger.

Chapter Nine

His last cast was removed in the morning, but Nick didn't realize how much bigger his body had gotten until he got dressed that night to go out with Ron.

The black button-down that had always fit him close was now almost obscene, the fabric gaping around each of the buttons where Nick had to strain to get the fabric closed, tan skin peeking out in each of the created marquise-shaped slits. Nick's chest pressed hard against the fabric, and he knew he'd have to leave the top three buttons undone – they just would not close – though his nipples were still clearly apparent, the cloth pulled close over them. His biceps strained the sleeves; he could see the sinew of each muscle through the black fabric as though the material were instead his skin. The black jeans he pulled from his closet cupped his ass tight, hugging him above where his thighs flared out, each leg an hourglass, the denim bunching and narrowing down to the knee before angling out and stretching again for his beefy calves. The only constant was in front, where his dick had always created a pronounced bulge against the fly. When Nick checked himself in the mirror, he reached for the phone and called Ron, who answered on the third ring.

"I've got a handful of hair gel here, sweetie." Ron skipped 'hello.'

"How about Score tonight?" Nick asked, naming the club that had always intimidated him, all the guys there seeming twice as hot as he'd ever be, sipping fifteen-dollar martinis in a cucumber-cool setting and looking, whether accidentally or on purpose, as standoffish as possible.

"You never want to go there!" Ron replied. Nick knew Ron would be delighted, as Ron always suggested the place and Nick had, before tonight, always refused. "So, why tonight, sweetie?"

"You'll see," Nick said, still looking in the mirror as he hung up and headed out.

Nick turned onto Lincoln Road and navigated the sidewalk between the storefronts and the café umbrellas, dodging dog leashes and restaurant wait staff as they darted between outdoor tables and indoor kitchens, trying not to sweat through his shirt before he hit Score, though he knew that, like so many guys there, he could just take it off and keep dancing.

Nick recognized the club from the look of the crowd just outside it – extremely attractive, if nearly identical, muscular men packed close enough to each other that Nick knew from the lack of discomfort on their tanned and tweezed faces that they were all gay – but Nick always looked for another type of sign outside Score. He looked for the equivalent of a roller coaster warning: *you-must-be-this-tall-to-ride-this-ride.* At the entrance to Score, Nick thought a notice that *you-must-be-this-good-looking-to-get-past-the-door* would be appropriate. Nick didn't know how a barometer like that would work, what one could measure one's attractiveness against to know whether entry would be allowed or prohibited, but knew there was no need for one. As far as appearance was concerned, most gay men knew where they stood, and a grouping of guys like the ones outside Score was enough to keep men who knew they didn't measure up from even thinking about going in; it had certainly kept Nick out until tonight.

This made it all the easier to spot Ron in the crowd. One of the things Nick loved about Ron was that he was fearless. Ron wasn't stupid, and he was surely self-aware; he knew he stuck out in a crowd of guys like the ones at Score. He just didn't care.

Nick made his way to Ron, liking how the crowd parted to let him through, heads turning, admiring eyes following, faces folding in on him as he passed. "I'm not ready to go back to Twist yet," Nick said, which was true but not at all the reason he'd decided on Score tonight.

"Oh honey," Ron said, sizing up Nick and shaking his head, "I don't think Twist is ready *for you.*"

Nick surveyed the bar and found still more reasons for Score to intimidate him; the interior design looked like the kind of work he wanted to be doing at the firm, like the Miami he'd imagined before moving here. The décor was on-trend – appropriate to a club for gay men obsessed with looking not only their best but current, though Nick was sure the interior would be overhauled before being allowed to look even a millisecond behind the times – the palette edited to only black and white and red. Walls glittered with black mosaic tile or the flow of a glassy waterwall. A boxy banquette was covered in a bold black-and-white damask, the created space within its L-shape filled with round red leather ottomans and stainless steel cubes. The bar was equally boxy, its white quartz counter separating the ripped, shirtless bartenders from the patrons in clear red-topped piston stools, both caging and framing the bartenders like animals at the zoo or art at a museum: do-not-feed-the-bartenders, do-not-touch-the-masterpiece. Nick figured the bartenders probably couldn't eat much and keep their abs as cut as they were, and wondered if touching them was like being pinched in a dream, for surely no one really looked like that.

Nick remembered then that, more and more, *he* looked like that. So did the well-muscled man with the shaved head Nick usually saw at Twist. Nick saw him in a corner and locked eyes on him, forcing the man to ignore the two guys that had been chatting him up, until Ron grabbed Nick's elbow and broke his focus.

"I'm going to get a drink and find the dance floor," Ron said.

"Sure-okay-fine."

"I'm going to marry the next woman I meet, have a couple of kids, and vote Republican," Ron said.

Nick grinned widely. "Sure-okay-fine," he said, this time more consciously. "Sorry, there's just something about that guy over there."

Ron was a decent wingman, and he knew better than to point. Not that he needed to; with Nick and the buff bald guy eye-fucking each other the way they were through the crowd, Nick figured everyone could sense their attraction.

"His name is Marco. The rest, you're going to have to find out for yourself," Ron said before plunging into the pack, looking like the kid at an amusement park who, though not tall enough to ride-the-rides, was determined to have a hell of a good time anyway.

Nick was working up the nerve to go talk to Marco when Marco saved him the trouble and waved him over.

"Haven't seen you out for a while," Marco said once Nick was within earshot.

I wasn't sure you'd ever noticed me, Nick thought, too stunned to speak.

"You been hiding?"

Nick nodded.

"Not hiding from me, I hope."

Nick shook his head as though in a hypnotist's trance. *When I snap my fingers, you will open your eyes and see the most gorgeous man,* Nick thought, his humor finally relaxing him enough to smile.

"Looks like you've been bulking up."

Nick didn't think he needed to nod, just puff out his chest a little more.

"Looks good on you," Marco said, smoothing his hand over Nick's shirt, pressing the cloth against Nick's tensed abs.

Nick still hadn't said anything, and though he knew it would have been polite to say 'thank-you' after receiving the compliment, he was more concerned with Marco discovering he was well-hung than well-mannered.

"What I can see of it, anyway," Marco said, his hand now up Nick's shirt a little.

"Maybe I can show you the rest sometime," Nick finally dared.

Marco grinned. "I'd like that. And I'd like 'sometime' to be tonight."

# # # # #

Carrie was all over Mark at the club, cooing into his ear when they were close and seeming to wag her ass at him, only him, from across the bar. Mark's gaze only strayed from her to eye Rob, make certain he was catching this, ensure that Rob saw that he could still get a girl like Carrie all over him, that being concerned about what they'd done to the man in that alley in South Beach didn't mean he'd gone soft. *Or queer, for that matter,* Mark thought, when he wasn't thinking *damn she's fine* about Carrie, or just thinking about what they'd do later.

Carrie worked her set on stage to two songs Mark thought she could have chosen knowing how much he liked them, and seemed to be dancing just for him, sweating under the hot lights until her skin had the sheen of polished brass. When her set was over, she pushed away the guys who pled to take her to a private room – Rob included, Mark noted – to search out Mark and drag him by his collar to the back.

Mark had seen Carrie give lap dances to guys lots of times, either through the beaded curtain that separated the back room from the main bar or from one of the other sofas in the back room, daring his eyes away from the girl he'd given sixty bucks to grind on his lap to see this girl – this hot, smart girl who intimidated him so much he couldn't talk to her, much less ask for the dance he wanted – do the same to another guy. Mark knew what a lap dance was, either performed by Carrie or another dancer. What Carrie proceeded to do to him was no lap dance.

Where Carrie worked, a lap dance was two songs, one fast, one slow, just like on stage. And, just like on stage, the girl usually waited as long as she could – even through the first song – before removing so much as her top, dragging it out, teasing her audience and waiting, making sure she was naked for as little time as possible. This meant that the club was, by the small town's standards, a class joint; in other bars, the girls were out of their tops even before their set started, and flashed the crowd everything while working the room for tips.

Carrie was out of her bra before Mark had completely sat down. She had looped it over his head and around his neck like a yoke or Hawaiian lei before he had settled into the sofa, and now that they were both in it, she used the bra to pull his head closer, into her chest, his nose between her breasts. Mark took a deep breath, inhaling sweat and the perfume Carrie wore when she worked, heated up, sweeter and stronger than he figured she'd choose for normal wear, for when she wasn't 'Diamond.' No touching was involved in a lap dance, but when Mark's hands found Carrie's back, fingers lacing between the protruding vertebrae of her spine, neither she nor the bouncer made any move to shoo them off her like flies. Carrie wasn't bothering with any music, but her rhythm was fast. She bucked up and down in Mark's lap, getting him hard almost instantly and making sure she could feel it against her sex. Mark tightened his grip around Carrie's torso and tried to control her rhythm but couldn't, her need for him was too strong, as was her will. He let his hands rest there but relaxed them, letting them slide a bit against her sweat-slick flesh. When she slowed, Mark reached his hands around to cup her breasts, still amazed that no one had come to break them up, stop him from setting such a bad example for the other patrons of what was acceptable to do to one of the girls for sixty bucks. She was coming down on him hard now, using her thighs to muscle herself against his rigid prick. Mark was close, and could tell that Carrie was, too. Mark glanced through the beaded curtain and saw Rob looking on; Mark knew that Rob, too, could tell how much Carrie was into it, into Mark. Carrie took Mark's right hand off her breast and drew it toward her face, molding his hand in hers until his middle and index fingers were pointing like a gun at her head. She put his fingers in her mouth, like she was going to blow her brains out with the mock-gun she had formed, and sucked and salivated on them enough to get them wet. She pulled his hand out of her mouth and away from her face, let his fingers quickly graze her nipple back and forth, before pushing them lower, to the waistband of her G-string, then inside it, then inside her.

"You're soaked," Mark blurted out.

"To the bone," Carrie replied, looking down at Mark's cock-strained zipper and his fingers inside her before coming, her sex convulsing onto Mark's hand.

Mark looked away, his eyes finding Rob's through the beaded curtain before he came against his jeans, so close to being inside Carrie.

# # # # #

Nick had seen Marco without his shirt plenty of times at the club, but seeing Marco's chest in front of him, at home with him, was quite another thing. He was sure every guy who went home with Marco marveled at his muscularity, and as much as Nick wanted to do something that would set himself apart from the guys that seemed to wait for Marco to notice them, he couldn't help himself. Every inch of Marco, from his neck to his waist, was delectable and looked delicious;

Nick drooled over the meaty slabs of Marco's pecs, the rib-like fingers of his obliques below them, the perfect ravioli-squares of his pronounced abdominal muscles lower still, like a starved man looking at so much food.

Nick's hands were all over Marco's chest, pressing his pecs, pinching his nipples playfully, running his fingertips through the crevices between his prominent abs. Nick's eyes were open wide, he didn't dare blink, for fear he'd miss some detail of the perfect musculature before him. Marco, in turn, didn't respond much at all to Nick's touch, as though this appreciation, this worship, was familiar to him.

"Wow," Nick said, unable to help himself. *Wow, wow, wow,* he thought.

"Like my chest, huh?" Marco asked, as though the line and its inevitable follow-up were much-rehearsed.

"Mmm-hmm," Nick responded as though his mouth were full, then filled it with Marco's nipple.

"Wait 'til you see my ass," Marco said, the line again automatic.

Though Nick wanted to see Marco's ass, and to kiss it and eat it and fuck it hard, he could, indeed, wait. He was nowhere near done working over Marco's chest. "Mmmf," he breathed out against the smooth skin around Marco's nipple. Nick licked the peaked bud, crazily slobbering all over Marco and not caring how it felt to him.

Marco just leaned back and let him.

Nick moved on to Marco's other nipple, pinching and licking and nibbling it a little, trying to hold back from devouring the guy, hurting him with too hard a bite, turning him off. Nick wondered if he even *could* hurt a guy Marco's size.

Nick took a break from Marco's chest to take off his own shirt.

"Not bad," Marco said appreciatively. Nick thought that was nice of him, knowing his body was nothing next to Marco's. Marco then gave Nick a taste of his own medicine, going at Nick's chest with his mouth, teeth, and tongue, laying into Nick until he was soaked.

"Feels good," Marco said, encouraging Nick to return to Marco's chest ASAP. Nick dove for Marco's abs face-first, and nuzzled them before licking into the deep contours there, even tonguing into Marco's belly button before popping Marco's fly and reaching down the front of his underwear.

Marco was hard and wet in Nick's hand.

"Feels good," Nick mimicked back to Marco, the words nearly-silent, barely breaths up Marco's core.

"Tastes even better," Marco said, and pushed Nick's head toward his cock.

Nick pulled Marco's pants the whole way off and caught his breath. Marco was wearing a jockstrap. Nick wanted to remember the way this looked on his sofa.

"What a vision." Nick said, before carefully stretching the jock around Marco's erection and pulling the loops of elastic down his legs.

Like Nick had worked over Marco's chest, he gave him wet and sloppy head, too, taking brief breaks to look up not at Marco's eyes or face but at his amazing torso, how the mounds of his pecs hadn't flattened out in recline but remained well-defined. Marco's muscles were huge and powerful, but his cock was manageably sized – if just as delicious, Nick discovered – and Nick could easily get it all in his mouth at once, though the tip of it kissed the back of his throat. He slurped and sucked at Marco noisily, nodding into him as he moved his head up and down and against him, faster and faster with each repetition.

Nick looked up at Marco's face; Marco's eyes were closed. Nick, by contrast, wasn't willing to risk so much as a blink; he wanted to see every moment of his time with Marco, to remember it later, play it back in his mind over and over.

Nick was into Marco big time, and though he was pretty much all-top, if Marco had positioned Nick to bottom for him, Nick wouldn't have said 'no.' *Had a bottle in there, what harm could a dick I can deep-throat do?* he thought. But Nick couldn't help smiling when Marco flung himself onto the bed back-first, kicked his legs into the air, and asked, "You wanna bone me?"

Do I ever, Nick thought to himself, then realized he was licking his lips. "Fuck yeah," he said, almost already inside Marco before he'd torn open a condom wrapper and rolled on the rubber with the dexterity that comes from being both entirely well-practiced and a little bit drunk.

"Smooth." Marco said.

"Just like you," Nick said back, and slid into Marco just as smoothly.

"Fuck yeah." Marco echoed as Nick bottomed out inside him.

Nick stayed all the way inside Marco for a moment, savoring the look on Marco's face as his body adjusted to Nick inside him. Nick locked eyes on Marco for as long as he could, too – making sure Marco didn't have his eyes closed anymore, was into it the way a bottom should be – before breaking the stare to allow his gaze to go further down, to Marco's chest and abs. Nick loved the way Marco's body looked with him inside him, and let his unconscious response to Marco power his thrusts. There was no toying with Marco's ass with just the head of his cock; each thrust was all the way in, and almost all the way out, giving Marco everything he had.

Marco gave as good as he got, tightening his glutes and using the strength of his thick thighs to pull and push Nick in and out of him deeper than Nick could thrust on his own.

"Squats are paying off," Nick said.

Marco merely grunted at Nick.

"Nice and tight," Nick added.

Marco grunted again, and Nick did, too, the strain of the powerful fucking he was giving Marco making him sweat.

"Deeper," Marco cried out, but Nick was large and already all the way inside him.

Fuck, this guy's insatiable, Nick thought, knowing he couldn't go any deeper but trying, praying to God now more than ever for even an extra millimeter.

Nick pressed harder into Marco until the man cried out "yes" in a voice so uncharacteristically high-pitched that it seemed to need to come from a much smaller man, and then Nick knew Marco was his. Nick began boning away in Marco, staying inside him but backing out an inch or two before slamming into him hard again, then repeating, pounding the last measures of himself into Marco again and again until Marco shot his come all over his perfect abs.

Ravioli Alfredo, Nick thought.

"Come for me," Marco said when he was done twitching and shuddering under Nick.

Nick tried to ignore him, tune him out, keep plowing away, but Marco resisted, letting Nick fall all of the way out of him and quickly lowering his legs, making it tough for Nick to get back in. Nick peeled off the condom and started to jack his dick, kneeling over Marco and watching Marco ready himself.

"Hit me," Nick said.

"What?"

"Hit me!" he said more forcefully, and Marco threw a light punch toward Nick's face. It landed soft against his cheek as Nick squeezed his dick hard.

"Harder! In my arm. Fucking punch my left arm!" Nick yelled, realizing he sounded nuts, still jacking himself on top of Marco.

Marco threw a real punch this time, and it landed hard against Nick's left arm, but it just stung his skin and made the muscle there throb.

"Harder. Right there. Hit me again right there." Nick's rhythm was frantic, his cock a blur in his hand as he looked down at it, trying to figure out where his come would fly if he just let go.

Marco did it again, and it hurt again, but it still just sounded like knuckles on skin above their breathing and bucking.

"Again. Fucking break it. Break my arm." Nick was so close he was fighting it back, holding it in.

Marco took Nick's left wrist and guided his hand toward his own ass. Nick instinctively pressed three fingers together and let Marco guide them into his ass. "Break me off," Marco replied to Nick's request and hit him again, harder than before. Nick felt it more in his fingers than in his arm, Marco's just-fucked ass holding his hand in place against the blow. Nick realized Marco wasn't going to hit him any harder than that, and that it wasn't going to be enough force to push through the muscle there and break the bone.

Both defeated and elated, Nick shot off all over Marco, the first blast of his come arcing over the guy's perfect body and landing on his confused face.

# # # # #

Back at Carrie's apartment, Mark saw the shirt he'd left there last time balled-up by her pillow and smiled, knowing that she was sleeping with it next to her, inhaling his scent as she dreamed.

Mark knew his face was betraying him as he opened the nightstand drawer, responding to the quantity of condoms there without judgment, as though Carrie were simply a prepared and responsible modern girl, and Mark knew they were cheaper in the value pack anyway. His eyes widened a bit more at the tube of lubricant, Carrie seemingly taking preparedness to Boy Scout lengths. Mark covered a guffaw with a cough as her vibrator rolled forward in the drawer. *The length of the Boy Scout,* he thought, remembering the Scouts' vertical three-finger salute and scaling the width of three of his fingers pressed together against the girth of the sex toy.

Carrie's face showed no embarrassment. "I get lonely."

"Good thing I'm here," Mark said, still turned-on and relieved that the vibrator was human-scale and not ridiculous, that he measured up well, though the locker room had taught him he compared favorably to most men.

"Let's hope it's good."

Mark pulled a condom from the nightstand and left the drawer open, not knowing if Carrie needed lube all the time or only sometimes and for certain acts. The thought of 'certain acts' sent Mark's mind on a tangent. Mark figured a girl with lube would be down for anal sometime, and Carrie was a stripper to boot; the thought of his dick drilling into Carrie's sweet, heart-shaped ass got Mark so hard he knew it was nearly time for the condom, his hard bone already poking up against the waist of his boxers.

Mark's mind suddenly flashed to the man in the alley in South Beach, to inserting the beer bottle into his ass, the sound the man had made, the sound the act itself had made: glass against skin, the resistance of the man's body against Mark's force

Mark fought not to lose his erection and forced his face into Carrie's breasts, not worrying if this was doing anything for her, just knowing that if he didn't, he couldn't do anything for either one of them. Assured he was still hard, Mark focused back on Carrie, on pleasing her, at least enough to get invited back again.

He pulled down her panties and went to work, his nose rubbing where she was shaved-smooth for work, Mark using his tongue to sign his name across her clit like pissing in the snow, claiming ownership. Mark's thoughts shifted again to the alley, to pissing on the guy he and Rob had attacked after they were done. Mark found himself writing the word 'sorry' over and over again with his tongue against Carrie's clit, in curvy cursive that circled back on itself. *Sorrysorrysorry,* with Carrie about to come.

Once he knew he'd brought her there – Carrie's upper thighs pushed against his face and now shuddering, the pressure of her groin easing up – Mark wanted to get sucked a little, but feared that breaking the visual of Carrie – losing eye contact, the ability to see her mouth, her breasts – would let his mind wander back to Miami, so he instead poised himself over her to enter her.

Mark rolled the condom on over his hard dick and dove in.

Carrie cried out, more likely still riding-high on the just-finished cunnilingus than from Mark's initial entry, which was rougher than he'd planned and might have hurt her a little, but he needed to fuck away the memory of the night in the alley.

"Yes," Carrie sighed as Mark settled into a rhythm.

Mark's mind wasn't in Carrie's bed with the two of them. It was in South Beach, with the man face down against the asphalt, not saying a word, just taking it.

Mark tried to continue the rhythm but faded out, lost tempo, lost focus. He couldn't get the man out of his mind.

In his out-of-control thoughts, Mark's cock was replaced with a beer bottle, and though he initially tried to jam it into Carrie to drive out the thoughts of what he'd done, he soon started easing off the pressure, became gentle, trying not to hurt her with his beer bottle bone.

Carrie rolled him over and stayed on top of him, taking control. The sight of Carrie going to town on his dick was enough to shake him out of it for a while, bring him back to town, to this bed, to being with Carrie. Her breasts were high and firm, they trembled with each ride she took up and down his cock. Mark couldn't help staring at them and had to remind himself to look up, meet her hazel eyes every now and then, but she almost always had her head thrown back or her eyes closed, or was looking at his tensed abs when he tried to meet her thrust-for-thrust, pushing from below when she was coming down on him hard. This only lasted a few strokes, until he remembered coming down hard on the guy in the alley with his fists, punching at his face mercilessly. Mark fought to get back in the moment, and managed to meet Carrie's rhythm for a while, and they really got going, the bed starting to move with them. The bed bumped Carrie's nightstand, which sent a framed picture she'd had there – Mark hadn't noticed what the picture was, and hoped it wasn't an ex – to the floor, where the glass shattered. The sound sent Mark's thoughts back to South Beach, to the baseball bat breaking off the beer bottle, swinging shards of glass loudly into the street and silently into the skin of some poor man Rob had decided to pick on.

Back to Carrie, Mark thought, and looked up at her again, at the light mist of perspiration that had collected on her skin and was beginning to roll down her chest, between her breasts, shiny as the shattered bottle glass that had glinted against the man's flesh in the alleyway's dim light. The tears streaming down his bloody face had shimmered, too, sparkling and wet like the sweat that Carrie now dripped on him.

Distracted, Mark came inside the condom – inside Carrie – without even realizing he was close. His body had just had sex with Carrie, but he was hardly there. He caught his breath only to try to get himself panting again, to grunt and gasp as he clutched Carrie's hips tight. Mark wondered how many times Carrie had had to fake an orgasm.

This was his first.

Chapter Ten

"Well, that's a first," Ron said to Nick the following morning at brunch.

"What?"

"Your order. An omelet. Bacon. Actual *food,* sweetie. I'd ask if you hit your head, but after all you've been through, honey."

"Hungry, I guess."

"After last night with Marco, I'll bet you've got quite an appetite. Wore you out, did he?"

Ron wanted all the details about Nick's night with Marco, and though Nick was happy to oblige, his mind was somewhere else.

On his doctor.

Ron picked up on it soon enough, though not before Nick recounted every minute of last night's action.

"Haven't you wanted this Marco guy for, like, ever?"

"Oh-yeah," Nick said the two words quickly, as though they were one.

"So why does it sound like you were less-than-into-it, sweetie?"

Nick recalled asking Marco to break his arm and wondered that himself. *I was into it at the time, that much I know. This morning, though, Ron's right. It's like it never happened, or never needed to.*

Ron resumed the inquisition. "Did you have a good time?"

"Hell yeah."

"Of course you did, you're the top. All you do is come, and automatically, it's a great time. You did come, right, sweetie?"

Nick breathed out a long sigh. "All over the guy."

"Did he seem to like that?" Ron asked. "Did *he* have a good time?"

"Yes and yes, I think," Nick said, thinking about how Marco had responded when Nick asked him to hit him, to break his arm. Nick also thought about how he himself had responded to his own request, how the blows Marco struck were hard, though not enough to break his bones, but that getting hit felt different because he'd asked for it. He'd asked to be hit, taking control rather than surrendering it to an attacker. Marco was hot, and Nick had enjoyed every second, but it didn't feel good to have asked.

"Then honey, why aren't you counting the minutes 'til it's acceptable to call him again?" Ron nudged Nick. "Three days, *ring-ring,* then *ring-a-ding-ding.*"

Nick thought about it for a while, about swinging the mallet into his own foot as hard as he could, as hard as the baseball bat had struck him months ago, as hard as Marco had hit his arm three times. It wasn't that. It was the doctor; hot as Marco was, Nick would have rather gone to bed with the doctor. Nick decided to tell Ron all about him, concluding his description by asking, "You know the expression 'I could watch that man read the phone book?'"

"Yeah."

"Well, I could watch him read my medical chart all day long. Preferably with it printed on my body. In Braille."

# # # # #

Mark felt the raised lacing of the ball in his hands and knew how to position it for a throw blindly; without looking down, he fit a stitch of the teeth-like lacing between each of his spread fingers.

Everyone knew the rules in football, and everyone knew the penalties for breaking those rules. The penalties had to do with two things: injury prevention and going against the clock.

If the defense went after the quarterback when he had the ball, that was fine, understood, the defense was just doing its job trying to stop the play. Hit the QB after he had released the ball and this attack was without cause, cited as 'unnecessary roughness.' Same with the kicker of a field goal or extra point: hit him before the kick, no-harm-no-foul, but with the ball in the air, it was a penalty play. The defensive linemen could use their hands, but the offense could not. A player couldn't facemask a guy, chopblock, or horsecollar him: grab the back of his jersey the way Carrie did it off the field to drag Mark around to where she wanted him, namely to bed. On the field and among the players, Carrie's sexed-up move would be flagged.

If a player jumped out of the line of scrimmage before play began, he was going against the clock. If too much time passed before a play, or if one team had more players on the field than the opposition during timed play, those offenses would result in penalties.

Everyone knew these rules better than they knew the Ten Commandments, and for the most part, didn't risk breaking them. Off the field, these rules didn't apply, but Mark wondered if maybe they should. *Thou shalt not gay-bash,* Mark thought. The man in the alley in Miami was minding his business: a quarterback without a ball, and he and Rob had no cause to attack him. It was unnecessary roughness. As for going against the clock, Mark wondered how much time he had before it all caught up with him, or if, after enough time, he could learn to forget.

Distracted by all this thinking, Mark led the team to defeat after defeat against team after team in game after game.

# # # # #

Nick went home from brunch feeling horny as hell, surprised he felt like he needed to come again after last night but wound-up on remembered details of his time inside Marco and his fantasies about the doctor. Nick walked home briskly, scanning the sidewalks on Washington for any prospects to take home and get off with before deciding he was better off with just his memories, not taking home some inferior guy so soon after perfect Marco.

Nick was fully hard before he'd even opened the door to his place, and popped his shirt over his head the second he walked in, closing the door behind him with the collar and one sleeve still caught around his wrist. He let it drop to the floor and left it there, already working on the button and fly of his jeans. He kicked off his shoes and stepped out of his jeans, his sock-clad feet sliding against the marble floor as he raced for his bed.

Nick flung himself on the bed and pulled off his socks from the toes, the movement reminding him of pulling off a condom from the tip, the image of yanking off a condom so he could come on his partner getting him even more worked-up. Nick pulled his underwear over his cock and down, leaving them just past his ass and under his balls, pushing his dick into his abs.

Nick spat into his hand and grabbed himself, then spat again, mixing spit with the pre-come on the head of his cock and getting to work. Nick shut his eyes and only opened them when he needed to spit again.

Like any designer, Nick was primarily a visual person, and usually couldn't get off on his own with just his imagination, but today was different. With Marco still fresh in his mind and the smell of him still in the sheets, Nick didn't need any help. He remembered the erotic surge of Marco's first touch, still at Score, through his shirt and then under it. The feeling of Marco's approving eyes on his body, first in the shirt he filled out to nearly its breaking point, then later, here, when he took it off. The way Marco's chest had looked at the bar, how it had looked different in bed, not just different because it was lit differently and closer-up, but because it was his. His to touch, to lick, to kiss, to suck on, to come on.

Nick was close, he knew, his head now spinning with thoughts of every good-looking guy he'd ever met, picturing them in sexual situations whether he'd been with them that way or not. In a way it felt like cheating on Marco, but Nick knew there was no connection there beyond the physical. Nick thought of the collage of men on Ron's wall, then of Marco's sweet dick, then his hot doctor, then of asking Marco to hit him. Nick brought his knees closer to his chest, knowing he was about to come, knowing he'd let it shoot all over his chest and abs the way Marco had let his land on his own last night. Nick thought of his own come hitting Marco in the face, then of being hit in the face that night in the alley by the attacker with the class ring with the blue stone, of the attacker's handsome face and jock body, of the hard-on that caused the man's piss to shoot high in the air before it landed on him.

His eyes closed tight, Nick came all over himself, thinking of his attacker.

# # # # #

"Thirty-nine, twenty-three, four, hike!"

Mark caught the football that was snapped back toward him from between the center's legs and adjusted his grip to throw it quickly. His timing had been off since he and Rob had returned from spring break, and he'd noticed it getting even worse in the last games of the season. Now it was autumn, and the new season was starting. Mark was a sophomore now, though he didn't know how he had passed chemistry, and had done so, like all of his classes since Miami, just barely.

Mark spotted his wide receiver open twenty yards away, and threw a pass at him that had gone incomplete, his own throw coming short but mercifully not intercepted by the opposing team.

Mark huddled in, fell behind the line of players, and waited to hear the three numbers that would have meant more, if not much more, had he paid attention in the huddle, where Rob had done all the talking.

Mark loved the maintained morale of the football team – how what he and Rob had done in Miami had remained their secret and could impact only them. *Only me,* Mark thought. Mark knew it wasn't the morale of the team but its morality that confused things for guys like Rob. On the field, unlike in life, everyone knows the rules, and everyone knows the punishment for breaking those rules. Fumble: ten yard penalty. Try and fail too many times: loss of controlling the ball. The man in the alley hadn't known the rules, and neither, Mark figured, did he or Rob. They'd punished the man for nothing, and Mark figured he'd eventually be punished for that himself.

# # # # #

Whenever something went wrong in Nick's life, he figured it was because he'd done something wrong himself, that it was his fault: a penalty for sinning. Tell a lie, get lied-to. Hurt someone and feel pain. Masturbate to fall asleep on a restless night, have a terrible day the next day, particularly for having thought of men to get off. Nick wondered if being gay really was a sin – it had been as hard for him to come to terms with his own homosexuality as it had been for others to accept – but Nick didn't feel bad for bedding Marco or beating off afterward.

As far as sins were concerned, Nick estimated the worst thing he ever did was think about heaven. Certainly thinking about the afterlife was natural, but he didn't dream of it the way the devout did, or debate its existence in agnostic reflection. As a designer, Nick planned it in detail, assigning everything from the programmatic elements – a pool, hot-tub, king-size bed with someone to share them all with – to an architectural style – Nick was unfailingly contemporary – to the abstract space he was creating in his mind. Nick also figured he was wrong for doing so, for not trusting that where his spirit would dwell after dying was either far grander than anything he could imagine or built from nothing more than dirt and decay.

Nick's ideas of right-and-wrong were shifting, as he couldn't figure what he'd done to deserve what had happened to him; surely he'd committed no sin great enough to deserve being attacked. Nick found that struggling with the equilibrium of good and bad was as hard as balancing his weight on his arms between the parallel bars in physical therapy. Karma-wise, Nick figured he had a get-out-of-jail-free card, but didn't know any of the rules of play, only that such cards were dealt in a game, and that games were supposed to be fun.

Nick resolved to stop thinking about what he'd survived – and about sin and punishment, penance and forgiveness – and start having as much fun as possible.

# # # # #

Carrie was aggressive, and Mark liked that.

So did the other guys in the club, Mark knew.

When she worked the crowd for tips or drinks or the sixty-dollar fee for a private dance, Carrie didn't seem to Mark to give the guys a choice. If she caught them looking at her tits, she'd get a tip out of it. If a guy checked out her ass, she called him on it, and ordered a drink on his tab. But if a guy looked her squarely in the eyes, she seemed to know she had him on the hook for a private dance.

Occasionally, she was bold – or drunk – enough to catch the eye of someone else at the bar – someone she knew, like the bartender or owner, but never one of the other girls – and mouth 'cha-ching' at them while leading a guy to the back room. On the nights when Mark was there – which, since they started seeing each other, was practically every night – Mark's had become the face in the crowd to which she most often aimed the silent and blasé words.

It was that aloof countenance that Mark counted on to put him at ease. Carrie could be near-naked and all over a guy, but if she caught Mark's eyes and rolled her own, he was okay with it.

Mark tipped her enough to be polite but no more than he would if she were another girl there that he liked. He didn't want her to think he was paying her to be his. But Mark stopped tipping the other girls altogether and hoped Carrie would at least notice that.

She had left with him most nights, too, and they had sex, her always climbing on top of him and releasing her frustration, running high on the sexual power of commanding the attention of so many men all night, before passing out on her bed. Tonight was no exception; Carrie left the bar with Mark half an hour before closing time. Happy as he was to be leaving with her, Mark hoped his being there – and her leaving early – wasn't getting her into trouble.

They went back to Carrie's place; they invariably went to Carrie's without there ever being a discussion about it. There was no way Mark was bringing her to the frat house to be eyed and talked about by the other guys, and Carrie didn't seem eager to subject herself to it – or to Mark's rarely-washed sheets and shared bathroom – either.

Sex with Carrie was as invariable as going to her place was. On the rare occasions when Mark found himself on top of her, he never stayed there long, always getting distracted by something – a memory of what he'd done in South Beach, or something that he'd done that day but hadn't focused on because he was thinking about Miami – and Carrie wasting no time to, once he was lost in thought, roll Mark over and ride him. Lately, they hadn't bothered with him on top at all; she pushed him onto the bed, back-first, and climbed on top.

Carrie let Mark's prick graze her between her legs but kept moving higher up on the bed, off his cock and onto his torso, his chest, his neck, until her sex was inches from his mouth. Mark's cunnilingus was clumsy but sincere, knowing he wouldn't last long inside her, trying in earnest to get her off before he entered her. *In earnest and in vain,* Mark thought, as she didn't keep her slit in front of his face long enough for him to get her as close as he was. She zigzagged her body back down his, Mark getting a good look at her firm breasts as they responded to her jockeying about, their subtle, unconscious motion always a moment after her every move, like an echo after a sound or an aura trailing behind a gesture. Mark's dick poked her ass, and he was afraid he would come right then and there, or when she rolled a condom over his cock – Mark hadn't realized she'd opened her nightstand drawer, removed a condom, and closed it, while she was up on the bed, her sex in his face – he felt as if he would blast a load into it before she'd even sat down on his dick. But he staved it off, holding back and trying to think about anything to keep himself from coming before she'd had at least ten minutes of up-and-down. Mark closed his eyes, not wanting to see how hot she looked: her mouth open, wet and panting; the breasts that had echoed and trailed her movements a minute ago shaking and shuddering – despite their size, they were too taut to bounce or sway much – more as she got into it; the crazy look in her eyes when she was putting just the right pressure on both of them; the way those eyes rolled back when she got close. Mark shut his eyes against all of those stimuli, thinking instead of Dr. O'Malley's class, how poorly he'd done in it, recent practices and games, how poorly he'd done there, too, of the frat, of Rob.

"Where are you?" Carrie asked.

Mark didn't reply.

"Open your eyes. Look at me."

Mark didn't, couldn't. His thoughts went where they had gone so often now, and he came, his dick deep in Carrie, his mind nowhere near her.

"Where did you go?"

To South Beach with Rob, Mark thought.

Chapter Eleven

Nick had never been to Bongo's on Ocean, and arriving that night with Ron and seeing the line, wondered if Saturday night was the best night to try to get in. But in bed with Marco, he'd realized that he couldn't get a guy who liked him and wanted him to hurt him badly enough to break his bones, and thought he'd try a night at Bongo's, a tourist trap of a bar known for the shows put on by the good-looking wait staff, who took breaks from taking drink orders and serving salty pseudo-Cuban food to dance on tabletops. Nick had never paid much attention to the clientele before tonight, his focus always pulled by the muscled Latino waiters and bouncers in their sleeveless most-of-the-way-unbuttoned animal-print shirts and tight black pants. Tonight, he would leer at them lasciviously, deliberate and obvious, not caring if they caught him looking, hoping in fact that they would. Nick knew but couldn't admit to himself that they were used to it, and it was the women who worked there who would likely notice his eyes were where they were for not being on them.

# # # # #

According to an internet search at the school library – Mark had found a terminal a student had forgotten to log out from, so no one would know he'd even typed in the keywords – the closest gay bar to campus was nearly an hour outside town. A couple of clicks later, Mark found one that was even further away to reduce the likelihood that anyone in the bar would recognize him.

Though there was a parking lot right next to the club, Mark left his car a few blocks away and darted in and out of unfamiliar alleys – alleys that reminded him of the one in South Beach – not knowing where he was going but wanting to duck into the bar unnoticed. Mark wasn't used to paying a cover and winced a bit as he handed over the crisp twenty he had just gotten from the ATM. Mark guessed that under the great quantity of her well-applied makeup, the older woman working the door probably looked very much like his grandmother, sharing her wholesome smile and tightly-rolled curls. She handed him what he thought was his change with a wink and the order to "have a good time tonight." Mark looked down and saw that the woman had simply handed him back his own twenty and looked up, puzzled. "They're gonna love you in there," she said.

"Thank you," Mark said, and meant it sincerely, though he had no idea what she meant and looked just as bewildered as he must have moments before, blindly navigating the alleys.

Mark figured that to everyone else in the bar, the confused look was familiar. They had all likely worn that look at some point, too, on their own first trips to gay bars.

Their intentions, Mark knew, had surely been different.

Mark took two steps into the club and stopped, trying to get oriented. Moments later, he took one more step to the side, to get out of the way of those coming in after him.

The club was dark and then it wasn't, quick hits of very bright light suddenly illuminating everything before the light went out again, and Mark's memory took over, piecing the club together in his mind from the elements he remembered. A bar tiled in black ceramic squares that read dark green or dark purple or dark blue, depending on the color of light that was hitting them at the time. Glossy vinyl barstools of the same quality: varying colors, consistently dark. Walls painted a similarly impossible-to-identify color – dark, but not as reflective as the bar's ceramic or the stools' vinyl.

The music was loud and throbbing, the same decibel level as at the strip joints he was used to but altogether different in tempo and tone. The beats of the bassline came at him rapid-fire, as much of an assault as the décor and lighting had been. Within a minute, Mark recognized the song from the radio, just sped up twice over, the pop starlet's strained vocals reduced to the background, added-in synthesized melodies mercifully drowning her out.

The lights brightened for a time and stayed that way, and Mark noticed something else; every man in the bar was staring at him.

There was a man with a thin face and even thinner eyebrows that arched dramatically on his otherwise plain face, their tweezed and penciled ends tapering to point to his diamond stud earrings. The man next to him wore earrings as well – small silver hoops – but his face was more filled-out and sported a few days' of stubble, as did his close-cropped head. An empty barstool separated them from an older man caught mid-sip in his drink, unable to set it down on the bar without looking away from Mark, so he simply stared on, clutching the drink so nervously Mark could see it shaking in his drawn, lined, and spotted hand. Two more empty stools were between him and a group of men who dressed a bit like the guys on the football team might, except their shirts were tighter over smaller biceps, with more buttons left undone than he or his buddies would dare, in more intense versions of colors Mark liked. Mark guessed the group had been talking to each other before he walked in from the way they were huddled together, but now, Mark noted, they all faced him without speaking. Another's legs were planted facing away from Mark, toward talking to the guy in front of him, but his upper body had twisted to get a look at Mark and stayed that way. The guy he'd been talking to didn't seem to mind and locked on Mark as well. On the dance floor, the action had all-but stopped – not that Mark blamed anyone for not wanting to dance to the accelerated girly pop playing so loudly, but he knew they likely had been doing just that before he got there – the only motion that of the shadows the moving and multicolored lights cast off the newly-still bodies on the floor, all facing him.

Where were the straight guys? Mark wondered. *The ones who preyed on these men?* These were the ones he was here for, but no one looked like that.

No one looked like *him.*

Mark figured he needed a prop, and went to the bar for a beer. Without him even ordering it, the bartender set a bottle in front of him and popped the cap.

"On the house."

"Thanks, man," Mark said without looking up from the beer.

"You wanted something else? I figured – guy like you – bar like this..." the voice faded away. "You're not in AA or anything, right?"

"No." Mark laughed and relaxed a bit before looking up at the bartender. The bartender's dark hair and muscular build caught Mark off-guard and, for an instant, Mark felt more or less like he was looking in a mirror. *Someone looks like me,* he thought. Although the mirror stopped at the neck; that *someone* had his shirt off.

"Then what else could you want?"

Mark shrugged.

"You're not lost, are you? You know where you're at?"

"I live about an hour from here, but yeah, I think –"

The bartender interrupted, saying distinctly, "I mean you know you're in a gay bar, right?"

Mark laughed again and nodded. "Yeah."

"Cool. Have fun. My name's Ted if you need anything else."

"What's your name if I don't?" Mark said, but Ted was already off serving another customer, and from the look of all the pointing in Mark's direction, fielding questions about the stranger with the bottle of beer.

# # # # #

Once inside Bongo's, Nick and Ron got separated almost instantly, Ron finding the one skinny and effeminate guy in a crowd full of girls and rushing toward him as though they knew each other; Nick doubted they did, but the guy looked to Nick to be Ron's type and, based on the crowd in Bongo's, Ron and the guy were each other's surest bets for hooking up tonight. On his own, Nick pressed toward one of the bars on the main floor and ordered, intending the whole time in line to order something fruity and flamboyant, but settling at the last minute – half chickening-out, half figuring that in a club of such bright lights, garish colors and lively, tropical music that there wasn't much one could order that would be overly out-of-the-ordinary – on a Mai Tai.

"Can't make one – out of pineapple juice," the bartender, a well-built man whose every muscle tested the club's tight uniform, shouted across the bar. "Try the other bar," he added, aiming a meaty hand – still wrapped around a bottle from filling another order – across the club to an even more crowded bar.

Nick turned around to follow the guy's hand, saw the line at the other bar, and turned back to shrug at the bartender helping him. "I guess just give me a beer, then."

"How 'bout I make you something else…festive." The man was friendly but still shouting. "On me. If nothing else, you can drink it while you wait in line at the other bar for…what was it you wanted in the first place?"

"What does it matter?" Nick shouted back, finding out for himself how hard it was to sound friendly with a raised voice. "Thanks."

Nick couldn't help ogling the bartender as he went to work on what Nick figured was a margarita, watching the muscles and veins in his arms press hard against his tanned skin as he worked. Nick loved the way a guy's relaxed musculature couldn't help responding to his every movement – pecs that hop up in an unbuttoned shirt just to shake hands for business, the left cheek of a tight ass lifting as a guy turned to his right – but the bartender's body was exaggerated and unnatural, almost cartoonish. Paired with the fact that the bartender kept looking back and smiling at Nick every time he caught him looking, and there was no doubt about it, Nick knew; the guy was flexing for his benefit.

"Salt?" the bartender yelled. "It's a margarita, to be clear."

"No, thanks. No salt, I mean. Yes, and thanks, to the margarita."

"It's loud in here and I caught about half of that." The bartender smiled wide at Nick. "The question is salt. Nod for yes, shake for no." The bartender's smile didn't let up as he demonstrated nodding and shaking.

Nick smirked back and shook his head slowly, like a naughty schoolgirl taunting a dirty-old professor she'd caught looking down her sweater.

"I get off at three," the bartender offered, his voice now trying for suggestive above the loud music.

"We'll see about that."

# # # # #

Mark figured after a while the men at the bar would lose interest and stop staring at him.

Mark figured wrong.

One speeding-out-of-control pop song crashed into the next, and Mark tried to nod his head in time with the music, sip his beer at regular intervals, survey the crowd, do anything to appear to everyone there as though there were nothing special about him, that he belonged.

Convincing the crowd that he belonged might have been possible, but watching the men in the bar eye him – their looks lingering on his arms, his eyes, his lips – Mark knew they thought he was special.

Half an hour had passed, and the bar was beginning to fill up. As subtly as he could, Mark scanned the arriving club goers for anyone like him – someone here for different reasons than the rest – but as each new man arrived, that man's focus would instantly find Mark and hold onto him, never letting up, letting go.

Mark nearly gave himself away when a large group arrived – mostly young men in their early twenties, with three women in the group. Mark would never have noticed two of the three in any other situation; they were overweight and overly made-up. But the third, with her long loose curls, low-cut shirt, and tight body, caught Mark's eye before Mark caught himself.

The bartender caught Mark sizing her up, too. "I'll ask again: you know you're in a gay bar, right?"

"She a lesbian?"

"I have no idea. Whatcha doin' *here?*" The bartender said the last word very clearly, then paused to think. "You bi?"

Mark misunderstood the question. "Oh sure, what do I owe you? And for another?" Mark asked, picking up his empty and cocking it back and forth in his hand. Every man in the bar eyed the gesture hopefully.

"I said it was on the house, and that's not what I meant. If you're looking for a job, they're always hiring guys here, if you're comfortable tending bar for a bunch of queers with your shirt off."

Mark looked at Ted quizzically.

"Well, it's not the best place to pick up a woman, so I'm trying to figure out what you're doing here. You're obviously not here to meet a guy."

"Says who?"

"Says you, nursing that beer and sitting by yourself. You could have left with any of them by now, and if you're thinking the crowd's going to improve as it the night goes on, you're in for a long one," Ted paused, "and not the 'long one' these guys would love you to believe they have for you."

"I'm here to meet someone like me," Mark said, and meant it.

Ted looked around playfully. "Guess I'm yours for the night, then," Ted said. "But I don't suck dick."

Mark had been sipping his beer when Ted said his last remark and choked on it when he laughed, then remembered Rob saying the same thing at Club Madonna.

"And, no one here thinks for a minute that *you* do, either," Ted added, before leaving Mark to tend to a customer's order.

# # # # #

Beach scenes and sexual symbols were painted in simple strokes on the walls of Bongo's in glow-in-the-dark paint, the scenes like cave-paintings or hieroglyphs, meant to tell the story of what the people in the club – presumably mostly tourists – had done that day, before coming to Bongo's. A crude and crummy one-point perspective – the lines and angles and scale all askew – of a kiosk selling sunglasses and suntan lotion. An overlarge seashell. An ocean scene, the horizon line where the earth meets the sky a fluorescent orange, the sea a glowing green, the blue sky as bright as Nick's memory of the stone in his attacker's ring. *The evolution of tourist.*

There was also a seahorse. A mermaid. With starfish on her breasts.

The look of Bongo's definitely kept your focus where it belonged: on the people working there. In the center of the club was a platform where a couple of employees danced – or rather, a woman who worked there danced, in a short red dress that flared out and flew up as she twirled, revealing her black thong, while a solid-looking man stood there for her to lean and drape herself on while he checked her out, the direction of his eyes calling the bar's attention to her thong in case anyone had missed it.

Nick used another bartender to get another margarita, knowing it was only because he was staring at the dancing man's face that he'd noticed the girl's thong at all. *Maybe if I stare long enough,* Nick thought, *the guy will come hit me.*

# # # # #

The scene at the club continued as it had – men scoping out Ted and Mark in ways that seemed alternately hopeful and hopeless, Mark planted in his barstool, too afraid to move, Ted coming back every ten minutes or so to check on him when the pacing of the customers' orders allowed.

"How do you deal with it?" Mark asked the obviously straight-like-him bartender.

"With what?"

"The..." Mark paused, thinking up the right word, *"...attention* from them."

"I work with these guys five nights a week. They may stare at me, reach over the bar to try to touch me a little, grab at my ass when I'm bending down to scoop ice or reach for some bottle of something so obscure and rarely-used that I think they ordered it just to watch me squat and search for it. And yeah, that makes me..." Ted's voice faded out as he found the words, "not sick, but uncomfortable sometimes. Yeah, there are times I want to tell them all to knock it off, but it's how I make my living, and it's not like I want to see any of them hurt for it."

"Live and let live," Mark said.

"More like 'serve and let drink – *and tip,'*" Ted countered. "I make five times more in tips working here on a slow Tuesday than I did in regular clubs on a busy Saturday. I'm sure they all know by now that I'm straight, but every now and then, probably when I know the rent is due, I admit, I throw one of them a bone and flirt a little. Do the same, and you could make a killing here."

Mark thought the word 'killing' was appropriately violent. "So it's all money to you."

"It was at first. Now I know a lot of these guys – they tell me what's going on in their lives, and I listen, just like any bartender. Some of them are more like you and me than you'd think." Mark watched as Ted checked his face for a response. "And yeah, some are so far out there that it's more entertaining than an *Entourage* marathon just listening to them talk. And that's cool."

Mark nodded.

"So after all this, are you at least gonna tell me your name? All the boys at the bar are dying to know"

"It's Mark," Mark said but instantly regretted it, wanting to remain anonymous here, adding, "but you can tell them all it's 'Rob.'"

# # # # #

Nick always thought 'Nick' – or 'Nicky' – was a great 'drunk name.'

For those who partied a lot, and publicly at that – like the roster of well-kept and well-heeled lookalike Latinas who routinely landed in *Ocean Drive* magazine's social pages – a 'drunk name' was one they could give out if they were ever in a bar that was off *Ocean Drive*'s radar, and they didn't want to get caught slumming. For those who partied too hard, a 'drunk name' was one they could use with their friends to signal I'm-so-drunk-I'm-calling-myself-the-wrong-name-so-maybe-it's-time-to-get-me-home. For those who partied with people they didn't want to see again, a 'drunk name' was a blow-off to a guy they weren't interested in. Hounded by him for a name and a number, it was easier to say 'sure' and hand him a cocktail napkin with someone else's name – sometimes an enemy, or an ex best friend, a even an ex –

scrawled over a meaningless combination of digits – or the enemy's or ex's number – or to program directly into his cell some fake name and random Three-Oh-Five whatever.

Nick envied the men and women whose real names weren't Nick, because 'Nick' was such a great 'drunk name.'

Men, of course, could use it, Nick thought. *Turn it into Nic-or-Nicky-short-for-Nicole and women could use it, too. And instantly, you were anonymous, still signaling to anyone who cared about you that you'd had too much and to anyone else that you couldn't care less.*

But, when your real name actually was *Nick,* Nick wondered, *what do you do?*

"I'm Ron," Nick said to no one in particular, a little too loud over the crowd and music at Bongo's.

# # # # #

The action at the club was dying down. The more average-looking men – their proportionally fit bodies in plain T-shirts and loose jeans, their neither pale nor tan faces neither blemished nor noteworthy, their uncolored hair cut in styles that were current but not trendy – at the bar had, after being ignored by Mark for so long, paired off and left. Now the slighter-built and overweight men – in sparkly tank tops and plaid flannel, their unnaturally orange or pasty pink faces painted and plucked or pockmarked and grizzle-bearded, their hair bleached out and spiked or overgrown and almost mangy – were starting to leave one-by-one alone. 'Last call' came and went, and after wiping down the bar and placing conical paper cups upside-down on top of each bottle's open pour-top like little dunce caps, Ted gave Mark his full attention.

"So, *now* will you tell me what you were doing here tonight?" Ted asked. "You didn't hook up – not that every guy here wouldn't have followed you into a firing squad if you'd so much as winked – but I don't think you were here to hook up. And yeah, I think every guy here could tell that much from the moment you got here."

"I thought I might meet someone, talk to them."

"You got a term paper due on homosexuality or something? You *are* a college boy, right, Mark?" Mark knew Ted was frequently dropping his name into conversation as a reflex, that in the service industry, using the customer's name made him feel special, personalizing the experience and yielding as bigger tip. Ted had comped Mark's drinks and wasn't likely hankering for a tip, but Ted was still at work and hadn't shut this off, if he even could.

"Sophomore at State."

"On the football team?"

"QB."

"Good for you, Mark. Having kind of a crap season, though."

Mark swallowed hard.

"Don't worry, I didn't recognize you from the sports pages, and I don't think anyone else here would have, either."

Mark's mind flashed to the men's rooms at the strip clubs back home; regardless of which club you were in, above the urinals was a bulletin board, and posted on that board was the sports section of the day's newspaper. Mark hadn't used the restroom at the club tonight – he was scared to leave his stool, much less enter a small room and pull out his dick – and hoped they didn't do the same thing here. *Maybe it was the style section,* Mark hoped, though from what he'd seen of the men at the bar tonight, he gathered their interests varied far more than he'd previously imagined, and surely included sports. *Shit,* he thought.

"And that crap season, if the local sports writers are to be believed, has just about everything to do with you, Mark."

"I've been off my game for a while."

"What's up with that?"

"It's kind of why I'm here."

"You think you might be –"

"No," Mark didn't let Ted finish. He didn't need him to.

"Didn't think so," Ted said. "Nothin' wrong with it, but yeah, I didn't figure you for that."

Mark didn't know what he should volunteer, and Ted hadn't asked another question.

Ted paused for a minute, then asked, "Coach thought you had low self-esteem? Said coming to a place like this would have you feeling like a god with all the attention – albeit unwanted attention? Man, coaches do some crazy shit."

"I – I wanted one of them to hit me."

"Like I said, the coach – or you – decided you don't get hit on enough by girls, so you thought –"

"No. Not hit *on* me." Mark cleared his throat and looked down at his bottle. "I wanted one of them to hit me."

"Whoa." Ted let a beat pass before his next single syllable. "Why?"

Mark told Ted everything. The trip to South Beach. Club Madonna. Rob buying a bat. The guy in the alley, who he still couldn't get out of his head.

"I thought there might be a guy here like me," Mark said

Ted pointed to his own face and smiled, raising his eyebrows.

"No, a guy who preys on them."

"A basher? Not that in a small town like this we wouldn't know one on-sight – and exactly what to do with him – but what would finding one of those accomplish?"

"If he thought I was gay, and maybe I left with him or right before, he might attack me in an alley and –"

"And that would make it okay? For you to pretend to be something you're not, lead a guy on, not the way you might have with these guys just by walking in tonight, Mark, but make yourself seem like something else, something this basher hated, and he could attack you?"

Well, when you put it that way, Ted, Mark thought. "Yes," he said soberly.

"It sounds like you weren't the one pulling the strings, Mark. This guy Rob – wait, that's the name you told me to give out for you, right?"

"Yes." It was all Mark could say now.

"I'm not even gonna try to figure out why you did that. But this whole attack was all his idea."

"Yes." Mark knew that word wasn't going to cut it. "But free will. I acted."

"That's good – that you're not letting yourself off the hook just for acting under this guy's influence. Not good what you did – far from it, Mark." Ted paused. "I'm not some old, wise cliché of a bartender giving sage advice to my customers. I'm your age, Mark, and I've done and said more stupid shit behind a bar than Woody Boyd. But Mark, it *is* good to realize when you're wrong, even if it's after, even if you think it's too late to do anything about it."

Mark looked up but didn't smile or nod or so much as breathe too hard. He just waited for Ted to say something else astute. He had come to the bar for abuse, not answers, but would take what he could get.

"You attacked someone for living his life. Statement of fact. And that's wrong. Not a judgment, Mark, but again, statement of fact. But it's just as wrong to think that pretending to be something you're not – something like him – in the hopes of eliciting the same hate response from a stranger is going to even things out on some retarded cosmic score card."

"I know."

"So why are you here?"

"I know that now. After tonight. After seeing these guys, and talking to you."

"Look Mark, you fucked up. Did the unthinkable. And yeah, I'm looking at you a little differently now than I have for most of the night." Ted locked eyes on Mark. "But if you're looking for what to do next, maybe you've done all you can by just saying it aloud. I mean, it's not like you can go find the guy, can you?"

"Wouldn't know how. Wouldn't know what to say if I did."

Ted waited a moment before speaking. "Apologizing for it doesn't make you a pussy. But admitting it at least makes you a man."

#

By the end of the night, Nick had done everything he could think of to get attention from the guys at Bongo's.

The wrong kind of attention, he thought.

He had been obvious in ogling the men working there, in their tight black pants and second-skin and nearly sheer shirts of animal-print on fleshtone. He had gotten handsy with a couple of them in the hopes that they'd haul off and hit him, or at least get a bit rough in their refusals. But the men had simply smoothed their hands over the tops of Nick's and removed them, the way one would pick an errant shed hair off a jacket.

Nick figured the employees were likely trained to handle this situation exactly as they did – this was South Beach, after all – and since the guys who worked at Bongo's were far-and-away better-looking than the guys who went there, Nick shifted his focus onto the male club goers with great reluctance.

Just like the people who worked there, the clientele of the club seemed to have a uniform as well. For the women, it was too much metallic eye shadow, a short dress of an inexpensive-looking but brightly-colored stretchy fabric, and high-heeled sandals with shiny vinyl straps. For the men, it was a button-down dress shirt buttoned-down to mid-chest with the front – only the front – tucked into loose jeans. Though Nick's shirt and jeans fit his body closer than the other men's, his outfit wasn't far enough removed from theirs to net him any attention on its own, so when his eyes or hands strayed to the bodies of the men around him, he just came off as a bit drunk and uncertain in the crowded bar. His eyes were met with an assertive nod of a spike-haired head; his hands were deflected, not usually just *off* the body of a man but *onto* the body of a nearby woman, a brush-up or grab that Nick would have apologized for profusely had he not been in-character and after a certain outcome for the evening.

Nick cruised and drank well into the night, growing more defeated as the night went on than he would if he were in a gay club and no one noticed him. He realized that what had happened to him that night in the alley had been immediate and impulsive, uninvited and unprovoked. Once Nick determined he couldn't set the stage for someone to bash him tonight, he sobered up quick. On his way out of the bar, he tossed his business card toward the well-built bartender who'd given him his first of what were now six margaritas, shaking his head, all schoolgirl again. The bartender looked up, flexed and smiled, but Nick still headed for the door.

"If I can't get bashed, at least I can get laid," Nick muttered under his breath, though he could have screamed it in the loud club and been just as heard.

Chapter Twelve

"Hey faggot! **Fag-got!**" Nick heard the call down the alley and knew exactly what to do.

He turned around and saw his attackers, two young men with broad shoulders and big arms, their shirts and jeans loose where Nick wore his tight. "Hey yourself." he said calmly, seeing one of the men fan a baseball bat in his hand, the movement as natural and provocative as jerking off.

"**Fag-got**," the one with the bat repeated.

"You boys out enjoying a romantic evening?" Nick teased boldly. "Care to make it a threesome?"

"Oh yeah, we're going to give you what you want."

Nick just shrugged, shifting his focus off the one doing the talking to the one who had been silent, seeing his blue eyes widen with what was going on, as surprised by his friend's actions as by Nick's, seemingly not knowing which side to take. Both men approached, the talker doing his best to knock Nick down with the bat, the blue-eyed one hesitating, then balling up his fists, always a step behind the one with the bat, himself a step behind Nick.

Nick ducked and dodged every blow the men sent at him because he knew their every move, and their every next move. One swung the bat hard at Nick, his intent to hurt Nick clear from the closeness of the bat and the look on his face; the other swung his fists less convincingly, as though he were looking to strike nothing but air, his face registering no emotion to Nick. Unless 'handsome' was an emotion, Nick thought. They danced like that in the alley – the attackers leading, Nick deflecting and turning away – until Nick got close enough to catch the bat with his hand when it came at him. It hit his palm hard and stung, but he wrapped his fingers around it, gripped it tight, and pulled. It fell out of his attacker's hand, and Nick took control of the situation.

"You had your turn with the bat. Didn't anyone ever teach you proper threesome etiquette?" Nick asked the two men, both suddenly saucer-eyed and flush-faced. "Make sure no one feels like the action's too one-sided." Nick swung the bat at the one who did all the talking and made contact, the sound and feel of the bat striking the man reminding Nick of breaking his own toe with the mallet. The blow threw the man off-balance and he went down, hitting the pavement just as hard. "Make sure no one feels left out," Nick continued, now focused on the man who hadn't said a word.

Still silent, the man simply put his hands in the air, waved his open palms once, and knelt down in the alley next to his friend, not checking on his buddy's condition but joining him, then pressing himself flat against the asphalt. Nick knew that none of the man's blows had connected with him, landed on him where they looked to be aimed. Nick decided he would try to avoid hurting the man if he could.

Nick beat the bat against the other man's arms, ribs, legs – the movement like an axe chopping wood – hearing the bones crack in the quiet of the alley and smiling at the sound. Nick kept at it for a while, savoring the complete satisfaction of it, then playfully tossed the bat around in his hands, changing his grip, swooping it again from low to high, opening up the loudmouth's jaw like the opening of Carson. 'He-ee-ere's….Nick!' Nick thought, as his golf swing connected with the loudmouth's chin.

The jaw kept mouthing 'fag-got' over and over to Nick, as though he didn't understand the concept of surrender. Nick kicked him in the mouth to shut him up for a while.

Nick set the bat aside and made a big show of unbuttoning his pants. "Both of you, too. Take your pants down."

"I'm not a fag-got," the talker protested. Blood had collected in the man's mouth from where Nick had struck and kicked; the man was having as much trouble pronouncing his words as Nick had when he was first in the hospital.

"You will be tonight." Nick stomped a foot against the asphalt right in front of the man's face, the threat understood. Both men reached under themselves for their buttons and flies, and wormed their jeans down over their asses.

"Underwear, too. Get 'em down," Nick said, eyeing the men as they obliged, shooting a glance at the talker's bunchy plaid boxers before getting a look at the tight white briefs stretched over the silent one's glutes and letting his eyes stay there. Nick licked his lips as the boxers and briefs came off, too, and he took a minute to admire the two perfect jock asses now fully exposed in the alley.

"Damn," Nick said, wishing he'd said 'damn' instead of 'wow' with Marco.

The one who'd been talking was crying now, and cowering away from Nick. The other just lay there, calm and silent.

"Not so fast, baby," Nick barked to the one whimpering away, though even he wasn't sure what he was going to do next.

Nick eyed a beer bottle in the street and discarded the notion of using it, then debated pissing on the two men. Thinking about pissing, he looked down at his dick, saw how hard he was there, and decided what to do to them.

He stroked himself, making sure both men were looking up at him, at Nick, wondering what he'd do to them.

Beep

Beep

Nick's cell woke him up and he reached for it, taking his hand off the erection he'd been jacking hard in his sleep. He checked the time: 3:05. *Unknown caller.* Nick guessed at the identity and answered.

"Did I wake you?"

Nick had guessed right, recognizing the voice but not the decibel level: the bartender from Bongo's, talking rather than shouting as he had over the bar.

"No," Nick paused, then corrected himself, "Yes, actually, but I don't mind." Nick glanced down at the hard-on that the dream had given him, the way it always had, and thought *at least I can put this to some use.* "I was just thinking about you," he lied into the phone.

"So you know who this is?" the voice on the other end asked coyly.

Conceited little bastard, but he deserves to be, Nick thought, remembering his attraction to the guy. "I didn't catch your name, but I think you bought me a margarita earlier tonight."

"Care for another?"

Nick gave the man directions to his home and estimated it would take barely ten minutes for him to get there on foot, realizing only after he hung up that he still hadn't asked the guy's name.

# # # # #

Mark was doing things he never thought he'd do. He'd followed along and joined in on an absurd act of violence against a complete stranger. He'd been underperforming both on the field and in class, giving the school not one but two reasons to question his staying on scholarship. *I went to a gay bar, for fuck's sake,* Mark thought. *Hoping to get in a fight. Hoping to* lose *that fight.* Somehow in all this, he was dating – Mark wondered if he could call it that, as he'd treated Carrie to hours of cunnilingus but never to so much as dinner and a movie – an unbelievable girl. In all his quiet observation, absorbing everything he could about the world around him, he'd learned so much, figuring out more on the drive back from a gay bar – he hadn't planned on being able to drive back, hoping instead to get caught leaving the bar and beaten-up in the streets, and it disturbed Mark to be disappointed by a lack of physical pain – than he'd picked up in nearly twenty-one years of taking it all in. He'd come to know so much, but he didn't feel like he knew himself anymore, and felt at once *so* smart and *so* stupid. Mark hadn't been himself since Miami; it was disorienting to live a life that was familiar to him as a man who was not.

More than alien or merely unsettling, Mark admitted to himself, it felt awful.

# # # # #

Nick's skill with the Spanish language was passable at best, but he'd always had a weakness for men with the bartender's name. Always, until he saw the name written out for the first time.

In Spanish, the letter 'h,' unless preceded by a 'c' or an 's,' was silent. The greeting *'hola'* was pronounced closer to the phonetic 'olah,' for hello; *'haces'* like 'asses,' provocatively enough meaning 'you do.' The bartender's name was pronounced 'Umberto,' which sounded suck-my-dick sexy to Nick until he'd seen it written out the first time, but, with the silent 'H' in front, was Humbert-with-an-O-at-the-end on paper.

The bartender had said, "It's Humberto," when he rang Nick's intercom to be let in the building. Thinking of *'haces'* and exaggerating Humberto's accent in his mind, Nick pictured the bartender bent over, pointing to his own ass, imploring Nick, *'you do.'*

Still picturing Humberto bent over, Nick thought *now I know what to whisper in your ear when I'm fucking you,* but buzzed him in without a word.

After a knock, Nick answered the door half-hard in his underwear, trying not to smile at the sight of his body taking Humberto's breath away.

"Wow," Humberto said.

Nick remembered saying that to Marco, one 'wow' when he meant several. He wondered how many times Humberto wanted to say it, but pulled him through the front door by his waistband and said, "Thought I'd save us the time." Nick remembered his dream and reminded himself to say 'damn' instead of 'wow' the next time a guy's revealed body impressed him so much.

"I'm overdressed," Humberto said, popping the last two buttons of his mostly-unbuttoned shirt while he spoke so all he had to do was shrug the thing off and let it float, gossamer-like, to the floor of Nick's foyer.

"Damn." Nick tried on the word and liked it, and liked what he was seeing. "Can I get you anything to drink?" Nick asked.

"I thought I was the bartender in the room."

Humberto seemed intelligent and funny; communicating with him was going to be a welcome change from just grunting about with Marco. "You can be whatever you like in this room, so long as the pants come off, too."

"Sorry. Slow poke."

If that's how you like it, okay, Nick thought, laughing at his silent entendre while Humberto struggled to get out of his shoes and socks, still in the foyer.

"Have a seat. I'm sure it's easier sitting down."

"Thanks."

"Fun to watch, though," Nick paused, staring, "fun, and really hot."

"Thanks for that, too," Humberto said, following Nick's extended arm to the living room, saying, "Your place is amazing," before sitting on the arm of a sofa, looking out at the view, the bright lights of Bongo's still on but barely visible in the middle of Ocean Drive. "There's Bongo's," Humberto said, pointing out the window.

"I'd never been there before."

"I'd have remembered you. I was surprised you were local – we get so many tourists in there. Thought I'd be meeting you in a hotel."

Nick gestured about the room. "Sorry."

"No, man, this place is nicer than any hotel I've ever seen"

"No turn down service," Nick joked.

"So don't turn me down," Humberto said slyly. He pulled off his shoes and set them carefully and quietly on the floor, then rolled off his socks and let them fall just as silently. "Now when you look out the window and see it there, you can think of me."

"I'd rather think of you when I look at this sofa," Nick said to Humberto, staring at the sofa as Humberto stood up to pull off his pants. Once down to his briefs, Humberto flexed a little for Nick, who nodded his approval; Humberto was hot, but Marco had been hotter. Nick didn't flex back, his eyes on the sofa behind Humberto pleadingly. *Just lean into it, Humberto,* he thought, *I'll do the rest.*

Humberto caught on. "Oh no. I woke you up. Let's put you back to bed," he said.

Humberto had looked good at the club in his sleeveless shirt and tight black pants, but he looked even better to Nick peeling off his underwear, his dick pointing to Nick's bedroom as though he knew the way.

Humberto removed Nick's underwear, too, tugging it hard over Nick's dick and leaving the fabric pulled tight in his tensed hand, kneeling down instead of just pulling the fabric down, so he was on his knees in front of Nick at the foot of his bed with Nick's just-released member wagging up and down at his face. Humberto grabbed Nick's cock at the base and angled it into his mouth, up-and-downing Nick for a minute before letting his mouth wander, kissing the tip of it, then Nick's hip, then his balls.

Nick let his mind wander, too: to Marco, to the doctor. Nick closed his eyes, loving the feeling of Humberto taking him back in his mouth.

Humberto reached up Nick's body, squeezing his thigh and his ass on his way around to his abs. Nick tensed his abs as a reflex when he felt Humberto's hand there, and Humberto moaned a little, his mouth full of cock, Nick feeling the moan against his sensitive sex more intensely than he heard it. Humberto straightened his arm all the way out to smooth a hand over Nick's pec, then found his nipple and gave it a squeeze, too. Humberto flattened his hand out against Nick's chest and gave Nick a little push, releasing his dick from his mouth as he did. Nick fell gently into his own bed.

Smooth, Nick thought.

Humberto didn't stand up fully, just crawled into Nick's bed from the floor. They kissed for a while, Nick tasting his sex in Humberto's mouth and liking it, before Nick broke the embrace and kept kissing Humberto, inching his way down Humberto's smooth body one kiss at a time. Neck, *kiss.* Clavicle, *kiss.* Sternum between pecs, *kiss-kiss-kiss* on the way down. To the side for one nipple, a long kiss, the kiss turning into a gentle suck, Nick feeling Humberto's heart race, each beat pulsing against Nick's lips as he kept them there. Down further, to kiss Humberto's abs, waist, cock. Nick popped Humberto's dick into his mouth more out of a sense of obligation and going-though-the-motions than from genuinely wanting to give the guy head.

Humberto responded as though he couldn't tell, moaning like this couldn't feel better if Nick tried.

Nick let Humberto out of his mouth, and Nick put his dick back in Humberto's for a while, letting the wet vacuum of it get him hard enough for a condom, for sex. He pulled out and rolled on a condom, then squeezed lube over his condom-wrapped prick. "Want some?" Nick asked Humberto, offering the lube the way one offers to share half a sandwich.

"I got it covered," Humberto said, and Nick could feel him rolling around in the bed while he put the lube back in the nightstand drawer and closed it, wondering if he should take Humberto from the front and keep kissing him, or lean back and let Humberto climb on and ride his cock. He gasped when he turned to see Humberto position himself on his bed.

Humberto was on all fours and all-business. "Fuck me," he ordered.

Don't have to ask me twice, Nick thought, and got on his knees to enter Humberto from behind.

Nick braced his hands on Humberto's hips and pushed a bit, parting Humberto's firm glutes to best get at his ass. Nick took one hand off Humberto to guide his dick in, just the head at first, not letting up as he sensed Humberto getting used to him there, inching into him the way his kisses had inched down his body.

"Yeah," Humberto sighed as much as said.

Nick smiled, relieved he wasn't hurting Humberto, that they fit together. He went to work on his rhythm, letting himself all the way into Humberto, alternating his deep plunges with eight thrusts that were shallower, then seven, then six, all the way down until every thrust was all the way into Humberto. He stayed completely inside him until Humberto started to meet him thrust for thrust, working his ass back onto Nick's cock. Nick pulled out just to throw Humberto off course, remind him who was in charge, before teasing him again with just the head.

"Give it to me, Nick. I need it." It was the first time Humberto had used Nick's name; Nick had been wondering if Humberto even remembered reading it off his card, had matched the name with the face or just the number to his body.

Nick leaned into Humberto fully, bending at the waist, so his breath hit the back of Humberto's neck. He kissed Humberto there, then kissed around to Humberto's ear, finally breathing out "Humberto." Nick had his weight braced on one arm and used the other to wrap around Humberto, letting his hand clutch Humberto's pec, grab at it as he started to fuck him more forcefully.

"Oh yeah, Nick," Humberto said, louder than he needed to for how close Nick's ear was to his mouth.

They kept at it for a while, until Nick felt Humberto's ass clench around his cock and convulse, Humberto crying out louder still. Nick resisted the urge to shush him, instead taking his hand off Humberto's pec to slap it over his mouth, quiet him as he kept fucking. When Humberto stopped calling out against Nick's hand, Nick replaced it on Humberto's chest, not missing a beat of his rhythm.

Nick knew that Humberto had just shot his come onto the black sheets below him; he pulled harder on Humberto's pec to keep his body in place, keep fucking him, keep Humberto's chest out of his own pool of come.

"Are you close?" Humberto asked.

Nick knew Humberto meant that Nick was hurting him, so he pulled out, peeled off the condom, and started jacking himself like he had before Humberto had gotten here, before the phone had even woken him up.

Nick shut his eyes in concentration, picturing Marco coming on his abs a few nights ago, then his own come hitting Marco's face, then the doctor's face, with its frame of unkempt hair and days of neglectful scruff and glasses Nick was dying to steam up. Nick opened his eyes to see Humberto with his back arched, ready for Nick's come but in a position he wouldn't hold forever. Nick shut his eyes again and focused, trying to hurry things along.

Nick was remembering his attackers when his come finally shot out of him and onto Humberto's back, the arc of it reminding him of when his attacker – the second one, the one with an erection, had pissed on him. It landed on Humberto in a jagged white slash; Nick admired it for a minute before admitting that he'd have to wipe it off to allow Humberto to turn over again, not that he didn't want Humberto to stay in that position – ass-up, back arched, his weight braced on his forearms, *ready-for-it* – forever. Nick caught his breath, still in orgasm as he heard his dream's taunting *'Fag*-got' in his mind.

Nick never knew what to say after he'd come. He wasn't going to ask if the guy wanted a rag to clean himself off with because the answer would always be 'yes,' and half the time, Nick found himself wiping the guy off afterward himself, and enjoying it, cleaning off the damage he'd done in sweat and semen, when he'd worn the guy out and ruined his ass. Tonight, Nick cleaned off Humberto, and they both fell on the bed, avoiding the center, where Humberto had shot off, each finding a side of the bed, leaving space between them.

"Sorry about your sheets, man," Humberto said.

Nick looked at Humberto's ejaculate against the black sheet and was reminded of his X-rays, the linear white form that started and ended in knuckled curls against the black background, the come, like the bone, fading to translucency at its edges. Nick smiled, though not knowing Humberto well, he eyed the come with more fear and emotion than he'd ever regarded his X-rays.

Not knowing what to say, Nick just asked, "Sure I can't get you a drink?"

"I'm a bartender. I spend every night surrounded by alcohol."

"Don't tell me you're in AA," Nick said.

Humberto laughed. "Nothing like that. I just get used to drinking whatever I want because it's around."

"And, what would you want right now?" Nick asked.

"Water, if anything." Humberto paused. "Yeah, water. I'm exhausted, man. You wore me out."

"Sorry."

"Don't apologize, I loved it. *I* actually meant to apologize on the phone for how I was at the bar. I came on pretty strong."

"I thought we *both* just came," Nick said, rolling his eyes at his own remark.

"And it was – *awesome,*" Humberto said, "but I wanted you to know I'm not usually like that. I don't hit on every guy who walks in there, and I don't do this a lot."

"You're pretty good at it. I'd say you're an expert," Nick teased.

"I just didn't want you to think I'm usually so forward. Or so easy. But when you walked in, I dunno. You're not like our regular customers. And I'm just not myself tonight."

I haven't been myself lately, either, Nick thought, getting up to get them each a glass of water. *And it feels fucking great.*

Chapter Thirteen

Mark didn't think Carrie seemed like herself tonight.

Guess that means she's 'Diamond,' he figured. When they'd first gotten together, Mark had listened with interest when Carrie had explained the difference – what it was like to be at work, to be someone else, to even *need* to be someone else to get through what it was she did, not that she hated it altogether, but that an alternate personality had helped to get through some of the sleazier or more intimate aspects of it. Mark had wondered how much of it was true: how much of what she was saying was how she actually felt, and how much was a story she'd come up with to tell whoever she was dating, so they'd be okay with what she did. Carrie was a bright girl, Mark knew, surely smarter than most of the guys who came into the bar – himself included – and by extension, most of the guys who came into her life. A story like this could be calculated to her partner at ease, make stripping seem like a means to an end, not a lifestyle. Carrie had locked eyes on Mark when she told the story, but tonight, Carrie avoided Mark's eyes altogether.

She took her turn on stage in the rotation, dancing to two songs – one fast, one slow – that Mark had never seen her move to before.

During the fast song, Carrie had taken almost everything off, which was unusual for her. Usually she left her bra on throughout the first song and even the first half of the second. She was beautiful and moved well and, barring the odd outburst from a soon-to-get-bounced drunk ordering her to "take it off," she got away with it.

Carrie didn't seem to want to get away with anything tonight, and was topless before the first chorus of the first song.

The crowd responded, and Mark, seated near the back to both see Carrie and montor the crowd, keep her safe, couldn't see much of her for the mob of guys clustered in front of her, waving money at her, fanning an already-hot flame. She looked out at the crowd and smiled widely, though Mark remembered Carrie explaining that the lights were too bright, when they were aimed at her, on her, she couldn't see anything but the stage in front of her, couldn't see out to the faces she at least appeared to lock on and smile back.

When the first song was nearing its end, and Carrie had collected what looked to be nearly four-hundred dollars, Carrie raked her hands through her hair, ruffled her short bob, and grabbed the pole.

The song changed, to one that was slow and low, though Mark figured he could have been deaf and known that the songs had changed from how the accent of Carrie's body English braked from brisk babble to slow drawl. Carrie had her right hand around the pole and leaned back, allowing her body to arc down like a wilting flower toward the stage, then spun around the pole.

The only thing she seemed to bother looking at, or pretending to, was the pole. She angled her body out from it like a sports pennant, and twirled around like a party favor noisemaker. Her movements were slow, slower even than the lazy beat of the drawn-out song, as though she were coming down from a high, crashing.

When her set was done, men raced to line up for private dances with her, and one-by-one, she took them on, not once searching the crowd for Mark's face, not looking for anyone to face and mouth 'cha-ching.'

Mark, not knowing what else to do, got in line.

# # # # #

Nick needed a break from the 11th Street Diner and suggested that Ron come to his place for an evening coffee instead, to wake and sober up after sleeping most of the day, and share about Humberto.

"Had you ever been to Bongo's before last night?" Nick asked Ron.

"No. And never again. I had more fun at my own briss."

"You're not even Jewish."

"See, I had more fun when someone *didn't* throw a party for my penis than I did last night. That guy I moved in on turned out to be a total queen. After that, no one looked at me all night." Ron brought his coffee close to his lips for a sip. "You got ignored, too, I guess?"

Nick nodded toward his bedroom door. "Bartender just left," he said with a wide smile.

Shocked, Ron dropped his coffee, making an oh-my-God-I'm-sorry face as the cup left his hand and sped to the countertop, then an oh-my-God-I-don't-believe-it face when the cup didn't break.

"I thought you were serving me on the 'good' china."

"I am," Nick said, knowing Ron was teasing but a bit incredulous at the thought that he'd serve a guest – even someone he was as comfortable with as Ron – on anything less.

"I thought I'd just broken your best china for sure," Ron said. "Glad I'm not in trouble."

"And you'd be in trouble for sure, if you'd broken it. But that's the difference between *fine* china and *bone* china."

"Um, excuse me?"

"Fine china is nothing but porcelain clay. Bone china, which you're holding," Nick smiled, "or rather, you *were* holding until you started throwing things around like an animal..."

Ron's face changed from the oh-my-Gods to I'm-so-sorry.

"...contains crushed animal bone and bone ash. Makes it whiter and more translucent. Doesn't chip, is more resilient." Nick paused, thinking about what his bones were now, too, on one side. "Stronger."

Ron smiled at Nick. "Like you," he said.

Nick smiled back. "Hell of a mess, though," he said, eyeing the spilled coffee dripping off the granite counter to the marble floor but thinking about his own blood and his attackers' urine on the asphalt of the alley.

#####

When it was Mark's turn, he sat for his dance like just another customer.

Carrie didn't treat him any different, going through the motions professionally, distant. Mark was almost surprised she hadn't asked his name like she'd asked the others' when they sat down.

"Fucking boning is digging into me."

"Oh, sorry," Mark said, and repositioned himself under her, so his erection-through-jeans wasn't making contact with her as much as before.

"No, not that, this corset." Carrie said the words without looking at Mark, then, in marked contrast to the slow and sexy reveal she usually used to remove her clothes and toy with the man she was dancing for, practically ripped the corset off and threw it to the side, grazing Mark's cheek with it as she did.

"Fucking *corset* boning," she said, and finished her dance without connecting to Mark at all.

Chapter Fourteen

Mark saw his victim everywhere.

Or rather, he thought he did.

When Mark hit the showers with the team after practice, he noticed a player he hadn't seen before. *Freshman,* he figured, but continued to eye the player as though he knew him from somewhere. He couldn't look away. Wet from the shower, tinged with the foam of soap, the player looked still more like his victim – when he and Rob had pissed on him, and their urine had glossed his face and frothed tiny bubbles where it collected in his eyes and nostrils. When the freshman caught Mark looking, he played the role of the victim before playing Rob, nodding at Mark and smiling before remembering that they weren't alone, that any of their teammates could be looking on, and beating them to the punch by tossing a breezy "faggot" at Mark, turning so Mark could either check out his ass or look away.

When Mark went to see Carrie perform – and make sure none of the guys in the audience got out of line – faces in the crowd reminded him of his victim. They looked at her the way the man in the alley had looked at Rob and Mark: lust confused with circumstance, desire yielding to disappointment and defeat.

When Mark met Carrie at her hairdresser's, he did a double-take at the man wielding the blowdryer. Besides his victim, the stylist was the only man Mark had seen in leather pants and a largely-unbuttoned button-down. When the stylist saw Mark stare, he smiled wide. When Mark realized he wasn't the man from Miami, he quickly sat in the waiting area and tried to be interested in a months-old *W* magazine.

At the first game of the season, Mark thought a player on the opposing team had his victim's eyes. It was tough to tell under the helmet, and the Lady Gaga rectangles of black under the player's eyes made him no more identifiable. Mark reasoned he was more likely to recognize the pop starlet without her wig and costume – *just how intently was I reading that* W *magazine?* he wondered on the field – than he was to recognize his victim from just the slice of his face visible through the helmet's mouth guard. He also realized that he didn't well-remember the face of the man he and Rob had humiliated in the Miami alley.

Just the tattoo.

Mark had seen plenty of tattoos around town. Strippers – particularly at the low-rent clubs he and Rob went to when they were just blowing off steam, more likely to make fun of the dancers than to try to get them to go home with them – sported them. A career stripper toward the end of her dancing years might tattoo her body with names; just one name was usually a husband or boyfriend, more than one name always meant she had kids. Girls who worked at the nicer clubs had small flowers decorating the small of their lower backs or fairies dancing lightly around their ankles. The guys on the team would brand their upper arms or chests with eagles and Superman insignias, or get inked so they could wear their player numbers even after they'd taken off their uniforms. But the man in the alley had just a small design on the fleshy part of his hand between the knuckles of his thumb and forefinger. An upper-case 'A,' the horizontal bar of the letter filled with smaller all-caps letters: K-R-A-M. The letters spelled his own name backwards, and like Mark looking into a mirror since the attack, burned into him.

Distracted by remembering this, Mark didn't see the player from the other team – the one he had thought looked like his victim – charging toward him after Mark had barely caught the ball that was hiked to him. He didn't see that he was unprotected, either – that his teammates were all running away from him, trying to get open for a pass he hadn't yet thrown. Unfocused but unconsciously able to do what he needed with the ball, Mark changed his grip, spreading his fingers to mesh with the lacing, shake hands with the ball. It felt familiar-enough in his hand to trigger in him what to do next, and he whipped his arm back to throw to any of the teammates who had abandoned protecting him to get open. What felt unfamiliar was the force against his throwing arm when the opposing team's player plowed into him. It had sounded out-of-place as well, the Rice Krispies jingle of his ulna snapping, the toughened cartilage of his elbow cracking, the broken bone popping through the skin of his forearm.

Mark fell to the ground and stayed there.

The team crowded him despite the coach's orders to give Mark some air. Mark saw what they were seeing, the bone broken through the skin, milky white around the tips of the bone circled in red like a wrong answer on a test. *I've seen plenty of those lately, too,* Mark thought, knowing his academic slide had already garnered him some unwanted attention from the school's dean. Tough guys bulked-up to twice Mark's size with muscle and gear covered their mouths, face masking themselves to swallow back vomit. One even passed out, but a stronger-stomached teammate caught him, kept him from hitting the ground and joining Mark. Mark saw Rob push through the macabre huddle and stare at Mark, more look-what-you've-done than are-you-okay. Mark divided his glance between his arm and Rob's reaction to it, himself fascinated by how the skin had slit open in such a straight line, the flesh flaring out from the center, the thickness of those layers of skin surprising him, looking like lips around his milky white bone. To Mark, the gash on his arm looked like what was between Carrie's legs. Mark spent a while staring at the injury and smiling, and kept smiling when he finally looked at Rob.

Mark thought he should have been in pain like he'd never felt, but hadn't felt this good since returning from Miami.

Chapter Fifteen

Mark had learned more in the hospital than he'd learned in his three semesters at State.

He'd learned that what had happened to his arm was called an 'open fracture,' in which the force that broke his bone had been great enough to push the fragmented bone through the muscle, ligament, soft tissue, and skin around it. The bone had been set with a metal rod and would heal in about four months, but the muscle around it would require surgeries and physical therapy for months beyond that, and Mark would be chugging antibiotics – and not drinking – for longer still. After he finished out the week in the grey-green walls of his hospital room, he would be discharged, ordered to take care of the puffy cast around his arm that bulked it up well-past the size he'd always wanted it to be, though he knew the muscle inside would atrophy and shrink, go soft inside the hard plaster. The doctor had stitched Mark up, sewn the lips of flesh around the wound shut, skin swallowing up the broken bone like a kept secret. Mark would have to be silent about what had distracted him on the field.

He'd learned that the team didn't care enough to visit him in the hospital. This was a big change from when they were winning – winning largely due to him. He'd sprained his ankle last year, the injury so minor that he couldn't remember which ankle, right or left, but it had kept him off the field when he'd been routinely leading the team to wins. Half the guys had checked in on him then, when the damage had been light enough that his ankle was wrapped by a third-year Sports Medicine major rather than a doctor. Now here he was with two chunks of bone poking through his throwing arm, and the team was nowhere to be found, doubtless clustering around the second-string quarterback who was now first.

He'd learned that Carrie didn't care that much, either. She, too, hadn't visited, but Mark wondered if she even knew he'd been hurt, with no one he knew around him asking if they should tell her.

Mark had learned more in the hospital room than he had in college, which made opening the letter that had been hand-delivered to the room a little easier, though he'd needed help tearing into the envelope.

Mark hadn't received a letter from his college since they'd accepted him; the thick envelope he received nearly two years ago contained his official acceptance letter, the terms of his athletic scholarship, some brochures about the campus, and the course catalog. The envelope in today's mail was thin enough that Mark could tell without opening it that it contained just a single sheet of paper.

On the same letterhead on which his acceptance had been affirmed, his scholarship detailed, were the words 'We regret to inform you…'

Mark didn't bother reading on. His scholarship had been terminated, and without it, he could not continue at State.

# # # # #

Nick had received a great deal of mail related to his attack, mostly just the back-and-forth between Mount Sinai and his insurance company. The hospital had sent notice that they would bill Nick's insurance company, then the insurance company acknowledged that they'd received the bill and enclosed an explanation of benefits that had made Nick glad he hadn't quit the firm altogether just yet. About a month later, the insurance company had sent notice that they would pay, and that they were contacting the Miami Beach Police Department for details of the attack to pursue subrogation against the responsible party, not knowing that no party had been identified and that they, in fact, might try harder to identify Nick's attacker than the police ever did. More months had passed, and Nick figured the envelope he received today would be the last.

Unable to identify his assailant, Nick was on the hook for the co-pay of his hospital stay outlined months ago in the explanation of his benefits. In all, the total worked out to roughly what Nick would pocket for a decent-sized job he could design on his own, outside the firm. Such a job could raise Nick's profile in the local design scene to boot, and Nick received the bill almost happy to pay it, not quite grateful for what had happened to him, but thankful for the way he was coming out of it.

# # # # #

Girls always marveled at Mark's arms, the sheer size of them, flirtatiously asking him to "make a muscle" and flex for them. Mark could no longer count on just one hand the number of times he'd had one girl squeezing on his left bicep and another on his right, but to Mark, only the right arm mattered. That was his throwing arm, used to get the ball to the receiver to make the plays that would get him a pro contract and out of here. The cast would be on for a while, but he was more afraid of what would happen when it came off, of the flaccid, lifeless arm muscle he might be left with. Mark thought of the girls who used to drape themselves on his arms; 'flaccid' and 'lifeless' were not words he wanted to have describe him.

At least I jerk off with my left *hand,* Mark thought, and smiled.

Mark's cast, too, revealed a lot about how much had changed. A cast – littered with signatures and well-wishes like graffiti – was a sign of popularity, of how much the injured and healing mattered and to how many people. Mark's cast remained conspicuously white: the color of purity here signaling instead nothing but sin and guilt.

The letter from State had stated that his medical bills would be taken care of and that Mark could finish out the semester still on scholarship, but that after that, the school would wash its hands of him.

# # # # #

"Hey faggot" a voice called to Nick. "Fag-got."

The tone and the words were familiar to Nick, but they had been meant to surprise him. Nothing could surprise Nick anymore: not the youth of his attackers, the phallic power behind the way one of them wagged and swung the bat, the erection that seeing them yielded in him.

Nick tried to focus on details of his attacker to recount them for the police. He noted the bravura posturing of the man shouting and swinging the bat, keeping his distance. Nick lost himself in the blue eyes of the man who got closer, if only to punch him, the emotion in those eyes almost an apology. Nick focused on the detail of the class ring the man wore, its oval blue stone streaked with his own red blood after the second hard hit. Nick covered his eyes with his hand for a minute, seeing the tattoo there, then everything started to blur together as he was hit in the head again, the attacker's ring starting to resemble the logo Nick had tattooed on his hand, the mark on his hand looking like his attacker's class ring.

Nick woke up startled, the logo inked on his hand always making him jump as though a bug had landed there, though even before he'd been tattooed he'd woken up enough times with the back of his hand still stamped from the clubs the night before that he figured he should be used to it.

The morning after being inked, Nick hadn't remembered getting a tattoo at all. Ron had gotten him just-drunk-enough to cloud his judgment but not raise any we-will-not-tattoo-the-intoxicated invariably-pierced eyebrows of the staff at Miami Ink. He'd woken up that morning with his hand bandaged instead, and knew that morning's hand stamp wouldn't wipe away.

Nick had been doodling a company logo for when he would break away from the firm and go out on his own on every scrap of paper he could get his hands on for months, and when Nick had grabbed a cocktail napkin from under Ron's stir-straw speared drink one night and absently drawn over the last digits of the phone number a guy flirting with Ron had scrawled out, it had been the last straw for Ron. Ron had dragged Nick to Miami Ink to get it done, wadding up the napkin with its obscured numbers and upper-case A for Akram Inc. Nick didn't remember how long it had taken or if it had hurt.

It had always disappointed Nick that the tattoo, meant to be his signature black, had turned out the harsh blue-black of ballpoint pen ink or an art student's dyed hair. Nick had neglected to put sunblock on the tattoo too many times; in the intense bright of Miami, the blue-black had faded further, to navy, then lighter and bluer still, and was now not even navy but a dull admiral blue, not really black at all. Nick knew that the color blue was supposed make him feel calm and safe. The ocean was blue, as was the sky on a clear day; dress uniforms for Marines were blue, like those for daily wear by police officers. Nick's clearest memories of being attacked were blue – his attacker's eyes and the stone in his class ring – and the color now made Nick feel anxious and insecure. Now that Nick was on edge about all things blue, he wanted the blue gone, if not the logo.

At the office one day scrolling through blocks of outdated emails – Nick was still behind from when he'd been in the hospital, as the firm hadn't brought anyone on to fill his position, temporarily or permanently – Nick had doodled again, picking up an orange marker and stroking it over the tattoo, letting the orange complement and counteract the blue, blackening the angular A on his hand. Nick had requested to leave early, gone home and parked in the condo's garage, and walked to Miami Ink, not bothering to change out of his business clothes, not thinking how out-of-place he'd be in a tattoo parlor dressed like he was. *At least I'm wearing black,* Nick thought, hoping color alone trumped his outfit's conservative cut and designer pedigree. Nick noticed that the original Miami Ink was now a novelty shop, selling souvenir T-shirts and silver jewelry to tourists familiar with the famed parlor that didn't want something more permanent to take back home with them. Nick stepped in to Miami Ink's new LoveHate Tattoo next door.

"Can I help you?" a leanly muscled man with lacy scrolls of ink curling out of his black T-shirt at its neck and sleeves asked.

Nick explained that he'd like to get the tattoo on his hand covered over.

"What, this remind you of somebody? Ex-girlfriend?" the man waited a beat, changed his tone: "Ex-*boy*friend?"

"No, not covered up like that. It turned blue." Nick proffered up his hand like he'd been asked to dance. "I want it black."

"We can go over it with black again, but it'll turn on you again, for sure." The man was inspecting Nick's hand in his as though Nick were a newly-engaged woman and he wanted to check out the ring, turning Nick's hand in his as though the tattoo could catch the light. "You didn't keep it out of the sun, did you?" the man asked the question judgmentally, the invisible rock imagined in his mind an obvious cubic zirconia.

"No," Nick said sheepishly, "and no, I don't want it covered with black ink again."

"I don't get it." The man dropped Nick's hand, confused.

"I want it covered over in orange ink."

The man behind the counter shot Nick a look of still-more confusion.

"Orange and blue are complementary colors."

Nope, that hadn't clarified it, Nick thought, gauging the man's unchanged face. Nick didn't really blame the guy; Nick had shown up straight from work and hardly looked like he belonged in a tattoo parlor, and was now speaking what clearly came off as complete nonsense.

"They're opposites on the color wheel. When you mix opposites – red and green, yellow and purple, orange and blue – they turn brownish-black. I'm hoping –"

"That if we cover your blue-ish tattoo in orange ink, it'll turn black." The man paused, then gave Nick a wide smile. "I never thought of that."

Nick shrugged.

"Can't guarantee it'll work, but it sounds kind of genius. Let's have a go."

Nick was in and out of the vinyl chair in less than ten minutes, the needle passing over his hand feeling familiar, not that he'd remembered much of his time in the chair the first time, but the sensation of the buzzing needle hitting his skin not unlike a microdermabrasion treatment. Nick was sure he'd looked away when he'd gotten tattooed the first time, but now he looked on, the flow of blood and transparent orange ink reminding him of getting cut and pissed on in the alley.

The much-tattooed man applied a thick salve and a white bandage to Mark's hand when he'd passed over the existing design and walked Nick back to the front desk.

"What do you I owe you?" Nick asked.

"You local?"

Is there a discount if I am? Nick wondered. "Yeah."

"No charge. Just do me a favor and stop back in in a week or so, let me know if it worked out."

Nick nodded appreciatively. "Thanks."

"And try to keep it out of the sun this time."

Nick realized that before he'd survived being attacked, he'd never have had the nerve to go after guys like Marco or Humberto, even if all he'd done was let Marco feel him up in a bar and toss his business card on the bar at Bongo's. If he could recover from so many broken bones, he figured, he could recover from rejection, and risked it.

Nick had gotten a tattoo, gone to Score, gotten more aggressive with more appealing guys, and gotten off with them. Nick wondered what other risky behavior he might try next.

Chapter Sixteen

"You left some of your stuff at my place," Carrie started in after class with her voice not predictably cold or distant but as sexy and coming-on as if she were soliciting a lap dance. "You wanna come over and get it."

"So you're done with me?"

"Is that what it sounds like?" Carrie asked, her voice still a confusing come-on.

Mark went home with Carrie not knowing what she wanted, but not surprised when they both ended up naked inside of a minute after entering her apartment.

Carrie had taken a week off work to cram for finals but kept seeing Mark for sex. When Mark pulled off her panties to go down on her, he saw that she hadn't shaved in that time. The sight of the hair growing in around her shiny pink slit reminded Mark of the scar Rob shaved into his eyebrow, but Mark dove in anyway, going at it earnestly, in fact fueled by how it reminded him of Rob, the feeling of kissing into her against her stubble, Mark figured, not altogether unlike kissing a man.

Carrie tossed a condom at Mark, and he unwrapped and rolled it on as she crabbed down his body to sit on and ride his cock wordlessly to completion. She lay in bed with him afterwards, not collapsing on his chest but beside him, a distance between them.

"I have a bone to pick with you," Carrie said, her light words and lighter, playful touch belying the seriousness of what she was about to say.

"What's that?"

"I don't get it. I don't get you. You're supposed to be some kind of stud."

"What do you mean?"

"Star quarterback –"

Mark shrugged. *Quarterback: yes. Star: not lately,* he thought.

"– not that that guarantees anything," it was Carrie's turn to shrug as she continued, "but I have friends – girls you've been with –"

"Friends?" Mark asked, the word flying out of his mouth before it hit him how rude the remark was. Carrie might hear gossip about who's-doing-who around campus – it was unavoidable – but the girls Mark had had before Carrie were cheerleaders, sorority sisters, the Homecoming Queen; there was no way they'd be 'friends' with a stripper.

"I hear things," Carrie corrected herself.

"What things?"

"That you know how to lay it down. You know how to bone."

Mark had never heard any of the girls he'd been with before Carrie use 'bone' as a verb that way. He wasn't sure if this only served to separate Carrie further from the type of girl he was usually with or if it was revealing, that all girls talked like Carrie – like men – when they were alone.

"You just lie there, and I do all the work."

Mark raised his arm, still in its plaster cast, higher in the air, as if to remind Carrie it was broken.

"It was like this before you broke your arm."

Mark waited a bit. "I thought you liked it like that, on top."

"Every now and then? Sure. I like control, I admit it. I like to be on top." Carrie was mad but still sexy. Mark understood that Carrie knew how to play fair and win, not lose every part of herself a guy had found attractive in the first place the second she picked a fight. "But not all the time, and not when I have to hear every girl in school..."

Mark raised an eyebrow to raise an objection.

"...not every girl, but you've gotta admit, there have been more than a few..."

The eyebrow lowered, and palms below it were raised and fingers fanned out. *Guilty, but what did you expect?*

"...and those girls talk. About how big it is..."

Mark stifled a smug grin and a little laughter. *This is not the time,* he reminded himself, despite his swelling pride.

"...about how good you bone, how hard you bone."

Mark was flattered and mortified all at once. *Studly and stupefied,* he thought, *that's me.*

"But with me, all you do is lie there. It's all you've ever done."

Mark waited out her silence.

"Is it because I'm stripper?"

Mark didn't know how to answer, so he didn't, but noted that even Carrie called herself a 'stripper,' not a 'dancer,' at least when she was talking to a guy.

"I mean, how would you like me to just lay there, do nothing?" Carrie asked, though Mark had been with enough girls who did precisely that and nothing more, were just still, didn't give him back any friction of their own when he was fucking them. Carrie was right; he didn't like it, and never called those girls afterwards.

"Is it because I'm a stripper?" she asked again. "Because sex isn't a lap dance."

Mark gave it some thought – not wondering what the problem was, for he knew the answer, but wondering whether or not to tell her, and if so, how much to say.

"I just haven't been myself since –"

"Miami," Carrie said. "Since Miami."

Mark looked at her, befuddled.

"I'm not an idiot," Carrie said.

"No, you're like, the smartest girl I've ever been with."

"Is *that* the problem? That I'm *smart?*"

Mark silently thought of an old joke: *How do you get a smart girl into bed? Tell her she's pretty. How do you get a pretty girl into bed? Tell her she's smart.* Mark figured he didn't know what to say to Carrie, to a girl who was supermodel-sexy and *summa cum laude.*

"What happened in Miami?" Carrie asked, adding, "We weren't together then, so if there's some other girl, hey, I'm not upset. I wouldn't have a right to be."

Hot enough – and comfortable enough with sex – to be a stripper, smart, uses 'bone' as a verb, uses sound logic in an argument, and fights fair, Mark thought. *How did I fuck this up?*

"I'll tell you everything, but you won't want to be with me after."

Carrie fired back: "In case you weren't listening, I'm not sure I want to be with you now. 'Telling me everything' isn't going to hurt at this point."

Mark bowed his head, remembering details and deciding what to share, what to omit.

"There's no other girl."

Carrie nodded and opened her mouth as if to say something, but seemed to stop herself.

"But there was a man."

Mark told Carrie almost everything. He told her about Club Madonna, and Carrie listened intently as he described how it was different from where she worked. He told her about the walk back to the hotel, about Rob buying a baseball bat. He told her how Rob had used that bat.

He left out Rob's real role in all of this, as the instigator, the one instructing Mark to do what he did to the man in the alley, barking orders at both of them. Mark had included Rob's part in it when he had talked to Ted and was afraid it shifted blame for what he'd done. Above all things, Mark wanted to be accountable, and let Rob disappear from the story after buying and swinging the bat.

When he was done talking, the whole story taking nearly ten minutes, Mark looked up at Carrie, who was sitting across from him on the bed with her head in her hands. He lifted her face, half expecting her to tell him not to touch her, for her to recoil away from his hands and scream, yell some insult at him that would cut him to the bone. Her eyes had teared-up, but she wasn't crying yet. Mark had told the story without emotion and was nowhere near tears.

In the same come-hither voice Carrie had used to initially seduce him and more recently, less congruently, to tell him he needed to pick up his things, Carrie breathed out two words: "Get out."

Mark wanted to tell her more, about how he felt now, after; how it had destroyed him. He wanted to tell her that thinking about it, remembering, had been what had distracted him on the playing field and gotten his arm broken in the first place. He wanted to tell her about his trip out of town to the gay bar where Ted worked, how he'd gone there trying to get bashed but had left knowing that that wouldn't solve anything, take back or undo what he'd done. He wanted to tell Carrie that he had no idea how to get back to the man he once was, the man those other girls had talked about in front of her: the stud, the quarterback with the athletic scholarship that the school was now going to pull, the man he wanted to be when he was with her, inside her. But without another word, Mark did as he was told, shutting the front door behind him as quietly as possible, as though he was never there.

# # # # #

Ron dragged Nick to Art Basel events every year. *Or was it the other way around?* Nick wondered, knowing how much he enjoyed the mix of good art and bad, of connoisseurs and conned suckers, the tasteful restraint of old money clashing with the outrageous and outlandish displays of the newly-minted. The annual artistic affair drew literate aestheticists to its contemporary exhibitions and a see-and-be-seen crowd from all over the world to its cocktail parties and happening scenes. Nick came to tonight's party fêting a fashion photographer who printed his black-and-white images on blue stock to look for work; with this kind of money in town but once a year, now was the best time to find a noteworthy project or two to complete on his own.

Everyone at the party was drinking the host's signature drink: a Blue Lagoon, which contained Blue Curacao and, like all drinks made with that liquor, looked to Nick like a glass of glass cleaner. Further, the color of the drink recalled his assailant's eyes and ring, and he was pointedly avoiding all things blue.

Nick ordered a Cosmopolitan.

With Ron distracted by a group of hot young Latin guys in the corner, Nick began eavesdropping on the conversations around him.

"...maybe buying art tonight isn't such a great idea. I'm thinking of leaving my wife, and I need to hide..."

Nope, Nick thought.

"...so my hairdresser just chopped it all off, and I thought, what is it costing me to be your vision? I mean, four-hundred dollars, and look at this color..."

Next.

"...just bought in Icon and need to find a designer to..."

Jackpot.

Nick listed toward the conversation as he listened in.

"So, how did you get stuck drinking that?" Nick managed to interject to the man with the new condo.

"It tastes better than it looks, which I suppose isn't high praise for what looks like a Windex-itini." The man paused. "Why is it we're all drinking this? Not to sound a decade behind the times, but is our host big-fat-and-Greek?"

"It's an international arts fest, but I think the Greeks are the least-represented ethnicity at Art Basel. Where are you from? I can't place your accent."

"I didn't know I had one. New York. And now, Miami, I guess."

"I overheard – Icon, is it?" Nick asked leadingly.

The man didn't take the bait. "Yeah. So, how did you get away with having some other drink? You're just about the only person here without something blue – that sounds like a bride's good luck charm – though I'm not sure I'm man enough to admit I'd rather have the pink drink than the blue one."

Part of Nick was trying to figure out if the guy was straight or not to know whether or not to flirt, but this part was drowned out by his interest in a project – any project – on his own, and at Icon, no less. "At least it's a deliberate pink, rather than an accidental one."

"Excuse me?"

"A deliberate pink. Bold. Strong, at least as strong as pink can be."

"And an accidental pink is?"

Nick paused, letting his muscles go slack as he shrugged at the man. "Wimpy."

"Kind of always thought pink *was* for wimps – and women. But you said 'deliberate' versus 'accidental.' I'm intrigued. What did you mean?"

"You know that pink that a load of whites turns when there's one red sock in the wash with them?"

"Uh-huh."

"That pink. It's an oops, an accident."

The guy nodded. Nick could tell he had the man's interest and attention, and continued.

"You get a paper cut while reading, forget it's there, lick your finger to turn the page, and look down: the little bit of blood, plus your saliva, on the white page."

"Accidental pink."

"Exactly. Accidental pink is light pink, pale, 'baby' pink – though a baby can be an accident for other reasons altogether."

The guy laughed a little. "I get this – and I like this. And, if it's not too forward, I think I 'get' you and like you, too. But what's 'deliberate' pink, then?"

"It's purposeful. Strong. Meant to shock or have an effect. It's the fuck-me-right-this-second shade of lipstick a woman applies when it's long past the third date and the guy still hasn't touched her. And she wants him to. *Bad.* Or the one a woman puts on to become the mistress of a married man, recognizable to the wife later as the shade she finds on his collar –"

"Or on his cock."

"Exactly: deliberate pink." Nick locked on to the man's eyes and held his gaze. "If you're taken to jail on a drunk-and-disorderly, they put you in a certain cell to quiet you down before booking you. The cell is painted pink – a shade officially called 'drunk tank pink' for the color's psychological impact of soothing and calm on the body. It's a strong shade that serves a purpose."

"The color of pellet I always use when I play paintball is bright pink, not just because it shows up well on the camo of the guy I hit, but to add to the humiliation, emasculate him, make him wear pink." The man paused, then added, "Deliberate pink."

"You've got it. I just realized I've done all this talking – and used the F-word..."

"I said 'cock.' I'm not Mormon."

"Or Greek, we established. But I don't even know your name."

"Chad."

"I'm Nick." Nick extended his hand for Chad to shake it, reminding himself not to squeeze too hard, accidentally hurt Chad the way he'd hurt the dancer at Johnny's.

"Nice to meet you, Nick, by accident or deliberately. You must be an artist, talking as you do about color."

"Architect-slash-interior-designer."

"Really? You know I just bought at Icon and I'm looking for a designer." Chad seemed to just-then realize he was still holding Nick's hand, and looked down at it by way of apologizing before letting go. It occurred to Nick how much a businesslike handshake was like pulling at half the wishbone of a Thanksgiving turkey, with two people each hoping that when they let go, they get what they want. Nick looked up and saw Chad's face as he saw the freshly-blackened logo tattooed on his hand inside Chad's and took a deliberately drawn-out drink from his cocktail, silently celebrating the idea that he already had the job.

# # # # #

No matter what noise was happening around Mark for the rest of the day – a game cranked up full-blast on the frat's big screen, loud rock blaring upstairs from the guys who said it helped them study, crass and crude conversations shouted at testosterone-amped decibel levels to be heard over it all, above any other man speaking – all Mark could hear was Carrie, telling him to get out. Though Mark was about to start packing to leave the frat, no one had ordered him to go; Mark was guessing at his own actions these days, and figured he was trying to beat them to the punch.

# # # # #

"I'm in with Steven and Christophe at Palm Beach Salon!" Ron announced to Nick over the phone.

"Could you sound *more* like a woman right now?" Nick asked and meant it, not resenting Ron for his feminine ways but thinking that Ron just didn't understand things the way he did, that emphasizing the masculine, rather than the feminine, sides of himself was going to make life – from getting the job done at work to getting laid – a whole lot easier.

It hadn't always been that way; Nick hadn't always had this figured out. When he was young – still a boy, really – he found himself attracted to men, but didn't know how to attract them himself. All he knew was how a woman attracted a man, the parts of herself that she presented or even exaggerated to get his attention, and these were the feminine parts of herself. Nick noticed that a woman walked differently when she was trying to catch a man's eye than she would if she merely needed to get somewhere, dressed differently to meet a man for a drink than to go out with her girlfriends, spoke and sat and even breathed differently when there was a man around to be drawn to her. He partly blamed the women he saw doing this in-person, but held women in movies and television far more responsible, how a femme fatale was irresistible to any man around her for her dramatic vamping and feminine élan. Nick initially explored those affectations, trying on the posture and persona of a woman in sexual need the way a teenager tries on different identities, trying to see what fit, what worked.

But Nick had thought his way out of these attempts when he realized that none of the men he was interested in played this feminine role; there wasn't a single effete trait in the men – athletes and outdoor-types, jarheads in fatigues or blue collars – that interested him. Knowing this, Nick set about trying instead to be what he himself desired, exaggerating the masculine parts of himself, hitting the gym and keeping his hair short. He didn't blame men who got it wrong – men like the nurse in the hospital, like Ron, like the man who maintained that short haircut of his – but felt more wizened than they were, as though he were in on a secret even though it seemed so obvious once he knew it himself.

It was this emphasis on the traditionally masculine traits, like consciously deepening his voice and communicating in a direct and to-the-point manner, that would serve Nick best on his new project at Icon. Chad, the client Nick had met at Art Basel, had hired the same contractor Nick had tussled with over the need for 'bone' versus 'biscuit' in a boring beige bathroom. Nick knew he was going to have to fight like hell to get this job installed the way he envisioned it.

"Steven will do the cut and Christophe will do the color," Ron said, returning Nick's thoughts to the fact that he was even on the phone with him.

"Color?" Though Nick had been tempted to tweeze the stray silver strands he'd seen sparkle through his otherwise brown crewcut – when he was already holding the tweezers to clean up his own brows, he admitted to himself – he had seen very few men's dye jobs he approved of. Nick also had to admit to himself that he'd often seen them close-up, looking down on bad highlights or a rinse as a man more fey than his liking went down on him. Having just now been with guys like Marco and Humberto, Nick wasn't going to settle anymore.

"I'm thinking red."

Though they were conversing over the phone, Nick was sure Ron knew he was rolling his eyes.

# # # # #

For Mark, packing to leave the frat house forever was little different from packing to leave for spring break. He didn't know if he'd miss it, but he would certainly miss the sense of accomplishment that living there gave him, given how much harder it would be for him to achieve much in his current condition.

Certainly being accepted by all these guys was a huge achievement for Mark, and the apex of this was his relationship with Rob. For a year-and-a-half, they did everything together, on the field, in the strip clubs, and in an alley. After all the time Mark had spent avoiding Rob, he was surprised to have Rob now avoiding him, preserving his popularity, not getting too near someone on his way out the frat's front door.

Having a stripper for a girlfriend could go either way, but with Carrie, it was clearly a coup. Usually, guys would congratulate the initial score, say that she was 'totally hot' or something similar, then tease that they'd all seen her naked, imagined doing things with her, even suggest that they had. But Carrie was above that, didn't socialize much with fraternity-types of guys, kept her distance and her reputation. Further, though she was indeed 'totally hot,' she was also truly beautiful, whip smart, and fun to be with. Mark knew getting with her was a triumph, to the degree that he feared she might well be out of his league, particularly now that so much was spiraling down for him.

Most of Mark's belongings fit in a duffel no larger than the one he'd taken to Miami. Mark didn't know if he should be relieved that there was so little to bother with moving or worried there wasn't more tangibly *to* him.

# # # # #

Most of the design firm's jobsites were middle-of-the-road Miami-Mediterranean, so the project at Icon was completely refreshing. Adding to the treat of it for Nick, of course, was the fact that the job was all his.

The Icon building sat against the bay between South Beach and downtown Miami, towering over the causeway that connected the two. The building was inhabited largely by wealthy and flamboyant Latinos, most of whom only lived there for a month or two out of the year, when Miami's weather and social scene were at their best, both of which started with Art Basel. The character of Icon was created by Philippe

Starck, an iconic designer Nick idolized for his eclectic mix of styles. In his industrial and furniture designs, Starck's vision was contemporary and often cheeky, and as an interior designer, Starck collected objects from various eras, from historically traditional to almost futuristically contemporary, with further irreverence and wit, all assembled to create a collaged signature style. If Nick asked nearly any resident of one of South Beach's many high-end residential buildings – from the Murano Grande next door to The Setai across town on the beach – where they lived, they would proudly answer 'South Beach' and smile, knowing that the area offered much in the way of nightlife and excess, and that the building they lived in helped create this mystique. If he asked this of someone who lived at Icon, they would answer 'Icon' with even more pride. Such was the building's spot in the hierarchy of desirable places to call 'home.'

Though Icon was widely viewed as the premier place to live, the chic building was far from the bright neon and Deco architecture that were the town's postcard-picture calling card. This drove Nick's design focus for the condo.

Or rather, the three condos. Chad had purchased three two-bedroom units in the building, identical condos that stacked on top of each other. Though the building was laid out to ensure the elevator lobbies on each floor were shared by only two units, this project's *program* – the list of spatial elements and features required in the remodel – was topped by a grand staircase unifying all the levels inside a soaring three-story volume. In laying out the space, Nick had devoted a huge portion of the available square footage to this singularly impressive open space, which overlooked the blue bay by day and the colorful city lights at night. But these were the lights of downtown Miami, not South Beach, and they lacked the latter's neon punch and animated exuberance. Downtown's lights highlighted the perpetually in-progress development of the skyline, tracing I.M. Pei's Bank of America tower in colors that changed with the seasons with the same intensity that illuminated the construction cranes seemingly permanently perched high above the city, metal monsters that loomed above new construction and derailed traffic and city life like Godzilla or King Kong: giant creatures ready to crush everything below them. The volume's view also included Fisher Island just below and to the left and Star Island further off and to the right, the wealthiest and most private of Miami's residential communities, the strife of the deflated downtown and unpopular, touristy Bayside poetically between them in the distance.

The ideas he had for the place were more creative than Nick even hoped for from himself, and after the bones on his right side had come back so strong, Nick wondered if his right-brained ingenuity was stronger, too. Nick had challenged himself to design the interior of the condo – reduced now to four bedrooms, one a sweeping master that occupied the entirety of the highest floor, and one large kitchen on the main level, the two existing kitchens on the other floors to be transformed into a wet bar and an expanded master bath – to build the drama of Deco Drive into the space, though the windows faced the opposite direction. He would do this with crystals and mirrors, with bright-colored textiles and low levels of lighting, with streamlined furniture and streaming dance music in concealed speakers throughout the project. Lacquered walls would mimic the Deco era's pastel Bakelite, sparkly quartz floors would bridge the gap between the asphalt of Ocean Drive and the terrazzo floors of the restored hotels that lined one side of it.

This would all happen soon, Nick knew, but not even the bones of his ideas had been built yet. For now, the acrylic-railed glass stairs that would link the levels existed only on the pages of the rolled-up blueprints he carried with him. All that had begun was demolition; namely, a fifteen-by-fifteen hole had been cut through the floors of the two upper levels, yielding a vertigo-inspiring view from the top that hadn't been railed-in, even by the scrap two-by-fours contractors relied on to keep clients and subs safe and potential lawsuits to a minimum.

Nick saw the openings in the floors as an opportunity and considered going for it. In his mind, he saw himself inching closer to the edge, waiting for the lazy, lax contractor to take charge of the conversation, lead the client to a detail on the other side of what would soon be a lofted living area, so he could fling himself down the opening, to the floor twenty feet below, pitching his body to land left-side down, surely breaking the bones in the half of his body that he still wanted to hurt, to heal stronger.

Nick eyed the opening and, despite his professional obligation to indicate the danger to the contractor and client, said nothing, wanting the opening to stay as it was, unguarded, dangerous as an open lion's mouth for him to stick his head – his whole body, really – in later.

Chapter Seventeen

Sleep came easy for Nick after visiting the jobsite at Icon, his dreams for once not filled with images of his assailants.

The even, monotone sounds startled him, as they had before.

Beep.

Beep.

Nick knew it wasn't his alarm clock this time, and smiled, remembering what he'd done. He blinked a few times to let his eyes adjust to the light – if they'd ever *adjust to those fluorescents, he thought – and checked his body for bandages.*

His left leg and arm were both Michelin-Man-sized-and-shaped, plaster-white and unmoving when he tried.

"Back again?" the voice was familiar to Nick

"Doctor Monroe, I presume," Nick said without turning his head. He had indeed tried to turn to see the cute doctor but couldn't, which made him happy he'd sustained injury there, too, but sad that he couldn't see the bespectacled and bearded face that he'd dreamed of so many times.

Nick reasoned that it was okay; he could have drawn the cute doctor's face from memory.

"So my favorite patient had a little accident, eh? It's like a party here at Mount Sinai, and you couldn't stay away." The doctor's joking affected Nick immediately. Not everything was broken; Nick could still get hard. The doctor continued, "Well the circumstances are better, I admit, though I'm afraid the extent of the damage is about the same."

"It's the lime Jell-O. Can't get enough."

"You know it's not a Jell-O shot, right? Nothing good in there. Not gonna get you high."

"I have morphine for that, Doctor," Nick said. *"Thanks to you."* Pronouncing the word 'thanks' with bandages close to his mouth proved a lisping embarrassment to Nick.

"Thanks to an unsafe construction site, I heard. They cut a hole in the floor without putting up a railing, eh?"

Nick couldn't nod, and it took him too long to discover that to suddenly agree audibly.

"Not that I'd ever encourage any litigious behavior, but it sounds like you've got a case."

That's a big part of why I did it, *Nick thought.* And to get to see you again. *"You're a lawyer* and *a doctor?"* Nick feared his attempt at light sarcasm might not have come through the bandages.

"We're a full service treatment facility." The doctor winked and exited.

"What the hell happened to you?"

Ron's voice was familiar to Nick, but the hair on his head was not. At Palm Beach Salon, Nick saw, Ron had gotten a decent spiky haircut with some rather loud highlights. *"I could ask you the same thing."*

"Cut by Steven, highlights by Christophe. You don't like?"

The streaks in Ron's hair were pronounced, very light and brassy, nearly orange against his dark brown base color. Nick remembered that he probably didn't look too good himself right now, particularly in the hospital lighting. *"It's a bit extreme,"* he offered, hoping the subject would change before Ron tested his diplomacy.

It didn't. *"I thought they were subtle."* Ron said.

"As a sledgehammer."

"Natural."

"As Cher."

"They're sun-kissed."

Nick smirked. *"The sun didn't* kiss *your hair. The sun* gave head *to your hair."*

"*Actually, Christophe gave me the highlights, and then* I *blew* him *before his next appointment.*"

"*A blow job for a bad dye job. What would you have done to him if you'd come out looking* good?" *Nick realized he was being rather mean but figured he was heavily medicated and could blame his words on that later.*

"*You're just jealous.*"

"*Of the fact that you're not half-cased in plaster and can stand up and walk around? Absolutely. Of your hair right now? Not on your life.*"

Ron stuck his tongue out at Nick.

"*Seriously, with the lighting in here you look like a porcupine drowned in a can of Orange Crush.*"

"*And how does your friend the doctor look under this lighting?*"

Nick got the subject change he was hoping for. "*Hot,*" *Nick guessed, as it was how he remembered the doctor from before but hadn't been able to turn his head to see him.*

"*Imagine him without fluorescents,*" *Ron said, pointing up and proving that he'd listened to Nick's many complaints about such lights, both in this room and in any application.*

Imagine him without pants, *Nick thought. Nick managed the most dramatic leading-lad sigh the constraints of his bandages would allow.*

"*Tell me you didn't do this to yourself just to see him again.*"

And what if I did? *Nick wondered.* "*Right,*" *he managed.*

"*You better ask him out this time,*" *Ron paused.* "*Or I will.*"

"*Can you be hospitalized for bad hair?*"

Ron took a long look at Nick, his hair alternately matted and standing on end around his white-bandaged neck, and said, "*Apparently.*"

Nick nodded appreciatively at the humor in Ron's pointed remark, then heard Ron say, "Glad to see you're okay," and exit, making room for the doctor to come back in and check on Nick again. The doctor rattled off the names of the bones Nick had broken on his left side, the severity of each injury, and how long each was projected to take to heal. Nick was unable to follow most of it; his hard-on was raging out of control.

"One last question, doctor."

"What's that?"

Nick hesitated, wondering how to ask as much as he wondered what the doctor's answer would be. "Do you want to go out sometime?"

"On two conditions."

Nick's eyes widened, hopeful but cautious.

"If you'll stop breaking your bones, and stop calling me 'Doctor.' It's 'Eric.'"

Nick woke up completely cognizant – and in one piece – and set about making three important phone calls.

The first was to the contractor for the job at Icon. Nick left a voicemail stating that he had observed a dangerous condition – the unrailed openings – at the jobsite and would follow-up with an email about the unsafe opening, cc'ing the client.

The second was to Ron, to try to talk him out of his hair appointment. "Call me crazy," Nick had said, "but I had a vision about it not turning out too well."

The third was to Dr. Monroe, whose hospital business card was on Nick's nightstand and whose first name, Nick consciously read off the card he'd only worried over before – felt the raised letters of the name without looking when he tried for sleep – *was* 'Eric.' Nick asked him out without hesitation.

Equally without hesitation, Eric said "Yes."

Chapter Eighteen

Nick picked Osteria Del Teatro, on Washington at Espanola, for his date with Eric, who he still thought of as 'Doctor Monroe.' Nick loved the food at Osteria, of course, but it wasn't why he went there. Nick figured the food probably wasn't the main reason *anyone* went there.

Nick loved the restaurant for its location. In South Beach, the restaurants on Ocean are usually thought to offer the best people-watching, as the nightlife-loving crowds walked by the restaurant guests looking for Bongo's and Wet Willies. But those crowds – both the passersby and the restaurant diners – were tourists, and the best people-watching in those restaurants was from their sidewalk seating; Miami weather wasn't reliably suited to alfresco dining. Osteria was located next to Cameo, one of the better-known night clubs that attracted C-list 'celebrities,' the attention of *Ocean Drive* magazine, and a mostly-local, good-looking crowd. Osteria didn't offer outdoor seating unless it was wildly overbooked, but its floor-to-ceiling glass separating restaurant from street corner afforded a great view – and a welcome barrier – to the odd homeless street person mixing with the obviously well-off, the valets struggling with the exotics rented by out-of-towners, the local girls in tight dresses queuing up at Cameo. Nick arrived early to make sure he got the table he wanted, in the window by the front door, for the best people-watching both in and out of the restaurant.

Another reason Nick so routinely chose Osteria was its host and manager, a more-cute-than-handsome man with a shaved head and huge brown eyes, disappointingly always covered up to the neck by a colored shirt and tonally-matched tie, making rounds in the small restaurant throughout dinner, shaking hands and kissing cheeks: forever flirting, with women and men alike. Nick knew he was straight, that his good-natured winking and teasing was just good business, getting all sorts of appetites going, but he enjoyed it nonetheless.

All thoughts of the host vanished when Nick spotted Eric through the window, crossing Washington from Espanola. Out of his scrubs, Nick could see that Eric had a smaller build than he usually went for, his narrow waist belted tight, a white dress shirt above and black pants below, both loose on lithe limbs.

Eric was more or less dressed like a waiter; Nick smirked, thinking what he'd order from him if given the chance.

Nick got up to greet Eric and then froze, not knowing if he should hug or shake hands or kiss his cheek in the restaurant with its mixed crowd. The last thing he wanted to do was be overly affectionate too soon, make Eric feel he was overstepping his bounds and keep every dismayed eye in the place on them for the whole meal. Nick clutched Eric's shoulder and gave it a squeeze, combining an acceptable-enough public greeting with copping a feel of Eric's frame – firm in his hand and not as bony as he'd feared – and sat down.

"So, you found the place okay?" Nick asked Eric.

"Yeah – I'd never been here before. Next person you have meet you here, just say 'It's the fishbowl on the corner,'" Eric said looking around, the eyes of people both in and out of the restaurant still trained on both of them for all the recent movement around their table until a low-slung car outside pulled up to valet, its loud exhaust note and red paint pulling everyone's focus out into the street.

"I love it here. I love being able to watch the crowd of..." Nick hunted for the right word, "...tacky people, locals who don't communicate primarily in English, and when they do speak English it's with a heavy accent. Their excessive tanning, disposable designer clothes –"

"Eurotrash."

"But they're mostly Latin – South American at that – the ones from other countries who seem so over-the-top. What's Spanglish for 'Eurotrash?' 'Brazilian *basura*?'"

Eric laughed, but the proximity of their table to the restaurant's other diners – many of whom fit Nick's description of 'Brazilian *basura*' – made him glance around to see if anyone was eavesdropping and offended.

"But you live here on the beach."

"Yes, you?"

"Aventura."

"Do you like it?"

"Not really, but it's on the water and quiet, at least for six months out of the year," Eric paused. "But the other six months, the traffic –"

"Snowbirds," Nick said, and Eric nodded. Certain areas of South Florida were all but abandoned for the warmer parts of the year, until it cooled off and people from up north descended on the towns. Aventura hosted a lot of people from Canada those six months, and was largely Jewish all year. Further north, Palm Beach was practically a ghost town for spring and summer, its famed Worth Avenue shops not even opening for those seasons.

"Do you like living here in South Beach?"

"Some days it has great energy. Others, it just has a lot of noise. But it's never boring."

"I can see that," Eric said, eyeing the sidewalk outside as a man walked by the restaurant with an enormous boa constrictor on his shoulders.

"And I don't like to be bored," Nick paused, "Or boring my dinner guest. Am I already?"

Eric laughed. "No, not yet. I'll let you know."

"Good. I'll do my best," Nick paused for too long, noting the way Eric's gaze had drifted down to his chest. Nick liked when that happened – and it happened more than ever now that he'd gotten so big – and never tried to snap a guy out of it, say something abrasive like 'my eyes are up here' when he caught a guy staring at his pecs like he was some busty businesswoman trying to be taken seriously. He was born with his eyes; he'd worked hard for his chest, and harder still to get a guy like Eric to notice it. Nick smiled and continued. "And now, I'm stumped for dinner conversation. Can't ask what you do for a living, given how we met."

"What about you?"

"Interior designer. It's not as gay as it sounds."

"How gay do you think it sounds?"

"You're a doctor. You save lives. I guess by 'gay' I mean 'silly' and 'unserious' as well as profession-routinely-associated-with-gay-men."

Eric smiled.

"Although I went to hear a famous designer give a seminar once, and he announced that he thought we as interior designers have the most important job in the world."

"Really?"

"And, I was so glad when everyone else applauded that, not because I agree, but because it covered up the sound of my own raucous laughter." Both men laughed, and Nick noticed Eric meeting his eyes now. "I mean, his point is that we create environments that allow people like you, who save lives or perform some other critical service, to go home and unplug in and go back to work so much more rested from being in such a well-designed place, so you can do the best job possible – saving lives or something."

"I never thought of it that way. Maybe you *do* have the most important job in the world."

"Hell no. If I create an escape or a place of respite, great. But, it's not brain surgery – by which I mean that it's not that serious, that studied, that life-or-death."

"You don't exactly sound like you love it," Eric opined.

"Oh I do love it. I absolutely do. And I'm doing absolutely too much of the talking."

"No, go on. For most of the time I've known you you've been unconscious. Or your mouth was bandaged so much that your vowels were pretty indistinct."

"You know you can *buy* vowels on *Wheel of Fortune*."

"How about I just buy you dinner?"

Both men smiled at each other. *Shit, he likes you, Nick,* Nick thought to himself. *Don't fuck this up.* "I can't believe I'm on a date with a doctor, and we're talking about *my* job."

"Nick, we're at an Italian restaurant, with a lot of red sauces and rare meat. You want to hear about what it looked like when I cut a bullet out of a cop the other day?"

Nick paused for a beat, but didn't need to think on it. "So the thing about being a designer..."

"That's what I thought."

Nick laughed and continued, "...is that you can't really escape. Like the guy said about us creating environments for people with, you know, *important* jobs to escape to."

"You can't escape in your home?"

"No. I'm always second-guessing my selections, comparing my furniture against something else I saw recently and liked. But that's actually not what I meant."

Eric smiled encouragingly. "Again, go on."

"You like movies? TV?"

Eric answered with an audible, "Yeah," the subtext clear to Nick, pairing *'doesn't everyone?'* with *'where are you going with this?'*

"You escape in them. Lose yourself for a couple hours."

"Apparently I have to. I've never hired an interior designer."

Nick smirked. *Cute, funny, and a doctor,* he thought. *Pinch me.* "I can't. I just can't."

"Why not?"

"Poor set design." Nick paused. "Let's say a character's supposed to be fabulously wealthy."

"Robert Redford in *The Great Gatsby.*"

"Right, or something more contemporary like Sharon Stone in *Basic Instinct* or Bruce Wayne in any of the *Batman* incarnations. So, they show the rich character's house, and every time – *every single time* – there's some sofa or other element that I know is only, like, nine-hundred bucks or something. Or I just recognize a fabric or a light fixture as something I've used on a job. Takes me out of the moment, thinking 'I've specified that.'"

"I think my sofa *was* nine hundred bucks." Eric shrugged. "I call it a couch."

"Maybe you have to at that price point. Maybe it's like pronouncing the word 'vase' as *'vaahz,'* meaning a vase that cost more than a couple hundred."

Eric paused to think. "I guess I don't own a *vaahz* then, either. Just a couch and a vase. I'm a simple guy."

"I guess we met just in time."

"Speaking of TV, I watch the decorating shows every now and then to get some ideas – and put myself to sleep – but my place looks like a bachelor pad. Like a straight guy lives there."

"That could be misleading to anyone you take home." *Like say, me, in about an hour,* Nick hoped. "Every gay guy wants a straight-acting guy, but a straight-*decorating* one? Hardly. My advice?"

"Hire a professional?"

"Or date one for a while." Nick wished he could take back the words the second they came out, thinking he came off too forward. "And turn off the decorating shows. No good can come from them."

"You haven't used the word 'decorating' before just then."

"A lot of designers are quite sensitive about that word, about being called a 'decorator.' The terms are used interchangeably by most laypeople –"

Eric nodded, guiltily and to continue the conversation while chewing.

"– but most designers find being called a 'decorator' insulting."

Eric had his mouth full, so he widened his eyes to keep Nick talking.

"It's connotative and dismissive. A designer is educated, licensed even, but a 'decorator' is someone who thinks he or she has an eye – or someone who watches too many decorating shows on TV."

Eric chewed and swallowed. "I never knew it was an insult."

"I've been called worse." *Fag-got for instance,* Nick thought to himself. "'Interior decorator' becomes 'inferior desecrator' by an architect who feels his 'vision' was compromised by the work of an interior designer," Nick used his fingers to make little quotation marks in the air when he said 'vision,' "but if they wanted to avoid that, and wanted a more cohesive project, architects would work in tandem with interior designers throughout the schematic stages of a job instead of judging what we do with the rooms and spaces they leave for us."

"Sounds like you're turning around and judging architects the way they judge you."

"Not at all. My degrees are actually in architecture, not interiors."

Nick met Eric's eyes to see if his doctor date looked impressed, but couldn't tell. Most people – most of Nick's dates, at any rate – marveled at an architectural degree, at the ability to turn ideas in his mind into works of mortar and stone – or at least drywall and two-by-fours – but Nick realized Eric had likely been in school longer and had the more-esteemed occupation. *M.D. diploma beats mortar-and-stone Master's of Architecture,* Nick thought. *Paper covers rock.*

"Even in architecture school, I noticed that we were almost *encouraged* to plan buildings that were impressive sculptural shapes first, and then worry about the functionality of the inside of the form we created. That seemed backwards to me. An impressive-looking building is great, but I think it's too often forgotten that the built form is meant to be experienced from within, and that perhaps the emphasis should be on creating livable or usable spaces first, then skinning them attractively." Nick stopped, then added, "Am I going to do all the talking tonight?"

"Yup."

"Great," Nick said, then was purposely quiet for a moment.

"A psychiatrist would enjoy contrasting your interest in perfecting the insides of things versus their outsides with the labor you put into your perfect physique."

Nick blushed. "Good thing you're not that kind of doctor."

"So it's safe to say being called an 'interior decorator' would offend you."

"By someone out of the industry, who doesn't know the difference? Not at all. I'm sure my grandmother probably tells the woman who rolls-and-sets her hair once-a-week that I'm a 'decorator,' and I don't care, but when some contractor who doesn't know primrose from puce thinks all I do is play in fabric swatches all day, then yeah, I throw a hissy fit." Nick paused. "But a very *masculine* hissy-fit."

"A straight-acting, straight-decorating hissy-fit."

"Exactly," Nick said, impressed with Eric's humor and hoping it was mutual.

"What color *is* puce, exactly?"

Nick affected a spooky voice, like someone from Hialeah talking about *Santeria,* "No one knows."

# # # # #

In a month, Mark would be old enough for a real ID and could retire his fake one, but by way of rights-of-passage, there was little left for Mark to do. The typical buying-a-sixer-and-getting-drunk or going-out-to-a-strip-joint were not only things he'd already done, but part of his routine. *Go-out-and-bash-a-gay-man,* Mark thought, *I've done that, too.* His build was clearly the product of years in the gym, and he'd had to shave twice a day since he was seventeen to not hazard sanding his dates smooth when he risked a good night kiss. He rarely got carded anyway, but with all that had happened, Mark was wondering what made someone a man. When people older than he was – his professors, his parents – talked about being his age, they excused much of their behavior, saying they were just kids, still growing, still turning into the adults they were now.

Ted, the bartender at the gay bar Mark had driven so far from town to go to, had told him admitting what he did – to himself, Mark had figured, for he didn't want anyone else to know – would make him a man. Mark instead knew that what he'd done was macho but hardly mature, not only the violence but the following of another man's lead, letting Rob be in charge for so much of his life and for the entirety of what they'd done in the alley. Mark shouldn't have gone along with it – should have spoken up, stopped it – but instead, went along like a child being led by the hand.

# # # # #

"Okay, I admit I read your chart more thoroughly than I would some other patient's. We're the same age, but you look –"

"Younger?" Nick hadn't meant to offend Eric and regretted both the word and having blurted it out so readily.

"Oh-yeah," Eric blurred the words together, like 'atta-boy' or 'oh-shit.'

Boo-yah, Nick thought, and smirked. "I damn well ought to," he said playfully.

"How do you mean? Most guys who work out so much end up looking older – more mature muscle mass, faces creased from the expressions they make under the strain of weightlifting."

"And all that tanning."

"Right. Why are tanning salons so popular here? This is Miami for Pete's sake."

"Pete who? I'm Nick," Nick smiled, hoping to sound more coy than corny. "But you must be very new to our area."

"I am – the lack of a tan gave me away?"

"That, and the fact that in Miami, you can practically get Botox at the gas station." Nick pointed his right hand into the shape of a gun, aimed it at the center of his forehead, and fired. "Fill 'er up," he said.

Eric laughed a little harder than Nick thought he would. "Fill 'er up, indeed."

"I've tried it, more out of a sense of experimenting than out of necessity. At least I hope I don't need it."

"You don't."

"I wasn't fishing, I promise," Nick said, "but hey, thanks."

# # # # #

Mark's hunger wasn't so great that it kept him from thinking about everything that had happened recently or how much his arm hurt, but it was enough to get him into the kitchen looking for something to eat. He thought how lucky he was that things with Carrie had been so easy at first, her all-but pouncing on him after he and Rob had gotten back from Miami, not like other girls, who wouldn't admit the attraction between them until Mark had shelled out for a fancy dinner at some out-of-the-way expensive impress-your-way-into-my-panties restaurant. Now that he was leaving State, he'd need all the money he had, and nuked someone else's leftover pizza knowing they wouldn't miss it, wouldn't likely admit it was even theirs, that they'd failed to finish the whole large-with-pepperoni in one sitting. Usually Mark would have pizza with beer, but he was on antibiotics, and found a flat two-liter of Pepsi in the back of the fridge that he was sure had been there since their last coed party, where just enough of it had been offered to girls who'd asked for 'just a soda' to cover the taste of the vodka some frathead had poured into the cup first.

Mark's things were packed, and in a couple of days he would leave, but he didn't know where to go. The only thoughts or images that were clear to him were those from the alley, of the man he and Rob had beat down and humiliated. Mark winced at the thought, though at first he thought the feeling was pain from his arm; Mark had learned a thing or two about humiliation since spring break.

# # # # #

There was no your-place-or-mine struggle after dinner. They went to Nick's place, which was mere blocks away and allowed Nick to show off a little.

Likewise, there was no top-or-bottom discussion before Eric pushed Nick into bed. They were into each other, and Nick thought it would figure itself out.

"You did all the talking, so why don't I do all the work?" What Eric asked didn't feel like a question to either of them.

"Huh?"

Eric lunged for Nick's belt, unbuckled it, and unzipped Nick's fly within the time of Nick's single short gasp of breath. Nick's cock, in turn, sprung up to meet Eric's hands, poking at the waistband of his boxer briefs. "Gimme that bone," Eric ordered. "I know *it's* not broken."

Eric hadn't so much as unbuttoned his own shirt before peeling down Nick's underwear, exposing Nick's rigid cock, and swallowing it whole.

"Wow," Nick said, then remembered being with Marco and Humberto and followed up with a fast "Damn."

Eric gave the kind of head that let Nick know Eric loved it down there. He released Nick long enough to whisper, "You like that, huh?"

"I fuckin' love it," Nick said, his voice carried on breath down his torso to Eric's face, letting his head fall back as Eric took him in again.

"Let the doctor nurse you back to health." Eric's lips were wrapped around the meat of Nick's cock the second he said the last word and stayed that way as he swallowed Nick from the head down the shaft all the way to the base. Eric inched back up again and licked around the wet, pink cap for a while, then put the whole head of it back in his mouth and just worked the tip up and down, occasionally tapping the slit of Nick's dick with his tongue.

"Oh God," Nick said, knowing if Eric didn't ease off the most sensitive part of him soon, he was going to come in his mouth.

Eric went all the way down on Nick one more time before letting them both breathe, licking up and down the shaft, then rolling his own lips into his mouth, wrapping over his teeth and gumming up and down Nick's sex with skin-softened bites.

"Fuck, you give good head."

Eric didn't respond, just carried on doing what he was doing. Nick couldn't believe how great Eric felt and tried to delay his inevitable coming as long as he could. Eric took him in again, still nice and slow, in no hurry to rush Nick's orgasm, Nick hoping he had a few in him. Nick felt the wet suede of Eric's mouth envelop his cock down to the base once more before letting go, licking around the head a while, and releasing him.

Nick usually closed his eyes when he got head as a reflex, but he couldn't picture anything hotter than his dick in Eric's mouth, so he opened them back up, just in time to see Eric dive for his balls and take both of them in his mouth at once.

"Jesus," Nick breathed out.

"It's pronounced 'Hey-Zeus,' remember?" Eric said back, muffled with a mouthful of Nick.

Nick laughed and looked down at Eric, who laughed as well and let Nick's scrotum fall out of his mouth. Eric then took turns lightly sucking on each of Nick's balls, smiling with his eyes up at Nick while using his tongue on the balls in his mouth, swirling around the skin, alternating his focus between where it was loose and where it was taut.

Eric let Nick's balls free again and licked up the shaft, to the head, and after taking him in all the way one last time, let him out and said, "Let me ride that bone."

"Fuck yeah."

Eric finally undressed, and Nick hastily pulled his own shirt over his head. Nick watched as Eric unbuttoned his shirt, slowly revealing the map of his chest hair, the dark peninsula of hair trailing down his abdomen to where his hands were popping his pants button and peeling down the zipper. Eric had a nice body but didn't look to Nick like he spent a lot of time working at it, and was pale from spending so much time making rounds at the hospital, particularly in contrast with the dark curls on his chest. Eric kicked his legs in place to work his pants down his legs, revealing the dark hair along them and a snug pair of navy blue briefs. As Nick wore only black, it always surprised him to see what color a guy's 'date night' underwear was. Eric's were the same color as Nick's tattoo had been before he'd had it covered-over orange, and though Nick liked the sight of Eric in them fine, he couldn't wait until they were off.

"Nice," Nick said encouragingly, thrusting his hips off the couch to take his own pants off. Once they were, he reached in his pocket for a condom, tore the wrapper off, and rolled it on.

"I wanted to do that." Eric said to Nick, disappointed.

"Next time." Nick pointed at the navy briefs and said, "Take those off and climb on."

Eric did as he was told, reminding Nick, "Just lie there, let me do the work."

"Yes, sir."

"Doctor's orders."

Eric lubed two of his fingers and reached behind himself, then positioned his ass right over Nick's cock.

Nick, ordered to stay still, didn't dare so much as blink.

Nick wasn't sure which one of them moaned louder when Eric sat down on his dick. Unlike the way he gave head, Eric didn't take all of Nick into his ass at first, allowing instead just the tip to feel the wonderful heat and clench of his tensed ass. Eric's breath was coming fast as he eased himself down further onto Nick, letting him in more and more, until Nick was balls-deep into him, all of Eric's weight on his knees and Nick's hips.

Eric raised his torso up and down, giving Nick's cock a few inches of up-and-down stimulation, before pulling up all the way, almost letting Nick out of him before sitting down again.

"God that feels good," Nick said, as he wrapped an arm around Eric's waist to hold him there.

"I said don't move," Eric said, but Nick didn't move his arm away. Instead, Nick's arm allowed Eric to change position a little, leaning back and letting his feet kick forward, his bent legs trapping

Nick's body in place on the bed while he used the strength of his thighs to jerk his weight up and down on Nick's cock.

"Fuck, you're amazing," Nick said, and meant it.

Eric kept at it for a while, the smile on his face as constant as the bucking motion of his body as he lifted and lowered himself on and off Nick.

Nick had obliged Eric's request to stay still as long as he could, but started thrusting his hips up to meet Eric's every downward ride of his cock.

Eric didn't seem to mind. "Yeah, give me that bone," he said.

That was all the encouragement Nick needed. He used his abs to push himself even deeper into Eric, matching Eric's rhythm push for pull. Eric began to stroke himself at rocket-launch speed as he rode Nick, not missing a beat of the rhythm they had created as his cock blurred in his feverishly-moving hands. The smile on Eric's face took a turn, twisting and perverting itself with crazily widened eyes and a wider mouth.

"Oh…yeah…" Eric nearly yelled out as he shot a thick rope of ejaculate all over Nick's chest and abs.

This was the moment of truth for Nick when he was with a guy. It was always disappointing for Nick when a bottom he was deep into came and decided that that was it; he had come and was done bottoming for Nick and would maybe get Nick off another way, usually with his hands, sometimes with his mouth, sometimes selfishly not at all.

Eric kept riding Nick excitedly, not even asking the leading 'Are you close?' or 'You gonna come?' or ordering 'Come for me' that always translated to Nick as 'Hurry up, I'm done and I'm only going to keep at this for so long.' Those instructives were all always counterproductive, serving instead only to frustrate Nick, break his focus and delay his release.

Eric's enthusiasm and technique amazed Nick, and moments after Eric used his fingers to pull his own ejaculate off Nick's torso and feed it to himself, passionately licking his lips as though this tasted better than anything at Osteria, Nick breathed out in bliss, "Watching you do that gets me so close."

"Come in my mouth. I want to taste you, too."

That did it. Nick's body tensed, signaling to him that he'd better move fast if he was going to oblige Eric's request. He pulled out of Eric. Eric crouched down and went to work, yanking off Nick's condom, jacking Nick's ready cock in time with his every rushed breath. He opened his mouth and took just the head of Nick's dick in, still jacking Nick with his hands.

Eric took one last lick across the head of Nick's cock before it blasted on his face and into his mouth. Eric stayed there, unflinching, letting Nick's come cover his glasses and extended tongue before swallowing. Nick looked down to lock eyes on Eric as he wiped his face with his hands and licked his fingers, one by one, before swallowing again.

"Fill 'er up, indeed," Eric breathed out.

Chapter Nineteen

The guys in the frat – Rob, mostly, Mark figured – threw Mark a party before he went away. No one called it a 'They're-Throwing-You-Out-of-School-Because-Your-Arm's-Busted-and-You-Can't-Play-Anymore,-Loser' Party, but as far as Mark was concerned, they may as well have. There was nothing to celebrate, nothing awaiting him after this experience, no plan in place for what to do if college didn't work out. College *was* the back-up plan; Mark had entered State thinking he'd only use his degree if he didn't end up playing pro ball, or if he injured himself too soon after turning pro to have made any real money. There was no plan for what to do if he injured himself before then, while still in school, trying to tread water academically and hopefully get picked an early draft.

Mark was going nowhere and had nowhere to go, but he had to leave the frat by Monday morning.

To mark the occasion, the frat would be packed with girls and kegs Saturday night after the game. The game itself was tough for Mark to watch; officially, he was kicked off the team, and couldn't even watch from the bench. Instead, he bought a ticket and sat in the stands, alternately rooting his team on and ducking his head lest anyone in the stands recognize him as having been on the field only weeks ago. The cast on his arm was hard to hide, but Mark did his best, draping a jacket over most of it, the plaster only peeking out when he switched the hands that held tepid beer and a hot dog. State won by a clear margin; Mark felt good for his team, but their victory without him – their first in some time   stung hard.

At least the team was in high spirits when the players descended on the frat house. Half the team belonged to the frat anyway, so it had the character of a house party, everyone feeling comfortable and at home. The girls seemed to be enjoying themselves as well, though most of them dodged Mark and his cast all night, not knowing what to say besides the odd "remember that time we..." that started off a story of sex from the girl's point of view – which Mark always liked hearing – to a wistful "I only wish we had..." to begin a story of longing, as though they'd always wanted to be with Mark – to have the former kind of story to tell – and his dismissal from school or the team or broken arm made him somehow crippled and unable to fuck.

To bone, Mark thought, remembering how casually Carrie had used the word he'd only heard guys use before in that way. Losing her hurt Mark more than anything tonight; it didn't surprise him that she didn't show up.

The party raged on well into the night, showing no signs of dying down at 2:00 am. Mark wasn't up to any of it, feeling weak, not physically but spent inside. He had found a quiet spot in the study – the frat called the room that despite the fact that no studying that he knew of had ever taken place in there, just the odd tryst or, in Mark's case, the remembering of attacking a man in an alley, of trying to be Rob's friend, of losing himself, and his morals, to Rob – and chilled-out, his face suddenly burning hot when it was hit with the red and blue colored lights that filled the room's few windows, the light itself seeming to find him alone. The study's quiet gave way to the whoop-wail of sirens. The police had arrived. *This is it,* Mark thought, *I'm busted.*

Or Rob and I are, he thought, knowing that any evidence he'd left in Miami could trace back to Rob, too, though there was less of it for certain. *It was only a matter of time, and it's timely in and of itself. Nowhere to go but to jail,* Mark figured, not upset at all that this was the moment he'd been found out. He'd lost everything because of what he'd done, and this ending suited him fine.

Mark walked out of the library and into the crowded party with his hands up, surrendering to what turned out to be nothing more than a noise complaint from a nearby house. When the guys in the crowd saw Mark's I-give, slap-the-cuffs-on-me position, they burst out laughing; someone shouted "Classic," and the party continued, Mark's 'wry sense of humor' now added to the few things anyone said they might miss about Mark.

# # # # #

Something about sleeping with Eric meant more to Nick than his conquests with Marco or Humberto. Marco and Humberto had been so overt in their orchestrating of events, setting Nick up to fall into bed with them as easily as he had gotten with the guys before them – lesser guys, Nick admitted – but Nick felt he had worked for it with Eric, making the first move in calling him, peeling away the layers of oversized scrubs and glasses to get to the cute guy underneath.

Though Marco and Humberto wore their sexual prowess like their tight shirts, Nick certainly hadn't expected Eric to be as good in bed as he was. Everything about Eric felt like a secret only he knew, and that made being with him that much more exciting. Nick purposely had Eric meet him at his condo before their next dates, hoping they'd skip the restaurant and just go to bed, whip up something in the kitchen if it came to it.

# # # # #

The stature of the team's new quarterback had changed since he'd advanced from second-string to replace Mark; he walked taller, his arms angled out wider, elbows almost touching Rob, who was seemingly always nearby. The two men had spent most of Mark's party in a huddle of conversation; the guy had been welcomed onto the field and into the frat without any real initiation or hazing, but Mark wondered if the QB would have to find a gay guy to beat up on to make his bones with Rob.

Mark couldn't get away fast enough, but hadn't known where to go when he drove off campus, out of the small settlement that existed primarily as a college town. He ended up at the airport, and paid cash to fly standby on the next flight to Miami, panic and weakness alternating in him like a bright light being turned on and off.

# # # # #

"Where do you wanna go tonight?" Nick asked Eric, feeling guilty that their last few dates hadn't gotten further than his own bedroom.

"Up to you."

Nick flashed Eric an I'm-the-top-and-I've-made-all-the-decisions-so-far-so-make-up-your-damn-mind-and-tell-me-what-you-want-to-do look.

"I'm not from here," Eric caught the look and continued, "Take me some place I haven't been."

Nick was at once challenged by the remark and relieved, not knowing quite what Eric wanted but wanting Eric to himself, and away from anyone he knew, from any of the guys he'd tricked with recently. "You've been up north to Wilton Manors?"

"I could either say 'no' or 'what's Wilton Manors?'"

"Got it," Nick said. "Bunch of little gay clubs and cute shops that sell anything from antiques to, um, adult 'novelties.'" Nick was sure Eric understood the euphemism, though he stressed the word just in case. "We could stop for lunch somewhere on the way up, spend the day browsing, have a little dinner, then dance it off."

"Dancing – are we dressed for that?" Eric looked down at what he was wearing.

"You really *are* new to Florida, huh?" Nick smiled. "I was like you once, dressing up to go to the store, out at night, to work even. My first boss here told me I should loosen up and wear shorts to work."

"Probably just wanted to see more of you."

"I don't think I was her type. But Florida is casual, anything goes. Flip-flops in the club, shorts to the office, not that I ever would. Sorry if that sounds contradictory, but you gotta draw the line somewhere. But someone would have to die for me to put on a tie again."

"To wear to the funeral."

"Right. And besides, Fort Lauderdale's a lot more, uh, low-pressure than Miami, especially at night. In Miami, I bust my ass at the gym four, five days a week, spray-tan once a week, get a haircut every three weeks, and I'm still an eight on a ten-scale."

"You look amazing," Eric said, shaking his head at Nick.

"But in Fort Lauderdale, I roll out of bed and I'm a ten," Nick said, instantly regretting both the conceit behind what he'd just said and the fact that he'd just put the thought of him rolling out of some strange bed in Fort Lauderdale into Eric's mind. It was already very clear Eric, for all his surprising ability in bed, was a lot less experienced than Nick.

"Which would make me..." Eric started.

"An eleven."

"Good answer," Eric said, and kissed Nick quickly on the mouth.

"So, you're game?"

"Sure."

"Buckle up, then," Nick said, though they weren't even in the car yet.

Nick had bought his car because he wanted it, but when he was honest with himself, he wanted it because it seemed impressive. To him and to many, it was: a loaded Mercedes SL, in his signature black with a black interior, both of which got hot enough in the Miami sun to almost make him regret the purchase. He also almost regretted thinking it was impressive, that it would stand out. After buying it, he realized how many of them were on the road in the area, and thought the police would be smart to purchase them as unmarked cars for how little attention anyone paid to the hundred-thousand-dollar vehicle on the road. Eric looked to Nick to be impressed, but Eric, Nick's questions had established, wasn't from here.

"Top down okay? We'll be taking surface streets – we won't go so fast that wind's a problem."

"No problem for me. You're not taking the highway?"

"I thought I'd stay on Biscayne the whole way. The path of no resistance"

"I think you mean the path of *least* resistance. The path of *no* resistance means you mix a drunk girl with a frat boy who has access to Rohypnol." They both laughed at that, though Nick reacted differently to the mention of frat guys after being attacked than he would have before: fearful, but still aroused. "But I still don't get what you mean."

"Ninety-five is sometimes smooth sailing the whole way, other times completely stopped up for no reason at all. Biscayne gives you stop lights and a lower speed limit, but at least you feel like you're moving. I'd call it 'the scenic route,' but unless you're into the architecture of fast food drive-thrus or like looking at the hookers in Hollywood, you won't find it scenic."

"I don't think I've ever seen a hooker before."

"Really?" Nick asked, doubtful that that could be true. "It's actually my favorite game to play in South Beach – next time we're at Osteria I'll play with you." Nick smiled that he had slyly created the need for another date with Eric.

"What game is that?"

"I call it 'Local Girl or Working Girl.' Girls walk by –"

"– in those skintight little dresses and hooker heels –"

"– and you try to decide if they're working the streets or just...*from* here. Local. The girls in South Beach, the ones who live here, nowhere else in the country do women dress like that, unless they're –"

"Working."

"You got it," Nick paused. "You sit in the window, and they walk by the plate glass, stop for whatever reason, and you think to yourself, 'this is what Amsterdam must look like.'"

Eric laughed. "You're hilarious..."

With the top down, Nick could barely hear Eric, and debated slowing down so they could take their time and talk on the drive north. Knowing there was nothing to look at on the way, Nick accelerated until he felt Eric's hand on his thigh. Nick then eased off the gas, not caring if either of them said another word or saw anything interesting so long as Eric kept his hand right there.

# # # # #

Mark didn't stay in South Beach when he returned to Miami. For one, South Beach was expensive; it was where everyone wanted to be, and they – the aforementioned 'everyone' – paid for the privilege, Mark learned. For another, Mark needed quiet, not at night, when the rest of the world was in bed, but during the day, when he planned to sleep to keep his nights free to stalk his victim.

These factors had ruled out Brickell as well, though an online travel site had recommended the hotels in Brickell, Miami's financial district, as being quiet. This they were, after dark, but during the day Mark knew they'd be jammed with conferences and conventions, far from the silent solace he sought. They, too, were expensive, and as he was footing the bill for this trip, not here on Rob's money – Rob, in fact, was completely unaware that Mark was here and would doubtless disapprove of what he was doing – Mark needed some place cheap.

Mark hadn't booked anything before leaving town, figuring he'd drive around the main roads until something caught his eye. He landed in Miami, retrieved the cheapest-car-possible from the rental agency, and hit Biscayne Boulevard, which the company's placemat-sized map showed him more or less paralleled the freeway – *not* that *'free,'* he'd thought, noting that two lanes of I-95 in either direction were express lanes that charged a toll – and started driving north. Downtown had yielded nothing but buildings resembling those at the edge of South Beach they faced – tall mostly-glass structures serving as either hotels or condominiums, predominantly vacant either way and, Mark guessed, expensive. Further north were Midtown and the Design District, and while each looked adequately dodgy and cheap, Mark noted, both were loud. The bustle of traffic there sounded little different from South Beach, but the locals – largely urban blacks proclaiming their presence with loud utterances and louder-still music – were largely unintelligible to Mark, who'd gone to a mostly-white state school only a couple of hours away from where he'd lived all his life, and served only to irritate, making what Mark considered a shitload of noise but not a bit of sense. Further still was an access bridge to Bal Harbour, which Mark recognized from the chi-chi magazines at Carrie's hairdresser as having numerous expensive boutiques; Mark guessed that meant any place to stay there would be well out of his range. Mark eventually pulled over in Hollywood, where the motels seemed as dodgy as they had in Midtown but were quiet from the street; Mark figured he could get some rest here, and could more or less afford it as well.

The motel names were bland or humorous – one, Mark noted with some irony, was called 'The Lucky Boy' – but did little to describe the joint to which they applied. Mark supposed that even 'The Lucky Boy' was a more appealing name than 'Small Random Concrete Box,' though he couldn't remember the name of the motel he checked into, handing over enough cash for a week's stay and signing in as 'Rob Diamond.'

The place was a dump, but since Mark knew this before even opening the door to his room, it didn't surprise or disappoint him. Instead, Mark threw his duffel onto the surely stained bedspread that was loudly patterned to mask this fact, pulled his flip-flops out of the bag, and put them on to shower; if he'd learned nothing else in college, it was to shower with your flip-flops on, and why. Wrapped in a towel and unable to wind down, Mark alternately lay down and stared at the ceiling, did push-ups against the dirty carpet, trying to keep his face out of it but washing his hands thoroughly after, and masturbated. Mark's mind couldn't fix on anything while he was beating off, and though he tried to focus on remembered details of his time with Carrie before she'd cornered him and ordered him to get out, other girls he'd fucked and all-but forgotten, and his favorite pages from dog-eared copies of *Playboy* and the Victoria's Secret catalogue, he ended up shooting his load while thinking about his victim in the alley. *Serves me right,* he thought, and showered again.

Mark had eventually dozed off without setting the alarm feature on his cell phone – this wasn't a place Mark figured he could request a wake-up call. Mark awoke to the sound of a woman calling out into the dusk's street traffic, offering herself into the night. *A hooker,* Mark thought, *great,* before figuring it was as good a wake-up call as any.

# # # # #

The walls in Bill's were painted a shade of red that blended blood with brick, and the crowd was mixed as well. Muscular if overweight men in tank tops or bare-chested mingled with just-plain-overweight men dressed in drag easily, seeming to Nick as though each respected the other's choices. Nick was used to much more judgment and exclusionary, cliquey behavior in gay culture – in every gay bar – and knew why this place was so popular; there was no attitude coming off anyone.

Anyone but himself and Eric, who Nick figured must have looked to the crowd at Bill's like they'd landed here from another planet.

Eric broke away from Nick to head to the bar, and came back with two beers.

"Seems like a beer kind of place," Eric said, handing one bottle to Nick and gesturing to the crowd with his other. Nick noticed that, in this crowd of such polar extremes of gay male types, even the lipsticked drag queens were drinking beer from bottles. *How ladylike,* Nick thought, and smirked.

"I think you're right. Don't know that that makes it *our* kind of place, though. But when in Rome," Nick said.

"Drink your beer."

Nick didn't know if Eric was finishing his thought or instructing him to shut up and just watch the crowd, sip, try to blend in. *Good luck with that,* Nick thought, realizing they had the most in common with the groomed almost-twinks pretending to shoot pool while eyeing the least hairy and most muscular of the shirtless bears. *Those twinks' attention will shift if they notice us,* Nick thought, and settled behind an interior window, watching the crowd like the girls loitering outside Osteria, separate from it.

Nick and Eric caught a glimpse of a particularly large drag queen in a small tight dress through the glass they nearly hid behind.

"Where does she think she is? *Who* does she think she is?"

Nick whispered into Eric's ear, "I can answer the where with the who:" Nick waited a beat, adding, "Amsterdam-Red-Light-District-Barbie."

The two men laughed so loud they couldn't hide any more, and the men whose glances they'd avoided found them, framed by the wood around the glass.

"Let's go." Nick said, knowing there was more to do across the street.

# # # # #

Barely awake at the motel, Mark let his thumb pulse up and down on the remote until he ran out of energy for even that, letting a half-finished movie about soldiers back from war play out as he fought the urge for more sleep. The soldiers onscreen were having trouble coming to terms with what they had done when deployed, stomaching the carnage they had caused. Mark invested a little into this feeling, knowing the soldiers were only doing what men at war do. In combat, men weren't guilty of anything more than acting on orders, of following someone else's direction.

Mark wished this applied to what he'd done in the alley – under Rob's command – but knew it didn't. Soldiers enlisted, agreed to surrender some degree of thinking and acting for themselves to their C.O. and for the greater good. Though Rob was always in charge of things, everywhere he went, Mark hadn't signed up for anything, hadn't agreed to act the way he had against the man in the alley than night.

Mark knew he had to find the man he'd attacked, but didn't know why, much less what to do afterward. He hoped that coming face to face with the man, with what he'd done to him, would set him on course for getting back to who he once was. If he found him – *when I find him,* Mark corrected himself, knowing that he couldn't stop looking until he had – *what then?* he wondered, not knowing if he should apologize, atone, or just finish the man off.

# # # # #

Alibi was a video bar, so there was a dance floor but no DJ, just a loop of music videos for obscure techno and sped-up pop acts playing on about a hundred TVs stacked throughout the bar. A very young pop starlet's video was playing, the girl dancing on screen in next to nothing, wearing more makeup than Nick thought a girl her age should wear and not nearly enough clothing, winking and blowing kisses at the camera between breathy and strained vocals, lipsynching lip-licking lyrics that said little more than 'fuck me, please.' Under the makeup, Nick knew, the girl was all of fifteen.

"What do you think of her new video?" Eric asked Nick.

"Gosh," Nick deadpanned, "so few porn actresses bother to sing the music that plays in the background while they perform. Good for her."

"You're too much."

Still eyeing the screen, Nick asked, "Seriously, where are her parents?"

"In a suburban McMansion their daughter paid for, one teenaged gyration at a time."

"Points for both 'suburban McMansion' and 'teenaged gyration.' I thought *I* was the funny one."

"You are, but give me a little credit: I'm quick. And you're a bad influence."

As far as influences go, I've got nothing on Ron, Nick thought, wondering if he should get the three of them together now that things were getting serious.

"And more than I can handle," Eric continued, grabbing Nick's ass and squeezing it hard.

That settles it, Nick decided. *I am* definitely *not letting Ron around Eric.* Still in Eric's grip, Nick turned to face him, breathing out, "Handle away."

"You're hot as hell." Eric leaned in to kiss Nick hard, then seemed to Nick to remember they were in public and got uncomfortable. "Really, you could give that teenage girl a run for her money," Eric added, seemingly trying to cool them both off, make them laugh out of the tight embrace.

# # # # #

Mark left the motel not knowing if he was late or early but still in a rush, wanting to get to South Beach as soon as possible, but there was only so fast a Chevy subcompact, bright red or not, could go. The drive down Biscayne was quick enough, most of the traffic lights turning in his favor, as though trying to help Mark's plan along. He noted congestion and noise where he had expected from the drive from the airport, and turned after Design District at a curved blue building to head over the bay, to South Beach, to set his as-yet-not-fully-formed plan – he knew he was looking for his victim, but had no idea what to do when he found him – into motion.

# # # # #

Back at Nick's condo, as they undressed, Eric noticed Nick's toe, still clumsily wrapped-up per the instructions Nick had found online.

"Uh, what happened there?"

"I broke my toe."

"I don't remember that from your list of injuries at the hospital."

"It's not from then," Nick replied, then tried to soften it. "It's nothing, really."

"It's a broken toe. That's not nothing," Eric said. "If that were nothing, I'd be out of work."

Nick shrugged.

"How did I miss that last time I was here? We were naked."

"Exactly; we were naked. I had my pants off and my *toe* is what you would notice?"

"I admit it took me a while, even now. There's a lot of great stuff to look at," Eric said, kissing Nick's chest. "And kiss."

"You keep your eyes open when we kiss," Nick started in with the doctor, taking the offensive in hopes of taking the focus off his toe.

Eric shrugged. "I like looking at you. Can you blame me?"

"And when I go down on you, you stare at me."

"Same answer. Insanely hot guy down there, I don't want to miss a millisecond of it."

Nick smiled at the compliment. "But, with other guys –"

"What other guys?"

"I didn't mean that you're seeing anyone else now. Before me. I mean, I doubt I was your first."

Eric gave Nick an I-will-neither-confirm-nor-deny face.

"Do you close your eyes?"

"Sometimes. Certainly when I started messing around with guys – this was years ago – I kept my eyes open and just stared, knowing I'd want to remember this later when I..." his voice cut off, Eric seeming to hunt for the right words.

"When you were alone."

"Exactly. I mean, when you're young, you're so curious about sex, how it's going to feel, what it's going to look like. And, when all you're ever told is what a man and a woman can do together, you're also curious about what exactly two guys are going to do."

"And then, later on, your eyes –" Nick wanted to get back to topic.

"What's this obsession about eyes?"

"Conversation I had with a friend of mine before I met you. Before any of it happened to me."

"Yeah," Eric said the word almost like a question, saying 'yeah' but Nick hearing 'And your point is?'

"So much has changed. Like you, I don't want to miss a minute of anything right now, but that's true whether I'm getting head – you're great at it, by the way – or just driving along the water or taking a first sip of a particularly good cocktail. I want to take it all in, to notice everything now." Nick said the words, knowing that what had happened to him was making him confront his own mortality like never before. "Why close your eyes at all, I guess, is my point. If I have one."

Eric nodded. "You do."

"So, what do you think about when you close your eyes during sex?"

"England."

"Ha. Seriously."

"Usually, I think about my exes. The cuter ones, or the ones I really got close with. I picture them doing what's being done to me."

Nick laughed.

"What's so funny?"

"If you've dated in your own league – before me, at least, and thanks for slumming it or being charitable or whatever it is you're doing with me," Nick saw Eric shaking his head and trying to interrupt, but kept going, "and the guys you've gone out with are *half* as cute as you are, I bet *I've* pictured them during sex, too."

"Enough talking. More kissing," Eric said, touching his lips to Nick's, silencing them both. Nick unbuttoned Eric's shirt and slid it off him.

"Mmm," Nick sighed. Nick popped his fly, let his pants drop to the floor, and pressed the bulge in his briefs into Eric.

"You're fuckin' huge," Eric said, stripped to the waist. He leaned his body into Nick's, their chests touching lightly, their groins grinding into each other hard.

"I thought you liked me for my sense of humor," Nick replied.

Eric stepped away and sized Nick up from top to toe, finally settling his gaze on Nick's crotch, his dick swelling the front of his underwear. "Ha," he said flatly.

Nick cracked a smile, and watched Eric's gaze move from his cock to his broken toe.

"Can I have a look?" Eric asked.

Nick looked at Eric in disbelief. *Here I am nearly naked, and you want to perform an examination?* "Never got over wanting to play doctor, eh?" Nick asked. "Go ahead."

Eric sat on the edge of the bed, and Nick lifted his foot into his lap, resisting the urge to nudge Eric's crotch – Eric's prick was rigid, stretching against his zipper – with the toe in question.

"How did it happen?" Eric asked.

After all that had been broken and now healed, no one had noticed Nick's toe before now, despite his having done this so long ago, so Nick hadn't planned a lie in advance. Besides, he didn't want to lie to Eric, ever. He really liked him. "I did it myself."

"You *what? How?"*

Nick looked down at Eric, who had gone from looking in earnest at Nick's toe to looking incredulously at Nick's face. Nick shot Eric a look. *Did I stutter?* he thought to himself. "I broke it."

"On purpose, it sounded like," Eric said leadingly.

"With a hammer," Nick said and Eric recoiled, letting go of Nick's foot altogether. "Well, a rubber mallet actually."

"Just swung right at it?'

Yup, Nick thought, alternately wishing that they could move on – finish getting naked – and that he'd kept his sock on. Still, he said nothing.

"Why?"

"When it all happened to me, the attack in the alley, I couldn't believe how much…" Nick paused, then stressed his next word, "…*stronger* I felt afterward."

"When a bone breaks, it does heal back stronger," Eric said. "The fibers more or less knit themselves back tighter, and an extra layer of bone grows over it, sort of like a callus, making it harder and less likely to break again."

"I had never broken anything before, so I didn't know that." Nick paused. "But that's not even what I mean. It's not just that the bones were stronger. *I* was stronger. I took on a job on my own, told off this lazy contractor I hated big-time, and I mean, I never would have dared to ask a guy like you out before –" Nick was glad he'd gotten through the explanation without mentioning Marco or Humberto.

"Before it happened?" Eric asked. "Why not, exactly?"

The question seemed ridiculous to Nick. *How is it that Eric doesn't see that he is so much better than I am?* he thought. Thoughts about how out-of-his-league he thought Eric was flooded him; Eric was a doctor – and a cute one at that – and Nick was a designer, such a stereotypically gay male profession that even Nick was a little embarrassed of at times. Again, he said nothing, just gave Eric a look that he hoped read as you're-the-most-perfect-man-I've-ever-met-and-I-don't-know-why-you're-with-me-let's-please-change-the-subject-off-this-unbelievably-crazy-thing-I-did-to-myself-and-get-into-bed-where-I-can-make-you-feel-as-good-as-I-do-just-being-with-you.

"So, why just the one toe?"

I did this batshit-bizarre thing to myself and that's *your question?* Nick thought, halfway relieved that Eric didn't find what he did absolutely senseless – or at least wasn't letting on that he did – halfway wondering what it would take to shock this guy, if he took someone he cared for hurting himself like this in stride.

"Did it hurt too much to keep going?" Eric continued.

"After what I've been through?"

"Good point." Eric paused. "I hope I didn't come off as insensitive, given what happened to you. It's just that this…is…*unusual."* Eric said the word 'unusual' as if asking a question: *Is this the right word?*

"Hey, I get it. Not every patient survives months of pain and rehab and lime Jell-O just to take a whack at his own toe. Maybe one in five, right Doc?"

Eric waited to respond. "Oh, you're teasing me, got it, sorry." Eric wore his confusion on his face like so much sexy stubble. "What was it like?"

"What was what like?"

"Hurting yourself. Intentionally. After so much pain."

"Different."

"Is that why you stopped?"

"I guess so, yeah. I realized that I couldn't do this to myself. I mean, I could, physically, but it wouldn't have the same psychological effect as having it done to me, surviving it, and coming back, healing."

Nick decided not to say a word about asking Marco to hit him, or about going to a straight bar to try to get bashed. He wondered if Eric would catch where he was going with this, and it seemed he did. "But, if someone else did it to you..." Eric started.

"Like, say, a doctor, who would know where to hit to break the bone without risking anything but a simple break –"

"Whoa. No. I took an oath, Nick. First do no harm. What you propose is in complete violation of that oath, that promise. I couldn't in good conscience –"

"Okay, I get it," Nick said, knowing in just saying that, he could be coming off as saying so much more. That he'd do more of it himself, *to* himself. That he'd find another way. Another doctor. Another guy.

"Whatever gave you the idea to break your own bones?"

"I thought we just established that. I felt stronger where I was attacked, and wanted to see if I could make myself stronger everywhere."

Eric's face was more unbelieving than understanding. "You didn't think it was strange that you wanted to hurt yourself?"

"Not really, no. I don't think it's human nature to second-guess your own thoughts. That's what society is for." Nick laughed a little, knowing it was inappropriate but unable to fight it. "Think about the first time you were attracted to another man. You didn't think anything of it, that there was anything wrong with it, or that it made you special. You just naturally thought of another man sexually. You thought it was something all men did, like worrying about hair loss or playing at being James Bond the first time they put on a tuxedo. It doesn't occur to you that the way you feel is in any way different from how other men do, or that there's anything wrong with it." Nick paused. "It takes someone else to make you feel bad about what you are, about the way you feel and what you've done."

"I didn't mean to make you feel bad."

Nick shook his head. "Let's make each other feel good, then," he said, and pushed Eric on the bed.

#

Mark parked in a garage across from Loews – fifteen bucks to leave the car from 7:00 pm to 5:00 am – because it was the only landmark he knew in South Beach and started walking, retracing his steps from the night it had all started. He found Washington Avenue and turned right, saw the gilt chair outside Club Madonna and turned around, knowing he and Rob had turned left when they left the club that night, found a souvenir shop, found the man in the alley. Mark found the same dark alley tonight and was surprised by its quiet. He caught his breath there, remembering the details of the attack, until he heard music playing and followed it out into the street, around the corner, to a short span of red carpet and a blacked-out glass door.

A small rainbow-hued sign above the door spelled out 'Twist,' and Mark saw that there were no women lined up to get in, only men: men that reminded him of the man he'd attacked.

This must be the place, Mark thought, guessing that the man he and Rob had attacked must have been here right beforehand.

A couple of guys in black T-shirts were checking IDs at the door, but didn't charge anyone a cover.

Definitely the place, Mark decided, knowing his limited cash would last longer if he only came here every night.

#

After days without talking, Nick called Eric and endured a few awkward minutes of small talk before thinking *to hell with it,* asking, "Look, what's up?" bravely, knowing the answer.

"You kinda freaked me out the other night."

"The toe thing?" Nick asked dismissively, as though he'd done nothing worse than pick at a scab.

"Yeah."

"Didn't stop you from –"

"From sleeping with you?" Eric asked. "I know, that was a bit tricky, and maybe I should have stopped myself. But, I really like you. I just don't understand how you could..."

Eric's voice faded out, and Nick waited out the silence, not looking to put words in Eric's mouth.

"...hurt yourself like that," Eric resumed.

Nick nodded into the phone but didn't say anything, knowing he wouldn't have understood, either, if he hadn't survived what he had and come out feeling stronger. Nick didn't know what to say about any of it, really, and wanted to leave things as open-ended as he could with Eric for a while, let them both figure things out on their own with the possibility of coming back to each other, not say anything damning that he wouldn't be able to take back if ever he got Eric back.

"I know, Eric. It doesn't make sense to you, and I can't make it make sense to you. It barely makes sense to me." Nick took a breath. "Maybe we should take a break for a while, cool things off, do some thinking."

"I'd like to try *not* thinking about things for a while, actually, but yeah, a break seems like a good idea."

It's amazing what you can live with if you don't think too hard, Nick thought, wondering where the thought had come from and if Eric could deal with the fact that Nick had done this to himself, wondering if he should volunteer that he didn't plan to do it again.

Nick didn't realize how long he'd been thinking to himself until Eric started in again. "If you're not going to say anything, that's fine. I need time to think – or not think – about things for a while. Maybe I'll call you, maybe I won't, but you're free to do whatever you like."

"Free to call you?"

"Free to do whatever you like with other guys, Nick. Don't call me. I'll call if and when I'm ready to try things with you again."

"I thought we had something pretty special," Nick said and meant it, their connection strong enough on so many levels that he questioned if a single broken bone, after so many others, would weaken it.

"We did. I think we still do, even," Eric said. "But I need time."

Chapter Twenty

The first couple of nights Mark had gone out, he'd covered his cast with a leather jacket. The first night he wore it over his shirt, the leather shrouding his body, hiding his muscles and lessening the attention he was getting from the guys in the gay club, and moreover making him sweat under the second skin, though Mark could tell from the way the guys at the bar paired off that a little sweat was hardly a deterrent. The second night, he'd arranged the jacket over his cast, waving it about with him like a flag he was about to drop. Tonight, he dressed in a plain T-shirt and jeans, and left the jacket on his motel room's one chair.

He hadn't realized until he was in the car, fit tight inside the subcompact, that the cast covered over much of his class ring; it only glinted in the glow of oncoming headlights when Mark grabbed the wheel from the top: *twelve o'clock,* he remembered from a Driver's Ed class that had taught him to keep his hands positioned at ten and two o'clock, not that he or anyone he knew ever did. *Twelve o'clock,* Mark thought, staring at the blue stone, then taking his eyes off the ring and the road to watch the digital clock on the rental's radio register midnight.

Mark knew there were plenty of gay bars in Miami – more in South Beach alone than there were strip joints back home, not that he really knew where 'home' was anymore, with no reason to ever return to where he'd come from – but Mark went only to Twist on the nights when he stalked his victim. That it was free to get in was a benefit Mark didn't deny, but he also figured this way he'd see him at some point, not miss him by being at another bar if his victim showed up at Twist.

Mark had gone to Twist every night for a week and a half looking for his victim, not that he knew what he'd do when and if he found him. Back home, he was confident he'd recognize the man, but at the club, and in South Beach in general, every man seemed to look like him. Every man had the same haircut, the same tan, the same manicured brows, the same clubby wardrobe – even during the day, the men in South Beach looked to Mark ready to party. Every man looked like his victim. And every man responded to Mark the same way, as though he was obviously an outsider, and just as obviously welcome anywhere he wanted to be.

# # # # #

Nick's new body continued to amaze him, and as he dressed to go out for the night, he felt just about physically perfect. He pulled a shirt that laced up the front from the back of his closet, and tied up just enough of it for there to be some point to it, a two-inch gap of his skin left exposed down the center of his chest, the black Xs of the lacing over it making him resemble a completed to-do list. *Survive a brutal attack? Check,* Nick thought. *Build my body back better than it was before? Check. Go to bed with the most desirable men I can find? Check, check, check.*

Nick paired the shirt with low-slung leather pants and boots. Nick had let Ron know he was going out tonight without inviting him along or telling him where he would be, so they could meet up. Ron, somehow, had acted like he understood.

After looking in the mirror and fingering the lacing provocatively – and downing three fingers of vodka – Nick finally felt brave enough to go back to Twist.

Nick got checked out a lot on the walk to the club, and he liked it, but he always checked out who noticed him right back, still thinking *check, check, check* and deciding if they were worth a slow burn of a look or if he should move on. Though he'd treated a couple of cute-enough guys to a bit-by-bit-building smile-and-stare, Nick made it to Twist in reasonable time.

The response Nick got in the street was nothing compared to the eyes on him inside. Nick realized that tonight, and from now on, he could have anyone he wanted. Nick found Marco's muscles through the thinner bodies that crowded him, then his face, his smile, and smiled back when he saw Marco try to get up, break away from the guys around him and get to Nick. Nick angled his hand, palm-out, toward Marco and patted the air between them a couple of times: *that's alright, stay where you are, enjoy yourself.* Nick then smoothed that same hand down the front of his shirt, toying with Marco. Nick knew how to find Marco when he wanted him again, and was glad to garner from Marco's struggle to free himself of the men that circled him that Marco was still into him, and Nick could seemingly have him anytime. Around the corner, Nick saw Humberto getting a drink at the bar and winked, but kept moving, kept searching. Nick felt Marco's and Humberto's eyes stay on him, watching to see what he'd do next, and was sure he'd end up in bed with each of them again – and was less confident if more hopeful that he'd do the same with Eric someday soon, though Nick knew better than to expect Eric in the crowd tonight – but saw someone through the crowd that he wanted more, and made a move. He caught the eye of the good-looking young man at the bar and, emboldened more by what he'd become than by any alcohol, moved closer and closer, discretely checking in with the guy's eyes, until he was barely three feet from the guy. The young man pulled the stool next to him out for Nick, a silent invitation to sit down.

Nick accepted.

Nick couldn't believe it – up close, the good-looking guy was gorgeous, not so much *his* type as *every* gay guy's type: All-American and athletic – athletic enough to have an arm in a cast. Nick characterized him as every gay's type because the guy seemed straight. Not that he said much. The guy seemed to look at him pretty hard, as though he were deciding something, and took a long time to answer any question Nick asked him.

"Haven't seen you here before. New in town or just visiting?"

Long pause. "Visiting."

"Where from?"

Longer pause. "No place like this."

"What happened there?" Nick asked, remembering how the dancer at Johnny's had said 'I should see the other guy' about his own bruises as he indicated this guy's cast with his hand. Nick watched the young man's eyes follow his fingers and widen upon noticing his tattoo.

"I'd rather not talk about it."

Nick felt him out cautiously, too attracted to just walk away but not getting enough back from the guy to believe it was at all mutual. "I can leave you alone if you want. I just saw the way you were looking at me and came over. If I read you wrong, I can just –"

"You didn't get it wrong. I just don't do this a lot. Ever, really."

Nick smiled for two reasons: because the guy wasn't some barfly who was out every night trying to get laid – surely an easy feat for a guy like this – and to put the man at ease. "What's your name?"

The guy paused long enough to make Nick believe he was making up a name, not that Nick cared. "Rob," the man answered.

"Well, 'Rob,'" Nick said the name thinking *'bullshit,'* "Welcome to South Beach. Can I buy you another drink?"

"Sure thing..." the man let his voice trail off leadingly.

"...Nick." *'Sure-Thing-Nick' would make a hell of nickname,* Nick thought. *Certainly a fitting one of late.* "Same thing," Nick nodded to the man's beer, "or something else?"

"Bartender here know how to make a Mai Tai?"

"This place isn't usually great for mixed drinks unless, well, unless the guy ordering looks like you. So let's ask him and find out." Nick said the words lightly, but felt that nothing about this man's outward appearance said 'I-drink-Mai-Tais.'

"What do you mean?"

"Something tells me they'll be a lot stronger if *you* order them," Nick said, noticing that the bartender hadn't looked away from the two of them – the guy he was talking to in particular – the whole time. "If stronger is better."

Nick saw the guy take in his bigger-than-ever muscles. "You'll have one with me?" the man asked, then added, "Alright, I know you asked, but let me get this round." The young man already had the bartender's attention but signaled him anyway. "Two Mai Tais." Nick noticed that the guy ordered the drink confidently, as though nothing could be more natural, as though every bar were stocked with the ingredients for such an offbeat order. The bartender's face registered barely a bit of surprise, his movement paralyzed by either a strive for cool in the face of such a handsome man or some aesthetician's injection.

"So, *Rob*," Nick again said the name as though it were genuinely false, as though he should follow it up with *'if-that-is-your-real-name'* although he admitted to himself that it didn't matter enough to him to push the topic, "what brings you to town?"

The man hesitated. "There are just some things I just can't do back home," he said, "so, I came here. And now, I'm sitting with you, having a drink, and I can –"

"Do those things you can't do back home," Nick said understandingly, assuming the man was closeted and only explored his truth when out of town, when no one he knew could see and judge him.

"Exactly." The bartender put their drinks in front of them. Nick noted that he hadn't said 'That'll be eighteen for the round' or even 'On the house.' It seemed the bartender wasn't going to collect from the young man who'd ordered them; he simply shrank away from the bar after setting the glasses down, glad to see a man like that up-close and have any interaction with him at all.

"What is it with this town and free Mai Tais?" the man asked neither the bartender nor Nick, and quickly followed up with "Cheers."

Nick doubted the man had paid for the beer he'd been nursing before, either. *Men like that don't pay for anything,* he reasoned, resenting the looks of the man sitting next to him before reminding himself that the man *wanted* to be sitting next to him, and that lately, he was getting to be a 'man like that' himself.

"A Mai Tai, eh?" Nick asked after taking a sip.

"I'm on vacation," the man said. "When in Rome."

"When in Rome? I've lived here for years and not seen anyone order one nor had one myself." This was true, Nick realized; he'd never received his initial order at Bongo's. "If you're thinking you should drink what the 'Romans' do here, try a bottle of water. Anything else messes with their meds."

"Oh, are you on –"

Nick laughed. "No. I'm not. Perhaps I'm not a true Miamian," he paused, before adding, "If you'd like to find someone else..." and just as quickly wishing he'd left it alone.

"Not at all."

"Friends?" *Romans, Countrymen,* Nick thought.

"More than that, soon, I hope." The man smiled at Nick weakly, took a drink, then winced and smiled again in quick succession. "That's awful," he said.

"You ordered 'em."

The young man's smile became a wince again.

"Pineapple juice. Not for everybody, though the pineapple is the international symbol of welcome." Nick wondered why he was even mentioning this, rather than trying to get this guy out the door with him before someone cuter walked in and distracted the guy, took him away from him.

"Tasting like that, I can't figure why."

"It goes back to a time when pineapples were rare in the continental U.S., before inexpensive air travel, so people and goods could only be moved by boat, which took a long time and a lot of money. It told your guest that you were worldly and that they were special: imagine-all-the-trouble-I-went-to-getting-you-this-pineapple."

"It certainly has been a lot of trouble for me."

Nick smiled. "Sometimes a little trouble can be fun."

"What do you say we get out of here, then?"

Nick's smile widened. "I'd say 'yes,' as a short answer. And I can serve you something better at my place, to answer your-place-or-mine."

Nick led the man out of the club and to his place, avoiding the alley he'd been attacked in. The man didn't walk next to him so much as behind him, to Ocean Drive and through the crowds, with Nick occasionally turning to make sure the guy was following close, and he always was. Nick noted that the crowd seemed to part right after him, making room for the man and admiring him as he passed. Nick was flattered that the man was always looking right at him when he turned around to see how he was keeping up, not distracted by the beautiful people swarming Ocean Drive. The man also occasionally tried to grab Nick, stop their rushed pace to just talk in the middle of the crowd. The man's face was deadly serious every time Nick got a look at it, but Nick figured the man was closeted and doubting himself, and that it would all work itself out at his condo.

Nick walked fast enough to break a bit of a sweat in the humid Miami night, and was glad for the air-conditioning of his building's lobby.

Once upstairs, Nick was surprised that the man didn't remark on his home at all, even to be polite. "I promised you a drink, what can I get you?"

"Beer, please," the man answered briskly, sounding to Nick as though he didn't really want anything and had answered as a reflex.

"Beer it is," Nick popped a Gordon Biersch for the man and poured a vodka rocks for himself, not bothering with a citrus twist, just needing something strong to steady himself.

"Thanks," the man said as he accepted the beer in its amber bottle.

"I'm sorry, did you want a glass?"

"Bottle's fine, thanks." The man fidgeted with his free hand and paced slowly about Nick's living room.

"If you're nervous, don't be."

The man's face registered fear and anxiety, as did his jittery actions, but his words were all-confidence. "Where's the bedroom?" he asked, though the condominium was small and easily navigable.

"Follow me."

"Huh-uh. I want you behind me." It sounded reasonable enough, hot even, to Nick, since the man had followed him for so many blocks on Ocean.

"Down the hall. Last door," Nick said, and followed closely, checking out the guy's ass.

The man walked in and stopped in the middle of the room, in front of the bed. He took a long drink from the bottle.

Nick smoothed a hand along the back of the man's shoulder, and he jumped away, some of the beer he was drinking dribbling onto the floor. "Don't," the man said, and stepped away from Nick. The man set the beer bottle down on Nick's nightstand.

"Sorry," Nick said. Nick had never been with a closeted guy before, someone who feared every touch so much.

"No, just..." the man's voice trailed away like it had at the bar, hesitance and fear seeming to mix with what Nick figured he wanted.

Nick leaned in for a kiss, and the man jumped away again.

"Don't, really. Just..." With the distance between them, Nick could see the tension and worry in the man's body, fists balled at his sides, his lip trembling with words he wanted to say but wouldn't. Seconds passed, then half a minute, then a whole minute, then several, feeling like hours as Nick waited out the guy's next word or move. The man hastily undid his button fly and yanked his pants down over his soft cock. "Just fucking bone me, man," the guy said, and bent over the footboard of the bed, his ass in the air, his eye on the amber glass beer bottle on the nightstand.

Nick didn't respond, but unbuttoned his pants and unzipped them, stepping his right leg out of them and letting the rest puddle about his left. He stroked himself a bit to get hard, for even though the guy bent over and asking for it was hot, his hot-and-cold act had done nothing to arouse Nick physically. Stiff enough, Nick bent down to pull a condom out of his pants pocket and stood back up, jacking his dick a little more before opening the wrapper and rolling the condom over his cock. Nick wished he could see more of the guy's body, or at least his face as he got ready, but ass-up, the guy was all-business – *no bullshit now,* Nick thought, *whatever-your-name-is* – and Nick did his best to remember the face and build of the man he was about to enter.

Nick knew the way the man had positioned himself – his pants still for the most part up with just his ass exposed, his legs close together – was not going to make fucking him easy, and that they were both in for more than a little pain. But after the way the guy had leapt away from his every touch, Nick wasn't about to try to pull the guy's pants down the rest of the way.

Nick positioned himself to enter the guy, and pressed the tip of his dick against the man's crack. "Fucking bone me." the man repeated his plea.

Nick did his best to oblige, forgoing anything he might have done purposely for the man's pleasure in order to just plow into him, plug into him, bone him. Though Nick breathed out heavily on his first thrust, and let out the occasional unconscious "yeah" and "God," the man he was inside was utterly silent.

Nick kept on boning the guy, concentrating on what had attracted him to the guy at the bar, since he couldn't see much of him now. He liked the guy's dark hair, the Vs of it at the sides of his neck where it was growing in telling Nick he didn't work too hard at his looks. Nick liked the guy's natural build, too; Nick could make out the muscles of the guy's back through his T-shirt. Nick steered his focus left to see the guy's arm, its bicep and triceps well-developed. Nick figured the other arm was built the same, but couldn't see it for the cast that encased it; with it stretched across his bed, Nick could see more of the guy's right hand peeking out from the plaster sleeve. Nick saw the guy's class ring, its blue stone twinkling in the room's dim light.

Memories of being attacked flooded Nick's mind as his brow dripped with the sweat of forceful fucking.

Nick tried to get a look at the guy's face, but only saw a bit of it, Nick just able to tell that the man was looking hard at the beer bottle on the nightstand. He saw the man's blue eyes, that he was crying, but Nick was too close to coming to care – or console or confront – the man he was inside, the man who may-or-may-not-have attacked him that night, and continued to hammer the guy's ass, harder with the possibility that it was one of his attackers.

Bliss blurred with rage for Nick as he reached orgasm, and he didn't ask if he should pull out, pull off the condom and come on the guy's ass; Nick just let himself explode inside the man, feeling his come swell up the condom around his erection. He gently pinched the condom against his cock to keep his ejaculate from spilling when he pulled out.

The man waited until Nick had stepped away from him to pull his pants back up over his ass. He walked past Nick without a word and left the bedroom, traced his steps to the front door, and quietly closed it behind him.

# # # # #

The quick click of the doorknob reminded Mark of his arm snapping on the field; he clutched the cast with his left hand and gave it a squeeze that he felt to the bone.

The Author

Sable Stone is an architect and interior designer with homes in Miami and Winter Park, Florida.